SAM CRESCENT

EVERNIGHT PUBLISHING ®

www.evernightpublishing.com

A SENSE OF DUTY

Copyright© 2023

Sam Crescent

Editor: Lisa Petrocelli

Cover Artist: Jay Aheer

ISBN: 978-0-3695-0778-5

ALL RIGHTS RESERVED

SAM CRESCENT

DEDICATION

To my readers for requesting this book. I hope you love it as much as I do.

SAM CRESCENT

A SENSE OF DUTY

Volkov Bratva, 2

Sam Crescent

Copyright © 2023

◆

Prologue

Adelaide

I always thought I'd live a long, happy life. Death wasn't something I ever thought about. What was the point? It was inevitable in old age. There was no way I saw my life ending early. I wasn't someone who ever made waves or caused any problems. I always helped where I could. For want of a better description, I was the epitome of a good girl.

Take the last few months, for example. My life changed completely with one greedy decision. My family were heavily involved in the media. Daddy considered himself a bit of a know-it-all when it came to what sells. Money made the world go around for him. It's how he landed my ex-model of a mother, where he was, to put it nicely, an asshole. They were considered to be like chalk and cheese, and to be honest, if it weren't for my father's wealth, my mom would never have looked at him.

She was a shallow person, still is. Age hasn't

changed her outlook on life—just her beauty—which has come at the cost of her ability to move much of her face. She looks youngish, if people were plastic. So, money was necessary in my mother's life, and then I've got to think about my father.

He loved money.

He loved power.

They were well-suited for each other in that regard, but while they were spending all this money, they were not making it. My father's family business slowly started to decline and rather than take the warnings his financial aides insisted on, he ignored them all, and just did what he wanted to do.

As far as he was concerned, there was no shortage of juicy gossip. But he didn't realize that people had so many other avenues to find what they wanted. My father's business went into the toilet very quickly. I'm not sure exactly when the harsh reality of what he'd been doing struck. It could've been when the debt collectors came calling. The expensive cars he'd never driven, but bought just to flash how wealthy he was, or not, in his case. Possibly the scene caused by my mother at one of those branded fashion boutiques because her credit card was denied.

I've also forgotten to mention another important piece of the puzzle: my lovely sister Bethany. She's not lovely at all. In fact, many would call her a spiteful bitch, but she's beautiful, and I've watched many men fall over themselves to impress her. She inherited our parents' need to spend money.

Why am I thinking about all of this? Well, as I look at my husband, his chest heaving as pain explodes in mine, I can't help but think about what led me to this moment. What drove me to this abandoned warehouse, where my husband Andrei Belov was hurting my best friend, Nathan. I don't know who sent me the details, but it came through as a text that my presence was needed in this place.

I am not an idiot.

From the moment my father called me back to his mansion and told me I was going to be marrying Andrei Belov, there was no hiding just how desperate my parents had become. Their thirst for greed and power led to this moment. He was supposed to marry my sister. She was the most beautiful, the loveliest. All my life, that was what I heard.

"Why couldn't you be more like your sister?"
"Why do you have to be ugly and fat?"

In the beginning, it hurt. No daughter wanted to hear those nasty words from her mother. How she'd pull on my hair in anger because I wasn't perfect. It's why I've been able to escape most of the press chasing after me. While my parents were happy to pose for pictures with Bethany, they kept me home, locked me up, like I was some dirty secret they couldn't get rid of.

Until I became their one saving grace. Bethany messed up big time. I was not exactly sure of the full details, just that her marriage to Andrei Belov was off, and well, the only remaining daughter was me, so guess what? I was the one walking down the aisle with him.

Bethany hated me for it.

My husband wasn't a good man. No, he was a man aligned to the Volkov Bratva. Ivan Volkov to be exact. I'd heard stories of how deadly they were. Again, I don't know how my parents got close to this deadly man, but here I am, pain exploding in my chest.

Before I fall to the ground, I gasp.

Pain.

Unbearable pain.

For some reason, I think back to my wedding

night. Bethany had told me how cruel Andrei was. How he'd make me bleed, cut me, make me wish for death long before he'd grant it. I'd never been so scared.

Pain was the one thing I couldn't stand.

Tears filled my eyes and the image of my husband went blurry. At some point, I think he caught me.

"Fucking kill them," Andrei said.

"I … I…"

"Shut the fuck up, Adelaide. Conserve your strength. You're not dying on me."

"I … I'm so cold."

My hands were like blocks of ice.

The world had already started to spin.

Sickness swirled in my gut, and the noise that had been almost deafening seemed to fade into nothing.

Peace.

That was what I wanted.

Was it so hard to ask for? To not be part of this world anymore?

I'd never longed for death. My life wasn't a great one, but there were moments of happiness, of joy, of … life. That's what I wanted. Not this marriage. Not to be connected to the Volkov Bratva.

I wanted to be alone, and as the world started to fall away, I wondered if death would be my one salvation.

Chapter One

Adelaide
Six Months Earlier

It wasn't normal to fear your husband on your wedding night. Not unless it was an historical romance novel, and trust me, this wasn't. Staring around the hotel room, I noticed it was far more luxurious than my bedroom last night, which had just a single bed. Bethany had demanded to be put in better accommodations, so our parents switched the rooms. Like always, I'm lucky to get anything, not that I'm complaining. It's easier to keep quiet and just let Bethany get anything she wants. If I don't, there's always a consequence where I'm the one who ends up paying.

Andrei hadn't said a word, but then, he'd not said anything to me for most of the day. Apart from, "I'm here now, pretend to be fucking happy."

I'm not sure exactly what Aurora said to him, but either way, his presence kept Bethany away from me, and for that I'm grateful. My sister is a spiteful soul. Even though she was the one who fucked up in this situation, our parents still treated her like she was a princess, rather than a disappointment, which was how I got treated. Between the dress and the cake, everything about this day had gone wrong.

Staring at the bed, I know there's no way I'm going to sit on that thing. I can't. With Andrei being his usual quiet self, I decide to leave him to it.

I'll figure some way of getting out of this monstrosity of a dress. I've never been the kind of woman to think in advance about her wedding. I never spent hours cooing over celebrity events, even the ones we were invited to. This wedding was all Bethany. The bride may have changed, but the dress, the cake, the band, the guests—they'd all been her choice. This wedding had been a nightmare. The only part of it I found deeply comforting was Aurora. Another woman married to a member of the Bratva. At least she'd looked happy. Could any woman married into this kind of life truly be happy? Was Slavik in love with her?

Love. This world didn't believe in love. It revolved around constant greed and desire for money.

I stepped into the bathroom and moved straight to the sink. I gripped the edge, closing my eyes, seeing spots even as I did this.

Breathe. Just breathe.

I counted to ten slowly, taking my time, filling my lungs with precious air, and slowly exhaled.

The panic attack today was the first one I'd ever experienced and once again, big surprise, that it was after my sister told me what a monster Andrei was in the bedroom. Tonight, we had to consummate the marriage.

I'd never kissed a man, or even hugged one.

Now I was expected to sleep with a total stranger. Whenever Andrei had been around with Bethany, I'd been out. My life didn't mesh with my family's. Their only demand on me was that I not work. For some odd reason they feared their reputation if I was to find a nice normal job. So, volunteering at the animal shelter I *was* allowed to do, and I loved it. Being around animals all day was heaven.

Once, when I was ten I think, I'd started to bring stray cats and dogs home. No one ever entered the basement, so that was where I offered them shelter. For several months I was able to help so many cats and dogs. Sometimes they'd leave, wander off for a couple of weeks but come back, looking for a nice warm place. My mother hated the cold—one of the few traits I inherited from her—so even the basement in our house was nice and warm, not that she ever went down there.

Anyway, taking care of them was my safe haven. Every single day after school, I'd run home to love them, to show them affection, until my sister discovered it. Within an hour, they were all taken from me. Rounded up by some animal control guy as if they were vermin or something.

I open my eyes and stare at my reflection. The dress is far too tight. My tits are almost bulging out of the top. It looked utterly ridiculous, kind of laughable. There were a few people at the wedding I'd overheard laughing about this dress.

Bethany ordered the wrong one. Ugh!

I hated how she was able to invade my thoughts and just dominate everything. Her place wasn't here. I refused to fall for it. My sister and I didn't have the best relationship at all. She preferred to be the center of attention. Her hatred of me was absolute. She even hated the fact I was younger than her by a few years.

If I had friends, she'd take them, turn them against me. Hurting me seemed to be a sport to her. Ignoring her never worked. She always found some way to humiliate me.

No. No. No. No. This was how she won. By getting inside my head even when she wasn't there. The truth was, for the past year, our paths rarely crossed, and my life had been bliss. Until the moment I was told I was marrying Andrei.

The dress was hideous.

I looked like a tank inside this dress. The horrible thing was two sizes too small. It made my breasts look enormous, and I looked stupid as if I were trying to fit into a dress that wasn't for me.

Bethany loved to point out how fat I was.

Considering how slender she was, everyone was fat to her. What Bethany hated most, I didn't care.

I mean, seriously, I went to a school notorious for bullies. One of our nannies was a strong-minded person and Bethany couldn't break her. The times I spent with her were the best of my life. Miss Nicole, which is what she demanded we call her, taught me to love myself. The world was far too cruel and evil, and life was too short to spend even a moment hating life or yourself.

So, I turned all of those cruelties around.

My body was my temple.

I loved my curves, my large tits, my too-rounded stomach, as well as my thick thighs. They were all part of me.

I miss her so much.

Taking a random trip down memory lane was not in the cards for tonight. I needed to get this horrible dress off and get in the shower to wipe the memory away.

Reaching around the back, I tried to find the buttons that had been squeezed closed. Turning this way and that, I couldn't find anything. The last thing I wanted to do was go back out there to Andrei.

Lifting the endless skirts, I attempted to find myself, but nothing. There was no end to this monstrosity. By the time I gave up, my face was red. This dress was clearly indestructible.

Stepping back into the main hotel room, Andrei sat on the edge of the bed with his phone in hand. He was sexy. There was no denying it, if women were into the big, scary, heavily tattooed giant. None were on his face, but staring at the cuffs of his jacket and the neck of his shirt, one could see them peeking out. Even his knuckles were inked.

I had no idea what they said. They were just little pieces of what looked like ivy on his knuckles. I also noticed a distinctive V in-between the flesh of each knuckle. Again, I'm not sure what it meant, and it would require me to speak to my husband, which I'd decided not to do. The less I knew the better.

He looked up as I entered. Freezing on the spot, I wasn't sure exactly what to do. He just stood there, looking all calm and collected, while I was terrified.

What would it be like to be the worst person in the room? To fill it with fear by a mere presence. I didn't need to think of that.

Pushing those thoughts to the back of my mind, I looked at Andrei. Of course he hadn't spoken. That would require effort.

"Er, I can't seem to..." This was so humiliating. Bethany had done this. *Stop that! She doesn't get to exist right now. I'm fine. We're fine. Everything is fine.*

It wasn't, but the longer I kept telling myself it was, the better chance I'd eventually believe it.

"I can't get out of the dress." Presenting my back to Andrei, I hoped he didn't see this as any kind of come-on or flirting. It wasn't. "Would you unbutton me, please?" There I was, forever the good girl with all my manners.

Clenching my hands into fists, I hoped he didn't notice them shaking. I'm not the kind of girl who is afraid of everything. Not that anyone would believe it right now.

I heard him move. The simple sound of clothes rustling was enough to set my teeth on edge.

At first, I didn't move. I couldn't. Even breathing was difficult. I was frozen in place. He stepped closer, and the heat behind him seemed to increase.

Ever since I'd been told Andrei was to be my husband, we'd not spent any time together. I'd been called to my father, where I'd been told what was going to happen. I was not sure whether others thought I had an opinion about what was going to happen in my life. That never happened. I wasn't asked.

No, I was told by my father with Andrei present and another man who made my blood run cold. He looked so terrifying. Ivan Volkov. Head of the Volkov Bratva. My father's new boss. My new nightmare.

I felt sick to my stomach just thinking about him. I gave nothing away to my husband who stood way too still. He didn't touch me. Other than the kiss in church and the few times he'd taken my hand, he never touched me. He often avoided it.

This was great. My husband detested me without even knowing me. This was how my life was going to end up. It probably didn't help that I might have flinched in church. He'd grabbed my arms and pulled me close.

The kiss was dull. My very first kiss hadn't made my heart sing or cause me to instantly fall in love with my husband. If anything, it made this whole marriage thing seem even more of a farce. There was no love between us. There was no anything.

He didn't touch me, but out of the corner of my eye, I saw the knife he'd pulled out. Fear raced down my spine. I didn't have time to run or move. He slid the blade between the center of my back and the dress. One tug, and that was it, the dress gave way and I had no choice but to hold it against my breasts to gain any modesty.

Tears filled my eyes and I hated them. I'd never been the kind of woman who constantly gave in to crying. I am strong. Being around Andrei, I felt anything but.

Without looking at him, I charged toward the bathroom, slamming the door closed. There was no lock. Nothing to protect myself.

I didn't have long before the door was pushed open. I stepped away from it before it could hit me in the face. Spinning around, still holding the dress in my hands, I backed away. Andrei advanced toward me.

He looked … dangerous. Not in a good way. He still held the knife in his hand. Without even looking at it, he flicked it away.

I kept moving back until the wall stopped my escape. Stupid wall.

His hands went either side of me, trapping me in place. "Don't ever run from me again. You won't like it."

"I … I didn't mean to run."

"Then don't."

He stayed like that, staring at me.

I couldn't keep looking into his eyes. They were a deep brown, all-knowing, penetrating. At times, I had to wonder if they were mostly black. He wasn't a good man.

"I won't. I promise." I'd do and say anything to get him the hell away from me.

He didn't leave right away.

Time seemed to stop for me the longer he just stood there. Did he like how he scared me?

I waited. I wanted to tell him to leave me alone, but in the end, he was the one who left. I just had to wait and I suddenly realized this was what our marriage would be like. No matter how uncomfortable I was, Andrei had all the power. He would do whatever the hell he liked and to hell with the consequences.

I didn't like this at all.

****

Andrei

Most men the day after their wedding are probably comatose from all the fucking they got done. Not me. Nope. My little virgin bride was still fucking pure.

She'd been shaking like a leaf when I finally finished in the bathroom last night. The bed had shaken like it was on vibration or something.

Raping women was not one of my skills.

I didn't want to start my marriage off by forcing my wife to take my dick. Even though Ivan expected it.

He was my boss, my Pakhan, the leader of the Volkov Bratva—the reason I'm one of the six men he trusted to control this State. Running a hand down my face, I stare out the car window, heading right back to my place where I had business to deal with.

Ivan had been present at my wedding. Of course he had. He'd been the one to change Bethany to Adelaide. There was no way I could have gone against him, even though Adelaide wasn't fit for this world.

She didn't understand the life she'd just entered. Like last night, Bethany would have enjoyed me fucking her. She'd have relished being part of the Volkov Bratva, the most feared Russian mob ever to rule the States. Ivan had taken us all into a new era. He changed the rules, adapted them to suit himself. It made me smile just thinking about it.

Life as a brigadier wasn't easy. Ruling over a state came with a great deal of problems, and enemies. My life was constantly in danger. It's why I had soldiers all around me. Every single one of us brigadiers had to. There were too many men and women who wanted us dead.

A little sniffle drew my attention to my wife. Adelaide was pressed as far away from me as any woman could get. I'd been the perfect gentleman to her last night, apart from the knife I'd used to rid her body of that awful dress.

At times during our wedding, she looked like she

couldn't breathe, the poor thing. Her tits looked close to bursting out of the dress, but then our wedding had been designed with me and Bethany in mind. Not much had changed.

It would have been like swapping the bride only, which was what happened at Ivan's request.

Bethany had been a slut, she still was a slut. I'd not been marrying her for her purity. Ivan had seen an opportunity with her parents, and, well, a union seemed to be the most ideal. They wanted money and power. Ivan had both in plenty supply. A deal was struck and the cost was a daughter, a marriage, a union that couldn't end in divorce.

Glancing over at Adelaide, I wondered if she realized her purity days would be over soon. Not only did I have her hand in marriage, but Ivan, the bastard, had informed me today that part of the agreement was a child within two years. She had to have a son or daughter inside her within two years to start the next generation of the Volkov Bratva.

I didn't need to point out to him that for the line to continue, he needed to father children. There was a great deal I didn't know about Ivan.

Unlike Slavik, one of the few brigadiers I knew, I'd not grown up with him. I wasn't entirely sure of the history, but Ivan and Slavik grew up together. I'm not sure where or how, seeing as both men were cast out of their families in some way. Like myself. My father couldn't stand to have me around. Ever since I was a boy, my father hated me. He would find any reason to take the belt or the boot to me. Many a night I was curled up on the floor, alone and bleeding at the mercy of the elements because he couldn't stand me.

After a severe beating, he'd toss me into the kennels where he kept the dogs. They were just as abused as I was, and so never attacked me. Sometimes he'd starve them and then go after me, making me bleed, in the hope of them eating me.

It never happened. Why? I fucking fed them, the stupid cunt. I was stupid. My father hated that about me. I figured out his plan to try and get rid of me. If I died because of the dogs, he could pass it off as some freak accident, kill the dogs as if to avenge my death, and he'd be fine and in the clear. Even before Ivan took over, the previous Pakhan didn't like when his brigadiers murdered children without his permission.

With the starved dogs failing, I overheard the plan he had. He was going to throw me into the dog kennels, and then one of his soldiers would take me out in the woods, force me in the dead of night to dig my own grave, and then kill me. If I disappeared, it could look like a kidnapping attempt.

Hearing what they planned, I ran. I ran so fucking hard that my feet were all torn up. I unleashed the dogs as well, and guess what, motherfucker? I was their goddamn alpha, not my dad. We ran, and we survived. That's what we did.

I became a man of the streets. The killer. The monster. I took that anger he'd built inside me, and I allowed it to blossom. I didn't give up or give in. I used it to become the man I am today.

When I heard of Ivan Volkov wreaking havoc, bringing down the old Bratva, I knew I had to side with him. Seeking him out had been easy. Swearing my loyalty had been a piece of cake, but earning his trust had taken a lot longer.

Ivan was a good man. He was evil, a monster to all those that crossed him, but he was fair and just. He was everything my father wasn't.

"How long?" Adelaide asked.

I glance over at her and notice the odd way she's pressing her thighs together. "Why?"

"No reason."

"Don't lie."

"I … I need to use the bathroom. Please."

My driver, Leo, raised his brow at me. He knew I didn't like unplanned stops. I nod my head letting him know he can find a safe location to let my wife out to go to the damn toilet.

Her family had already been waiting for us when we made it down this morning. Adelaide had gone straight to the coffee, not eating a single thing, just drinking caffeine. She hadn't slept at all last night, and I should know, I'd been lying in the bed beside her, watching her, waiting. The moment the sun began to rise, she was the first one out of bed.

Two minutes later, Leo brought the car to a stop outside a diner. Half of the sign was missing so it spelled IER. This was not a place I would stop.

"I'll only be a minute," Adelaide said. Her hand reached for the door.

I grabbed her arm, tugging her against me. "Don't ever get out of the car unless I say so. Understand?"

Her eyes went wide and she jerked her head, letting me know she understood. I highly doubted it, but I didn't scold her anymore. She would have to learn on the job. She was now a Bratva wife. Going out into the world was no longer as easy as it once was.

Leo was already out of the car, on guard, as he opened my door. Climbing out, I had one hand at the base of my back, waiting. I still held my wife, firmly, and without waiting, I marched her into the diner.

It wasn't busy, and Leo was already at the counter, talking to the man who was wiping out a glass. The scent of greasy food was heavy in the air.

I didn't eat in places like this, not for a long time. Living on the streets, I'd find odd jobs working in diners like this. After the first few weeks of running away, my father had sent some of his men to look for me, but I had a way of hiding in plain sight. Changing my hair and dress, I'd been able to blend in.

It also helped that I'd been a skinny kid. Someone people glanced over, but never took the time to care about. I'd used it to my advantage. Over the years, I'd come close to the previous Bratva men and I'd been so tempted to kill for them, but it was only when I joined with Ivan that I'd allowed myself the pleasure. The moment Ivan said I could, I did, and I relished it.

Killing was in my blood. It called to my soul.

"I can go on my own," Adelaide said.

Ignoring her, I shoved her into the bathroom. It had a single toilet, and there was writing all over the walls from previous customers. The place was a dump, no doubt about it.

Her face was a pretty shade of red. I wasn't used to being around women who blushed so easily.

"Pee," I said.

"No. I can't go with you watching."

"Then you don't have to go." I reached out to her but she stepped back, her shaking hands going to the belt of her jeans. "Could you at least look away?"

"Do you think seeing a woman pee is gross?"

"I … I know it's natural and all that, but it's not something you need to see."

I stared at her.

"Please," she said.

I wasn't turning around.

Her jaw clenched and she lowered herself to the toilet, after she cleaned it. She squirmed. Didn't she realize I found her reaction to my presence amusing? I wasn't going to tell her.

Adelaide was interesting. I'd never met another woman like her. The women I knew were only after money and position. They liked my wealth and status. Bethany had asked me endless questions about what being my wife would mean. Could she get away with murder? Could she have a slave? Could she kill? The woman was an evil bitch, much like her parents. Their only desire had been for what they could get out of life. Adelaide asked for nothing. She didn't even beg for her own safety.

I'm aware she wasn't given a choice in being my wife, and I accept that. She wasn't here of her own free will, but she wouldn't get the option of going anywhere else. I owned her. She was my wife, and the only way out was by death.

Adelaide peed and I was shocked that she was very desperate to go. The coffee had needed a way out. Her face was bright red by the time she finished. I could have fried an egg on her cheeks with how flushed she looked, even as she wiped. She wiggled back into her clothes as if she had a choice of keeping her nakedness from me.

Two years. Two years to put my baby inside her without raping her.

Adelaide couldn't even look at me. Her hands were constantly shaking. The ring decorating her finger was too large. It was a statement ring, a brand of ownership.

She was mine and I wasn't going to give her back.

Chapter Two

Adelaide

Andrei, of course, lived in luxury. He was a man who knew what he wanted and how to get it.

His penthouse apartment was in the nicest part of the city. I hated heights and he thought it was fun to have floor-to-ceiling windows. Just going within a foot of them made me feel dizzy.

I'd been married to him for one week. In that time, I'd seen him once. I think he came home at night. I'm not sure because I've been left in his penthouse to do nothing.

There was no guard, unless you counted the one outside my door, who wouldn't let me leave. I'd tried. Multiple times. I'd explored every single inch of his penthouse suite, boycotting his office and his side of the walk-in closet. I didn't need to see or smell more of him than necessary.

Wrapping my arms around myself, I kept my back to the windows that overlooked the city. I'd tried to get closer and that had been laughable. I got to the footmark and ended up on my stomach, attempting to crawl closer to see if I could stomach looking out the window. It didn't work.

My fear of heights was so strong I'd even changed his sitting room around. The sofa was placed so when I watched television, my back was to the window. If the curtains weren't open before I got up, they stayed shut.

All this time trapped inside the penthouse was driving me crazy. I was going out of my mind. Growing up, I'd never stayed indoors and always preferred to be outside.

I missed the animal shelter. This apartment was

boring.

Collapsing on the sofa, I stared up at the ceiling and wondered if it would cave in. Would I be able to make my escape? I'd even thought about baking a batch of brownies that had sleeping tablets in them, but I didn't have any tablets. Also, I'm not the kind of person to feed drugs to an unsuspecting person.

I was going to die of boredom. There was nothing to do, no one to talk to. I thought I'd at least be able to talk to Aurora, the kind woman I'd met at the wedding, but nope.

No cell phone. No laptop. Nothing. Just an empty penthouse apartment. I saw the small library he had, but reading right now felt like I was giving into temptation. I loved reading, but that wasn't what I wanted to do.

I wanted to go out and explore. Find a different animal shelter a little closer to home, and volunteer.

This was a prison. Worse than the one my parents tried to force on me.

At the sound of the main door opening, I jerked up, a little startled. No one had come home during the day. Fear clawed its way inside me. Should I stand up? Stay seated? He didn't give me any chores to complete. Nothing that would make my life worthwhile.

Andrei entered the main room and glanced over at me. "Get dressed. We're going out to dinner in an hour."

"We are?" I asked.

My voice sounded croaky even to myself.

"Yes."

Nibbling my lip, I had so many questions but the fear of being forced to stay in this apartment was too much. I needed to get out. To feel the sun on my skin, or what was left of it. I'd even accept the cold bitterness of nighttime, just so long as I was out of this apartment.

Scrambling to my feet, I rushed into our bedroom. When I arrived a week ago, I found my side of the walk-in closet had been filled with clothes that my husband found acceptable. I don't know if he shopped for everything or instructed a woman to do so. Looking through the clothes, I couldn't pick the right one, so I settled on a dark-blue dress with a low neckline and a split up one side of the skirt. A little risqué for my taste but the most modest one available to me.

I hummed to myself as I went into the bathroom, and took a quick shower. After washing my body, I blow-dried my hair to give it some bounce and body. I have long brown hair that falls to my waist. Most of the time, I pull it back in a ponytail. Just recently, I'd been leaving it down.

Entering the bedroom, I see the dress I picked had been changed. In its place is a red one that ends at the knee. There's a slit at the side, which would reveal a lot more thigh than I wanted, and it was figure-hugging as well.

One day I'd given myself a little fashion show to see how much I loved or hated the dresses, and most of them I hated.

This wasn't good. I didn't want to wear this dress. The lingerie I'd pulled out was also gone. In its place was a red thong.

What should I do? Should I put the blue dress on? Or this one? I didn't choose this one, so that meant Andrei had been in the room and changed it. He wanted me to wear this.

If I wore this, would he be in a good enough mood for me to ask for some concessions? How did this work? I was so far out of my depth, it wasn't cute or funny.

He could kill me easily, dispose of my body

without anyone finding out. His wife could end up disappearing so easily. The Bratva were capable of it. They had many people on their payroll. Lawyers, judges, cops, their reach knew no bounds.

Sticking out my lip, I pouted. My husband's life was now my life.

Reaching for the thong, I slid it on and up my body. I was a French knickers and briefs girl. I never wore a thong and this felt … weird. It slid between the cheeks of my ass, and I took a moment to glance in the mirror, checking out my ass. How could anyone call this lingerie? Sure, the main gusset fit nicely, but come on, it didn't keep the ass contained.

I shook my head. There was no point in arguing. I wasn't going to win. The dress had a zipper in the back and the way it was fitted meant I couldn't zip it at the front and wriggle it into place. I was going to need Andrei's help again.

With it settled into place, my back showing, I left the bedroom, and sure enough, Andrei was dressed again, looking every bit the wealthy businessman. The suit he wore fit him like a second skin. He had one hand shoved into his pocket, and the other typed away on his cell phone, without a single care in the world. His face was void of any expression.

I stepped toward him, cleared my throat, and he finally looked up. I don't know how he did it, but every time he looked at me, I felt myself freezing up and my cheeks heating. We'd not had sex. We'd not done anything.

I spun around, presenting my back to him. "Could you please zip me?"

Pressing my lips together, I held my breath waiting for him. Why did this have to seem like a hard request? He was my husband. I imagine wives ask their husbands this all the time. Even boyfriends or girlfriends. There was nothing wrong with needing help with a zipper. I only hoped it fit me properly.

His fingers grazed the base of my back and I tensed up. I'm not a machine like him. I hadn't spent a long time trying to school my face into doing what I told it to do. When I liked something, I smiled. When I hated it, I frowned. Something disgusting, my face scrunched up. This was who I was, and there was no changing it. Did he hate it? I had to wonder if he did.

He eased the zipper up my back and as he did, his touch seemed to set a path of fire along with it.

Again, I was still a virgin.

The day after our wedding night, he told me to pretend like he'd been fucking my pussy raw. I didn't know what he expected, but being awkward came naturally to me. So, I'm not sure if I succeeded in what he suggested but from the few sad faces on the women, I was guessing it worked. Yay.

He finished lifting the zipper, but his touch lingered. One of his hands went to my waist and I tensed up. I wasn't used to being touched. His breath fanned across my neck and my heart raced. What was he thinking? What was he doing? I didn't know what to say or do to make this situation stop.

"There are heels in the box," he said.

I glanced down and sure enough, to my left was a box. I bent down and didn't realize how close he was standing, and that my ass actually nestled against his crotch. Standing back up, I moved quickly, this time crouching down as far as the tight dress would allow. I opened the box and looked at the red, shiny shoes. I was not someone who knew fashion. They looked painful and expensive. I wasn't going to ask him for a pair of sneakers.

Walking in the small heels on my wedding day had been a challenge. Whenever I could, I'd snuck away to take the shoes off. When I realized how long my dress was, I'd toed them off and walked around barefoot. Until my mother realized what I was doing, and told me to stop being an animal and to wear the damn shoes.

Sliding my feet into these heels, I knew I wasn't going to make it past the night without breaking my neck. They were way too high.

"Perfect," Andrei said. He moved away.

Was I expected to follow?

With his back turned away from me, I chanced a couple of steps in the too-big heels, and winced. They were going to hurt my feet. The shoes were a perfect fit but for a woman who'd spent her life in flats, my poor feet would pay the price. I should have taken time growing up to learn how to walk in heels. They were the ultimate weapon, apparently.

"Move it," Andrei said.

Hands clenched, I rushed my steps, praying I didn't look like a penguin walking. Would it have killed him to at least be a little nice? I was trying here. At least he got to go out and explore the world. He wasn't trapped in a penthouse suite, dying a little every single day. I didn't demand this marriage, he did.

My lips remained closed. There was no way I'd have the guts to say this to his face. He'd kill me and laugh as he did it. All I could do was hope he'd be in a good mood later on so that I could request to leave the penthouse at least once a week. That wasn't too hard, was it?

****

Andrei

I didn't like when Ivan came to my city. Especially when it wasn't planned, out of the blue, and one week into my marriage. I had nothing to hide from him, apart from the fact I'd not fucked her.

Every day for the past week, I'd arrived home to find her fast asleep. I'd lain in bed and waited for sleep to claim me. I'd never been a hard sleeper. Years of waiting for my dad to come and take his anger and aggression out on me had done that. I always slept now with one eye open. Did she know how many weapons I had close by?

There was always a gun beneath my pillow, as well as two underneath our bed. Another in the drawer. Our penthouse was full of weapons to grab in case of an ambush.

Adelaide kept trying to pull the dress down. It had ridden up the moment she sat in the car, and that was how I liked it. Seeing that blue dress on the bed, I didn't want her to wear that, to hide from who she was. My wife had an amazing body. Curves in all the right places. To some, she might be considered fat, but to me, I happened to like looking at her curves. The only saving grace about her wedding dress had been what it did for her tits. They should be on constant display. My men knew to look away, and any man caught staring at my woman would feel my anger. Adelaide was all mine.

Now, some men might prefer their women to cover up, to hide their bodies for their own viewing pleasure. Not me. I didn't want to see her drowned in clothing. Adelaide hid enough as it was.

I'm aware she's pissed off. Did she know I watched her? Did she know I had cameras in every single room of the house? That all it took was a few presses on my cell phone, and I could see what she was doing every single second of every day? I doubted it.

She was going crazy. Staying in the penthouse all day, every single day, was starting to take its toll. Ivan was screwing with my plans. Ever since he'd changed

Bethany for Adelaide, his meddling hadn't been appreciated. A whore like Bethany knew of our world. Adelaide should never have been my wife. She wasn't made for this.

"Where are we going?" she asked.

I ignored her and stared at my cell phone, scrolling through the endless emails.

"So, we've been married for one week," Adelaide said.

"Shut up." I wasn't interested in knowing how long we'd been married. I was not stupid. I could count.

She tensed and moved a little closer to the door. Did she really think that would help her? Putting my cell phone away, I stared at her exposed thigh. Her legs were pressed together. The tempting white flesh of her knee was too good to ignore.

"Circle the block, Leo," I said.

I closed the distance between us and placed my hand on her thigh. She gasped, her hands moving as if to push me away. Bethany had warned her. I knew her vile sister would spread her gossip. Bethany wasn't wrong. I did like to fuck. I loved having a woman's cunt on my dick. I liked it rough. Hearing a woman moan as I pounded away inside her, holding her into place, marking her, was the best feeling in the world. What the bitch hadn't said to Adelaide was I'd never touched her.

I hated Bethany. Marrying her was all a business deal. I didn't want my spunk inside that nasty cunt. Nope. Ivan hadn't told me about the baby part of things. That had come after I put my ring on Adelaide's finger, and my name taking hers.

"Thank you for putting on the red dress," I said.

I had to wonder if she would fight me or give in. Teasing my fingers against her knee, I slid them between her thighs, or tried to, but she pressed them together tightly. That was fine. I stroked along her thigh, teasing the fabric of the dress where it lay. It looked to me like she had stopped breathing.

"What was wrong with the blue?"

"I didn't like it, Adelaide. You want to do things that please me, don't you?"

She didn't respond.

"What's the matter, Adelaide? Don't you want to talk to me?" I asked.

"I … I don't want to be … your penthouse, it's too much."

"You can change any part of the penthouse you want."

She shook her head. "That's not what I meant."

"Then tell me what you mean?"

Adelaide opened her mouth, closed it, opened it again. She had such lovely plump lips that would look so good wrapped around my dick. She was a virgin. Ivan made that perfectly clear. I don't know how he got those details out of her, but he'd been more than happy to let me know.

Stroking her thigh, I wonder if she would like fucking. I could teach her. I had the patience, especially when I'd be the one to reap the rewards. Having boring sex seemed dull. We're going to be married for a long time, unless it turns out she's got a mean streak we don't know about, or she's not loyal. Ivan makes sure everyone is loyal before they're marked.

"We're here, sir," Leo said.

Fuck.

The moment was wasted, and I couldn't keep Ivan waiting too long.

The valet knows not to go for my doors. The last man that tried it ended up with a broken wrist. I don't allow anyone to touch my car. Leo's already out of the car and opening my door.

I climb out, run my hands down my jacket, not a wrinkle in sight, then round the car to my wife. The title is still foreign to me. I'd vowed never to take a wife, but what Ivan decreed, I followed. Holding the door handle, I pull it open. Offering her my other hand, I wait.

Adelaide nibbles on her lip, hesitant to take my hand, but before a scene could be caused, her hand slides right into mine, exactly where it's meant to be. I help her out of the car, place my hand at her waist, and head inside.

Ivan's already at the table waiting. The maître d' leads us to the center of the room, where I'm surprised to see Slavik and his wife Aurora at the table. This isn't my first visit with Slavik, nor will it be our last.

I shook hands with Ivan and then Slavik, before taking Aurora's hand and giving it a kiss just to piss him off, in greeting. While I'm doing that, Ivan's already moving Adelaide close to him. Aurora's on one side, my wife on the other. He's done it on purpose, the asshole, but I can't say anything at risk of causing a scene.

"Now isn't this nice?" Ivan said. "Two beautiful ladies here to eat dinner with."

"I didn't know this would be a family affair," I said, looking at Slavik. He takes a swig of water.

Slavik and I don't trust each other. We never have, but that's our personalities. Surviving in this world is knowing you don't have anyone at your back. I didn't even trust Leo. People were fickle and could be easily swayed. The only person I did trust was the one person I swore my loyalty to—Ivan.

He'd given me the greatest gift of all. The ability to wipe out every single person in my family line, from my father, all my brothers, their wives, and beyond. The only living male heir with the Belov name is me.

"Surprises are all well and good," Ivan said. "These two lovely ladies need to know each other. They got along so well at the wedding."

I watch Adelaide, who offered Aurora a smile.

"Weddings do bring people together," Slavik said.

Adelaide and Aurora might become friends, but not yet, and not now. I'm not sure of my wife's loyalty to Volkov. She's an outsider. She doesn't know how the Bratva work, and until she has complete and total loyalty to me and Ivan, there will be no reaching out to others, not even Aurora.

Slavik has his own area to protect, and his place is not near mine.

I pick up the menu and chance a glance through it to see if there's anything I want to eat. I'm a steak man, have been for a long time. All those years of diving in dumpsters, I vowed that one day I'd never do that again. Good food was a necessity.

Adelaide reached for the menu, but Ivan took it from her. "I know this restaurant, sweetheart. Let me order for you."

I gritted my teeth. Was he doing this on purpose? I was aware he liked to play between Aurora and Slavik, but that was their own business. They had a history.

Other than changing my bride against my wishes, Ivan, as far as I knew, had nothing to do with Adelaide in the past. In fact, at all the family dinners, my current wife was never present. Bethany and her parents never talked about the other member of their family. She never attended celebrity events and was often kept out of the media.

I knew why. They were ashamed of her, often referring to her as the Ugly One.

The name alone angered me, for Adelaide was in

fact a beautiful woman. She had the sweetest smile and the sexiest laugh. I was surprised years of being put down hadn't affected her, but seeing her tonight in that dress, I'd already noticed a dozen men looking at her. They wanted to bed my virgin bride, but none of them were getting within touching distance.

I had the overwhelming urge to pull my gun out and shoot them all right in the eyes. Blood had always been a lovely sight to me, and the day I painted my old family home red had been a joyful day.

Some would say I'm a little warped, but that is a kindness I don't deserve. I know there's a darkness inside me. It's cold and part of me is dead inside. A man like me should never be near the innocence of Adelaide. For now, she's safe. This is all new to her. I've not exposed her to the real me, but the moment she realizes what I am, she'll hate me.

"She'll have the steak," I said.

Ivan chuckled. "Have you not gotten to know your wife?"

I clench my jaw. "Is there something wrong with steak?"

"I don't like it," Adelaide said after a few seconds of silence. "I never have." She looked down at the table, avoiding my gaze.

"Then she'll have the chicken," I said. I do not want Ivan ordering for my woman. Adelaide is mine. There were plenty of other virgins out there in the world. He wasn't having mine.

Ivan snorted.

Adelaide nibbled her lip. "I'm a … vegan. I don't eat any kind of meat."

"And that's why, Andrei, I chose this restaurant. They have the best marinated tofu. I cater to all tongues, including your sweet wife's."

There is a great deal I don't know about Adelaide, but a vegan? Why did he have me marry her? She would be eaten alive in this world. There was no room for her or for us. She was far too innocent and I knew I had no choice but to break her.

Chapter Three

Adelaide

I didn't announce my veganism to the world. What was the point? I wasn't doing it out of protest. When I was younger I stumbled onto an exposé documentary of what happened in the meat industry, and considering how much I loved animals, I stopped eating them. My mother loved the idea because I was on yet another diet in her eyes. Also, my parents didn't cook.

We had a chef, who happened to love the challenge, and so I was fed really well, much to my mother's annoyance. My weight fluctuated but I never changed my eating habits for weight loss. I like who I am. In fact, I love who I am.

Something Miss Nicole always said to me: *"If you can't love yourself, who do you expect to love you?"*

Or it was something like that. I found her words of wisdom to be completely wise. I missed her when she left, but her true passion had been to travel, and the moment an opportunity arose, she left. Not that I held it against her. I didn't. I remember how happy she was.

Cutting into the slice of tofu that had lovely grill marks and a slight smokey flavor was so delicious, along with all the vegetables dressed in a gorgeous seasoning. I was in Heaven. It was so good.

I didn't pay much attention to the conversation at the table happening between Ivan, Slavik, and Andrei. My husband didn't look happy. I'm not sure if I've ever seen him happy. He'd never smiled in my presence. He sipped at his wine looking rather concentrated.

Finishing off the food, I pressed the napkin to my lips.

Aurora declared she needed to use the ladies' room, and it was the perfect opportunity for us to get away from the men.

I wanted to get away from them. In the car, the way Andrei had touched me had sent a flame shooting right through my body in a way I'd never experienced before. Was I attracted to my husband? I don't know. There was a lot I didn't know. Just like he didn't know a whole lot about me.

Getting to my feet, I followed Aurora into the bathroom. The moment the door was closed, she crouched down and looked beneath each toilet stall.

"We're alone." She spun toward me. "How are you?"

"I'm fine."

"Are you?" Aurora asked, searching my gaze.

I nod my head. "Yes, I'm perfectly fine."

"Thank God. I've been so worried about you since the wedding. You've not gone on your honeymoon?"

"No." There was no mention of us going away together, and to be honest, why would we? "Our marriage isn't a love match, Aurora. I don't think we'll be going on a honeymoon."

Aurora frowned. "You know you can call me anytime." She pulled out a piece of paper from her purse. "I'll be happy to talk to you."

"Thank you."

"You know, you're nothing like your sister."

I couldn't help but laugh. "That's not exactly hard for me to do."

She giggled.

"We better go back to the table," Aurora said. "I just wanted to make sure you were okay."

"I'm fine." At the wedding, Aurora had been a lifeline, but now I'm not so sure. I don't know why I suddenly feel this way, but a sense of dread is washing over me. "I do need to use the bathroom. I'll join you in a minute."

"You're sure?"

"Yeah, I'm sure." I force a smile to my lips, hoping she doesn't see the fear in my eyes.

She wraps her arms around me, holding me close for a couple of seconds. "I'm so pleased we're able to see each other again."

I wished I believed her. Paranoia was a horrible thing.

Aurora left me in the bathroom. I don't need to use the toilet, but I do need a few minutes away from the table. It was just too much. In and out, I take several deep breaths. There's nothing I can't handle.

Dinner with Bratva men—piece of cake. Plans with Aurora—easy-peasy. The moment I allow myself to think of what my life has become—a fucking nightmare.

"You're taking too long."

Jerking up, I see Andrei has entered the bathroom. It's easier for me to want to shout at him and tell him what a horrible husband he's being when he's not in the room. He looks too scary right now.

"I just needed a minute."

"What's that?" he asked, pointing to the slip of paper Aurora gave me.

"It's her phone number."

"She's worried I'm hurting you?"

"No, not like that. She's just worried because I … the wedding and stuff." I'm rambling.

Since the car, I'm not sure I want to be alone with him. I'm not used to my body reacting that way. He took a step toward me. On instinct, I stepped back. I didn't mean to do it, but I felt I needed distance from this man.

It didn't stop Andrei, he kept coming until he'd

trapped me between the wall and his body.

I should feel fear, but I don't.

This man is used to getting what he wants. I'm not what he wants. Bethany is. Would he kill me to get to my sister?

"You know, if you want something, all you have to do is ask," he said.

"There's nothing I want."

He smirked as if he knew a secret I didn't.

"You're enjoying life in the penthouse suite," he said.

"It's … fine." I was bored and he knew it. I'm not sure how he knew, but the way he looked at me, there was an understanding in his eyes. As if he knew he was doing it on purpose and that alone was enough to piss me off. "What would I need to ask for?"

"That's up to you to tell me."

The tips of his fingers traced across the skin of my cheek. "So smooth." This was my chance. I wore this revealing dress, which I happened to like, but that was beside the point. I did what he wanted me to do. I didn't want to spend another day sitting around that stupid penthouse suite.

"What if I wanted to go out?" I asked.

"To shop?"

Shopping was boring. "Perhaps." It was a start at least.

"Then all it would take from you, Adelaide, is a kiss."

I frowned. "What?"

He cupped my cheek and the flesh of his thumb rubbed across my lips. "A kiss from those lips. Not a peck either."

"You want me to kiss you?" she asked.

This wasn't fair.

"It's all the payment I'd need, and I would grant you a single wish. Anything but divorce." He leaned in close, and I felt his breath fan across my face. He was so close. "Think about it."

He pulled away, and the moment was lost.

"Ivan's waiting for us." He went to the door and my alone time was over. This was his order.

Squaring my shoulders, I stepped out of the bathroom. I didn't get too far before his hand was on my hip, guiding me back to the table where dessert was already waiting for me.

"Is everything okay?" Ivan asked.

"Fine," Andrei said. "I have to wonder, where is your date tonight?"

Ivan laughed. "I don't have time for dates when I can enjoy the pleasure of your lovely wives."

Andrei's hand gripped me a little tighter. He let me go so I could take a seat.

A chocolate mousse waited for me.

"I hope you don't mind, Adelaide, the vegan mousse here is simply to die for."

On the outside Ivan may seem like a good guy, however, I got this sense that he was anything but. He was the head of the Volkov Bratva, the man my husband swore loyalty to, and took his orders from. It was because of him that I was now married. He wouldn't listen to my father's concerns that I wasn't the kind of woman destined to be a brigadier's wife.

Anyone else should have felt shame because of their family's constant put-downs, but not me. I was used to it, and I'd been able to build a very strong wall around myself. Their nasty comments no longer bothered me.

"Have a taste."

I swept my spoon through the dark mixture and took a bite. The moment the mousse hit my tongue, my mouth watered. There was no denying it was a delicious mix.

"Yum," I said.

Out of the corner of my eye, I saw Andrei shake his head. Have I embarrassed him? I don't know the proper protocol for a brigadier's wife. I'm surrounded by men who do bad things, but no one is telling me what the rules are.

Aurora seemed content to be silent and allow whatever was happening to go on. I'm not like that. Without knowing the rules, I fuck up. It's inevitable. All my father told me to do was follow my husband's orders, to not make waves, and under no circumstances was I to ever go to the police.

My family were not pillars of the community. They were not good people. I'd seen a great deal of crap at their parties—drugs, orgies—I was very much aware of it. I'm a virgin in body but not in mind.

"I'm glad you approve."

I didn't want to eat the mousse. The dress felt too tight all of a sudden and my throat felt like it was on fire. My time alone was way too short. Panic filled my lungs and threatened to burst.

"Just breathe. Whenever it feels like it's getting too much and you have no way out, practice your breathing. Slowly take it all in, and then hold it, and then release, slowly, with control. No one controls your breath, Adelaide, only you do." Miss Nicole's words were a security blanket to me.

At a time like this, I was the one in control. My father had taken my future, as had Ivan and Andrei. I was at the Bratva's mercy, but that didn't mean I couldn't have control over my body or the way I reacted.

Andrei may be embarrassed over me now, but I'd learn. I would find a way to fit into this way of life.

There was no way Bethany would be right about this. I wouldn't die at my husband's hands. I could live through this.

We finished dessert, had some coffee, and then Ivan made his excuses. He was the first to leave, and I noticed the four men that followed him out. I hadn't even noticed them waiting for the boss. They blended into the scenery so easily.

Slavik was next to go with Aurora. There was politeness, but nothing else. There was no warm welcome between the two.

Finally, Andrei and I left. He put his hand at the base of my back, leading me out to where Leo waited with the doors open. Andrei waited for me to enter before he climbed in beside me.

Trapped, alone in the car, I had to wonder if Andrei was telling the truth. Would he let me leave the penthouse if I kissed him? Why would he want a kiss from me? None of this made any sense.

The dinner had been far too stressful. The food had tasted delicious. I'd enjoyed it, but everything else had been a challenge. I wasn't used to Bratva politics.

I don't fit in. And I had a horrible feeling I never would.

****

Andrei

Screams filled the air and it was such a pleasing sound to me. Pulling out the fingernails of the piece of shit rat that squealed was satisfying to me. He'd worked in the finance department at one of my casinos. It was one of the places I used to help work the cash through to get it clean.

It made the most sense, seeing as a whole lot of cash could be won, and there weren't a whole lot of eyes on it. It was one of the many areas we worked. I'm a businessman, with a lot of businesses under my belt, some of them not even associated with the Bratva name, which was how Ivan liked it. Last night I got a call from one of my informants within law enforcement, and he gave me details of a meeting between this little rat and one of the cops determined to bring the Bratva down. It was not going to happen. The truth was, I was in the mood for torture, especially after the dinner I had the other night with Ivan.

He clearly has something he wants to say to me, or point out, but I don't know what. I'm married to the bride he fucking chose. Bethany was more than a suitable candidate, and sure, I hated the bitch, but at least she knew what she was getting into. She liked it as well.

There were times during our *dates* she'd ask me just how far I went, how much blood I'd spilled. She even knew of my deadly reputation and rather than terrify her, it excited her. Again, I didn't give a fuck. Bethany was a slut. When Ivan found out she was horrid to Aurora, I didn't expect him to change her position. He went so far as to lure her into bed with other men and film the sessions, then threw it in her parents' faces. Within a matter of minutes Bethany was out of favor, and suddenly, my intended was the sister. The young, virginal, sweet sister. The one who stayed as far away from me and Ivan as humanly possible without insulting anyone.

My annoyance wasn't being sated with torturing this asshole. Under different circumstances, the sound of screams and the dark spillage of blood helped to cool my mind. Not today. I'd already gotten all the information I needed, but I wasn't a man who was known for doing things lightly. If you crossed me and Ivan, then it was a guaranteed death sentence. Nothing more. Nothing less. There was no way out of it once you committed a sin like that. You were well and truly fucked.

Staring at the rat now, dripping with blood, stinking of piss and shit, I was done. Drawing out my blade, I slid it right across his neck, ending his misery way too soon.

Without a word, I left the warehouse, grabbed my jacket that Leo held, and made my way toward the car. No one said a word to me. They knew not to disturb me during a time like this. Once inside the car, I pulled out my cell phone, typed in the password, and found the security camera app with a view of my penthouse suite.

She still hadn't kissed me.

I found her within seconds, lying down, her legs dangling across the arms of the sofa, kicking them out. Her hands were pointing up, swaying back and forth, and she was looking so fucking bored. That's what I wanted—her desperate and hungry. Begging. Adelaide would look so cute on her knees, begging me.

I didn't turn up the sound but from the way her lips were moving, I could tell she was singing. The temptation to turn the volume up was strong, but I refrained from doing so. Listening to my wife sing would be far too much of a distraction, and I had more business to attend to.

I logged out of the app and ordered Leo to take me to the casino. I needed to make my presence known there first, and to also account for all the log books, while keeping an eye on any potential new faces.

The Feds had a way of appearing randomly. Some of them came to the casino dressed in civilian clothes, but I knew they were there to case the place. To see for themselves if I was prepared at a moment's notice for a possible invasion. It pissed me off, but again, it was all part of the fun and games.

Leo arrived at the private underground parking.

Climbing out of the car, I buttoned up my jacket, which hid the bloodstains. My hands were also tinted with it.

This was a risk, but I always got a thrill out of the prospect of showing who I really was. Getting caught didn't scare me. There was no way they'd be able to hold my ass for long.

We moved toward the elevator doors together. Typing in my code, I didn't have to wait for them to open. I stepped inside and pressed down to the basement.

"Terrance sent me a message. Adelaide tried to leave again today. She said you had agreed to it."

"Did he allow her to leave?" Andrei asked.

"No."

"Good."

I knew Leo didn't approve of my method of dealing with Adelaide. Other brigadiers would have chosen men they trusted to spend time with their wives, to keep them safe, and to keep other men away.

Not me. There was no man I trusted with Adelaide. No one I wanted to leave next to her, day in and day out. She was my wife. No one else would get the pleasure of her company. Not that I spent a whole lot of time with her. I hadn't granted myself the luxury.

"Sir, can I speak freely?" Leo asked.

"Not about my wife. No."

"Sir?"

"I'm handling her the best way I know how. If you don't like it, then you can leave." Which was a death sentence. Once part of the Bratva, there was no escaping it.

The doors opened and I stepped off. My presence made the room immediately freeze. Men and women, counting piles of cash, doing their job. Glancing over the people, I noted there were no new faces. Everyone here had been working for me for quite some time. They all knew not to fuck with me. Still, it didn't hurt every now and then to appear, to let them see me.

They had all seen me kill a man. Admittedly, it had been to save them, seeing as he'd brought a gun to this place in the hope of killing me and ending the Bratva, which was so fucking cute. There was no end to Volkov. No way of outing the best man that had ever come to this place.

I'd not been kind to the man who threatened to kill my staff. I'd been a mean motherfucker and they all saw it, and in doing so, they had sworn their loyalty to Ivan. Once I was satisfied nothing was amiss, I left the basement and went to my main office. Leo left me alone long enough to change. I stuffed my clothes into a bag, which I handed to Leo to dispose of.

Rather than leave the casino, I decided to check the basic running of the place. Sitting behind the desk, I logged into the computer, drawing up the emails, and reading through them. There was enough to keep me occupied.

Working my way through each one, the temptation to reach for my cell phone and to see Adelaide was strong, which didn't bode well for me. Women were a weakness.

Adelaide meant nothing to me. I had no reason to be so … intent on seeing her. I reached for my cell phone, but stopped myself from logging in to see what she was doing. She was just a woman.

My wife.

My still virginal wife.

Gritting my teeth, I tossed the cell phone into my drawer and continued with my work.

As I was about to reach for my cell for the fifth fucking time, my office door opened. I was about to yell at whoever dared enter my office, but I kept my mouth shut as I watched Ivan Volkov enter the room.

After years of being his brigadier, I knew he didn't want any special greeting. Even though he was the Pakhan, the boss, he never wanted to be treated as such, unless he requested it.

"Hello, Andrei," Ivan said.

"Volkov."

"How come you've not booked a honeymoon?"

I frowned. "A honeymoon?"

"It's what new couples enjoy after getting married." Ivan grabbed my hand and pointed to the band wrapped around my ring finger. I'd picked the ring out. It was silver, plain, and could have been mistaken for anything. "In case you didn't know, you're married."

"I know."

"So, what about the honeymoon?"

Ivan let go of my hand and I sat back, looking at him. "You've come all this way to berate me for dealing with work? I dealt with a rat this morning, who was quite happy to snitch."

"Ah, yes, but you see, you've got a very lovely wife at home."

"I know what I've got at home." A complication.

"I'd have expected this behavior if you'd married Bethany."

"Adelaide shouldn't be my wife."

"Not only is she your wife, but she will be the mother of your child, but then, you'd actually have to fuck her to do that," Ivan said.

I gritted my teeth to keep from talking. He knew I hadn't taken her on our wedding night.

Ivan smiled. "I like that you don't lie to me, Andrei. I do like that about you. It's one of your few rare qualities."

"What brings you here?"

"I've got some business to attend to in Slavik's territory. No matter what you hear, you are not to respond to it, am I understood?"

"I'm not sure I follow."

"Simple. You're not to move from your territory. I will call you with an update, do you understand?"

I didn't like this. Slavik and Ivan were planning something. I hated being kept out of the loop, but this was my job.

"Yes, sir."

"Good." Ivan tapped his fingers on the arm of the chair. "I've been thinking about Yahontov."

Yahontov was Ivan Yahontov, but we called him Ive so as not to confuse him with Ivan. Not that you could mistake the two.

Ive was a monster to the core. I heard his territory was dark and his men were cruel. One of the rules as brigadiers is that we never got involved with other territories. We ran our places the way we saw fit.

Ive was cruel. He was evil. But with a past like his, I could totally understand that. The fact he was able to attend certain functions without drawing attention to his oddness was a miracle. Ivan liked to have strange men running things.

I was an odd choice—the unwanted son of the previous Bratva, who was in fact a soldier's son. Yes, I discovered through torturing my *father* that I wasn't his son after all. My mother had an affair with a soldier, but they didn't kill me.

My father was ordered to raise me as his own, which of course he never did. He made sure I paid every single day for my mother's betrayal. That was her punishment to see my life ruined day after day, because she had fallen in love. It was just another reason why Adelaide would never have a soldier near her.

"What about him?"

"You and Slavik are married. I think it's time Ive has a woman of his own." Ivan sat back, running a finger across his lip.

"I thought you had women picked out already?" I asked.

Ivan smiled. "No. I like to make sure the women I choose for my men are tasteful. Those women would not make it in this world."

I didn't even have a fucking clue why he picked Adelaide for me, but poor Ive. If Ivan was going to marry him off, I didn't know who I felt sorry for more.

Chapter Four

Adelaide

I was fucking bored. I was so bored that I had even given boring a new name.

The curtains were open, and that meant a perimeter was nicely built around the penthouse suite. I'd already tried to ask my guard for one day out of the penthouse without Andrei knowing. Was I given that luxury? Nope.

Moving into the kitchen, I opened and closed the doors to the fridge, then the drawers. I glanced at the notice board and saw a marker. Without thinking, I grabbed said marker, made my way toward the edge of the penthouse, as far as I could go, and got to my knees.

I drew a line, and then I carried on, until I had gotten across the room to the far wall. The moment I had done it, I realized I had drawn on a very expensive-looking wooden floor, and my heart started to race. Andrei hadn't given me permission to change anything.

I didn't have a cell phone. Even the phone in the bedroom didn't work. I couldn't find a laptop. The outside world was cut off from me, unless you counted the guard at the front door, who wouldn't even tell me his name.

This sucked.

I hated it.

Rushing to the kitchen, I grabbed a cloth, wet it, and got back to the line I'd just drawn across the floor.

"Stupid fucking thing," I said, rubbing the cloth back and forth across the line. Of course, it was permanent.

Great. Now I was going to look like a child and any hope I had of getting out of this apartment was fading, and fast. Sitting back on my heels, I pouted, and I had a sudden overwhelming need to cry.

We'd been married nearly three weeks. He'd propositioned me a few weeks ago. A single kiss. Could I kiss him? I'd never been kissed before my wedding.

Covering my face, I cried out. Did he want me to go insane? Was this part of his plan? To drive me crazy so he could divorce me, because all he needed to do was ask. I was happy to end this farce. This was not love. This was not a good marriage. It was a fucking nightmare for me.

The sound of the front door opening and closing made me panic. Getting to my feet, I spun around, quickly shoving the cloth behind the pillow on the sofa to hide it.

I expected to see Andrei home. He rarely came home early, but it had been known to happen.

It wasn't Andrei. It was Ivan Volkov.

"Hello, Adelaide."

"Mr. Volkov," I said, bowing my head. Did I look like a moron? I don't know Bratva rules. I don't know anything. Did this have to do with my father's business? Get one of his men married to the daughter, drive her crazy, kill the family in some freak accident, and take claim of the company? My paranoia needed to be put in check.

"Ivan, please," he said, moving toward me.

He grabbed my hands, lifting them to his lips. His gaze landed on the floor and he tilted his head up to look at me. "Decorating?"

"I … no. I don't suppose you know how to get marker out of the floor?"

"Why would you draw a line?"

I take a deep breath. "I have a fear of heights. It's crazy and stupid, but I've had it since I was a little kid." I pull my hands from Ivan's. He might seem like a nice guy, but every single sense was going off in my head to be careful. "Would you like something to drink?" I stopped and spun toward him. "Am I allowed to give you something to drink?"

"Do you plan to poison me?"

"What? No, of course not."

"You'd be surprised how many people close to me would love to see me dead," he said. There was a sadness in his eyes. It was only there for a fleeting second, and if I'd not been looking at him, I'd have missed it. I saw it.

He was sad.

I had an overwhelming need to hug him. To offer him comfort, so against my better judgement, I did. I stepped up to this man, who put fear into me, and I wrapped my arms around him. "It's ... it's going to be okay," I said. I had no idea what I was saying.

"You're a sweet girl," Ivan said.

He patted my back. I didn't want to be known as a sweet girl.

I took that as my cue to step back, giving him the space he needed. I shoved my hands into my jeans pockets, and hoped I hadn't broken any rules. This was awkward and so far out of my depth.

"Drink. You want a drink." I turned my back on him and rushed to the kitchen, needing to put some distance between us.

My hands shook a little as I filled the kettle.

Andrei had offered to have food sent to me, but I was happy to cook for myself. It was nice not having my mother or a chef breathing down my neck. There were small freedoms here, but not a lot. I wished I could go outside. There was so much I missed, mainly volunteering at the animal shelter.

I didn't get a reprieve from Ivan's company for

long as he entered the kitchen.

"This is nice," he said.

"Andrei does have good taste."

"I'm not sure he's aware of just how good his taste is."

I wasn't sure what he meant by that, but I didn't comment. My life depended on me being able to bite my tongue and not say a word.

Ivan stayed silent as the kettle came to a boil on the stovetop.

"Do you like tea or coffee?" I asked, presenting a box and a jar of each.

"I'll let you decide."

Again, was it wrong of me to choose for him? I settled on coffee. With Ivan Volkov here, I felt I needed to have every single part of my senses and my wits about me. This man was dangerous.

With the kettle boiled, I poured our coffee and we moved toward the sitting room. I sat on the corner of one of the sofas, sipping at the scalding liquid. I'd used plant milk for both of our drinks and I watched Ivan take a sip.

"Not too bad."

"I'm sorry I didn't have creamer or whatever it is you use." I cringed. Was that disrespectful?

Ivan chuckled. "This is just fine. So, tell me, Adelaide, how is married life treating you?"

It was on the tip of my tongue to tell him how bored I was, and how Andrei and I weren't a good match. My life would be over if I even suggested a divorce. Not that I'd seen anything. Other than the one dinner, Andrei came home when I was asleep. Our paths rarely crossed. Sometimes I'd wake up in the middle of the night to find his arms wrapped around me. It was always so dark, I wasn't sure if I felt it or not.

Pushing those thoughts to the back of my mind, I

instead focused on the man in front of me, sipping his coffee.

"It's good."

He tutted. "I don't like being lied to. Even I can see that you're at your wits end." He pointed toward the markings on the floor.

"I'm fine. Honestly."

"You know, Andrei's not a hard man to understand."

"Really?" I asked. "Then tell me why he seems intent on boring me to death." I gasped and stood. "Crap, I am so sorry. I didn't mean to ... oh, my God." I put a hand to my chest, trying to tell myself not to panic, not to worry. I had just snapped at Ivan Volkov. "I'm so, so, so sorry."

Ivan chuckled. "You are so charming. I can see what he sees in you."

"I have no idea what that means."

"Oh, I know."

He wasn't going to kill me.

Sitting down so that I was perched on the edge of the sofa, I held my cup between my hands and waited, trying to find the right words. Ivan wasn't a good person. I knew that, but he seemed reasonable. I was a fool for even thinking it.

"I ... Andrei can't stand me," I said. "I think you chose the wrong sister. I know Bethany did something wrong, and I'm sure she regrets whatever it is she did." I'm not sure if they told me what Bethany did, or if I've been so consumed with my own life that I've forgotten. "I think ... don't you think it would be better if he married someone else?"

Ivan sipped his coffee but his gaze stayed on me.

There was the fear rushing down my spine. As well as the sick feeling that I had fucked up big time.

This wasn't good. This was scary.

"You want a divorce?" Ivan asked.

"Andrei hates me. I think this is … we're not a good match."

"A man who hates you doesn't keep a guard at the door all the time. My men are not known for being fools, Adelaide. Most of them would always have a guard by your side, and yet, Andrei keeps you home … alone."

I didn't like the way he said the last part, as if I wasn't alone.

"I'm not sure I follow."

"Aurora has a guard with her at all times. If Slavik isn't around, she has someone to protect her. Andrei won't allow another man to come near you. That is not a man who hates you, Adelaide. I am going to give you a piece of advice. He has probably already told you what he needs in order for you to have more freedom. Andrei doesn't trust easily. He's a hard man. Life hasn't been kind to him, but it is his story to tell, not mine. The man you married is complicated and cruel, but believe me when I say you are the best match for him."

He sipped his coffee, and I drank mine.

It wasn't exactly a comforting speech. No part of it made any sense. Nibbling my lip, I stared straight ahead.

"I think it's time that you talked to your husband."

"He's never home."

"He's home every single night. It's time for you to stay up."

I frowned and turned toward him.

"I have my ways of finding out what I need to." Ivan smiled.

That wasn't a good look on him. Averting his

gaze, I sipped my coffee and wondered how I had gotten to be part of this life. What had I done to end up like this? Tears filled my eyes, and I hated it. I'd never been much of a crier, and I wasn't going to start now.

Andrei had given me a chance to get out of this apartment. A kiss. Was that all he wanted?

"I can't wait to see little Andreis and Adelaides running around," Ivan said.

"What?" I asked.

"You and Andrei, having kids. I'm sure he will have a nice country house waiting for you." He winked at me.

Again, he shouldn't try to be the teasing sort.

****

Andrei

Ivan was in my home. Leo informed me and I brought up the penthouse suite on my cell phone. I was at the casino across the city, nearly an hour away without traffic from my wife. I left the casino immediately.

There was traffic, and it was a nightmare. Running a hand down my face, I kept glancing over at my wife. I couldn't stand her to be alone with him. I shut down the app and tried Ivan's cell phone, which went straight to voice mail.

Anger rushed through me. I couldn't kill Ivan for being near my wife. I continued to dial his cell phone, but he never picked up. In the end, I had no choice but to watch my wife and my Pakhan as they had coffee. I wanted to know what they were saying but with Leo in the car, I wasn't interested in turning up the volume. Trust only went so far.

We were still ten minutes away when Ivan got up, and I watched him leave. Before I had chance to sign out of the app, my cell phone started to ring, and of course it was Ivan.

"Are you nearly here?" Ivan asked.

I'm not a fool. I know Ivan has spies in every territory. He is a man known for being one step ahead of the game. No one could take a shit without him knowing about it.

"Yes. What are you doing at my house?" I asked.

"You saw quite clearly that your wife is still in one piece. You're welcome. Adelaide is spending a lot of time alone. Is your intention to drive her crazy?" Ivan asked.

"She hasn't earned the right to leave," I said.

"She has a right to a cell phone, a laptop, and a guard. You won't even let the poor woman shop. Are you aware she's afraid of heights as well?"

No, I wasn't, but I wasn't going to tell him that.

Ivan laughed, as he always did, which meant he already knew the truth.

"Don't punish her too badly," Ivan said. "I really like her. She's got a whole lot of fire inside her, and if you were to train her well, she'd be a good wife to you."

I didn't need him to tell me what Adelaide would or wouldn't be. She was my wife. I was the one who would take care of her. Instead, I kept my thoughts to myself because he was still my boss.

"We'll talk soon."

Ivan hung up, and the desire to crush my cell phone was strong, but I didn't. Changing cell phones pissed me off. I preferred to keep the same one that I knew how to work.

Arriving at my penthouse building, I didn't wait for Leo to park the car. I climbed out even before he'd finished, and was near the elevator. Pressing the button to my penthouse, I waited. The ride was taking too damn long.

The guard outside my door looked afraid, but I

couldn't kill him for letting Ivan in. He outranked me, but the thought of another man being near my woman angered me.

"Leave," I said.

Terrance knew not to fuck with me and left. It was why he'd been given the guard duty. He was a good man, loyal, and wasn't easily swayed by sweet eyes.

Entering my apartment, I stormed toward my wife and found her on her knees, scrubbing away at a hideous black line.

"What the hell did you do?" I asked.

She stood up, pushing her long brown hair out of the way. I loved her hair. She never had it cut. The length was glorious, and I couldn't wait to have it wrapped around my fist.

"I'm sorry," she said. "I … I need to get out of this apartment."

"You're not leaving this place."

"Are you trying to kill me, is that it? You hate me so much that you want me to do the deed myself or something?" Her hands were clenched into fists.

This I wasn't expecting.

"You're not going to die."

"Seriously? Can't you see I'm dying already? Do you have any idea what it's like to spend every single day here, doing nothing?" She yelled each word at me. "Before you I had a life. To many, it would have been boring, but I had a life. I enjoyed leaving and being free, but I can't even have that anymore. Your boss, or whatever the fuck he is, was here, and you know what, I was scared, because I don't know this way of life. I know you're part of the Bratva, but I don't even know if I'm supposed to say that. I didn't grow up in this life. Ugh, what is the point? You should have married my sister. I'm pretty sure you would have been far happier with her."

"Are you done?" I asked.

"Why? Bored of being in this place already. Trust me. I know I am." She threw the cloth at me. "And I don't care if you're pissed off that I damaged your precious wood. What kind of an asshole lives this high up?"

I'm stunned by her language, by her aggression, and most of all by just how aroused I am. I take a step toward her, then another. With her fear in place of the heights, she doesn't move, the line keeping her in place.

Sinking my fingers into her hair, I tug her close, not to hurt, but to guide. She gasped. Her hands went to my wrist. Her touch shouldn't do anything for me. I shouldn't enjoy it. There should be no happiness at having her hands on me.

When it comes to the opposite sex, I'm the one who's always in control. They do my bidding. They are not permitted to touch me. But Adelaide is my wife. She is not like other women.

"If you want to play the victim, carry on, but I've told you exactly what you need to do in order to earn rewards."

"Are you being serious right now? You expect me to kiss you to get out of this place? To have a cell phone? To even go shopping?" she asked.

I smiled. It wasn't a nice one, and she flinched away from me as I did so, but with the hold I had on her hair, there was nowhere for her to go. She was stuck with me.

Holding her close against me, I relished the feel of her curves. They were so soft and so close. She smelled good as well, like strawberries and cream. My mouth watered for a taste.

"Do you think kissing me is so distasteful? Do

you have any idea what I could have ordered you to do?" I asked. "I could make you go on your knees, take my dick between those fuckable lips, and choke on it. Force you to swallow every single drop of my spunk. Or I could have pounded your virgin pussy. Forced you to bleed over my dick for your first time. What about your asshole?" I grabbed her ass, pulling her toward me. "If your pussy and mouth haven't seen a cock, then I bet your ass hasn't either. Forcing you to take me there, just so you could breathe fresh air. So, the next time you think I'm a monster, why don't you compare my request to the other things I could have forced you to do?"

"I hate you."

"Get in line. There's a long list of women who hate me."

This time, she fought against me. I could make her accept me. Kiss her. Make her give me my due. My dick hadn't seen a pussy in a long time, and I was well past due emptying my balls. With Adelaide, I didn't even need to use a condom. She was supposed to be getting pregnant with my kid, but that wasn't going to happen until I fucked her.

I let her leave and run away toward our bedroom. I'd give her a few minutes to gain her bearings, and then I'd seek her out. Annoying the fuck out of her was part of my plan. Hurting and raping her was not. Nor was terrifying her.

Some men couldn't handle facing off with me. Adelaide was just a woman. I should have gone easier on her.

I moved toward my office, removed my jacket, and threw it across the chair. The scotch called to me. I made my way over to the drink, poured myself a generous shot, and drank it straight down, enjoying the burn.

A memory of my father flashed through my mind. I couldn't have been much older than six or seven. My mother had asked me to go and grab the photograph album she'd left in his office. I had been a klutz back then, and as I lifted the heavy book, I knocked his bottle of vodka off the table. The glass had smashed. He'd entered as I tried to clean it up, and as punishment, he'd grabbed the glass and slashed me right across the arm, three times. I was bleeding, he'd punched me in the gut, and tossed me out into the cold. Three days later, the doctor had come to fix me up. I'd nearly died of infection.

Pushing the memory to the back of my mind, I put the glass down and made my way toward the bedroom.

Adelaide wasn't there. I heard the sound of the shower running, and I walked toward the door. Her clothes were on the floor, and I saw the outline of her body in the frosted glass. My dick hardened. She was my wife. Mine.

After removing my clothes, I eased them onto the floor and stepped toward the shower. Opening the door to the stall, I stepped inside and heard her gasp.

She wrapped her arms around her body and turned her back to me, but I was a man who liked a woman's ass, and the one she presented me with was sheer fucking perfection. Rounded, juicy, almost a little too big, but a generous handful.

I closed the door, moved in closer, and she stepped forward to try and keep some distance from me. There was nowhere for her to go. Reaching past her so that our bodies touched, I grabbed the soap.

"What are you doing?" she asked.

"Taking a shower."

"I can't even have one of those alone anymore?"

I smiled, lathering up my hands with soap. "Tell me, Adelaide, do you want to live?"

"What kind of question is that?" she asked.

"A real one."

"Of course I want to live. Who wouldn't?"

Putting my hands on her hips, I pulled her back against me. She was so damn tense. "Then I will start to teach you tomorrow morning," I said. There wasn't much to teach, not really. Ivan liked to consider this new era of Bratva to be modern, thinking outside of the box, and making sure our enemies didn't have a fucking clue what to do.

Adelaide was too adorable to show disrespect, and I could imagine Ivan would find her cute as well. He wasn't a stickler for tradition unless he faced someone he hated, and then he made sure tradition was served.

I slid my hands around to her stomach, feeling the roundness of her flesh. I'd never been a man who liked a skinny woman. When I was younger, I'd been with a couple, and they'd always whimpered and complained about how I touched them. They couldn't handle a man like me. Adelaide was built to take me. To be mine.

I couldn't help but wonder what it would be like to finally father a child. To have my baby growing inside her. Adelaide would make a wonderful mother. She was a kind soul, which marveled me from the household she grew up in.

"As for the rest, Adelaide, all you've got to do is kiss me, and what you desire will be yours."

Chapter Five

Adelaide

A kiss.

That was all he asked. A single kiss. Not a peck on the lips, but a proper kiss. I remembered his terms and it was so easy to think that a kiss would be just a simple brushing of lips, nothing too hard or strenuous. But it wasn't that simple.

To most people with experience, it meant nothing. I had never kissed anyone, other than Andrei at our wedding, and did that really count? It was part of the binding. Husband and wife, that kind of thing.

This was … horrible.

The penthouse apartment was driving me crazy. It was a beautiful place to stay but I hated it. I needed fresh air. Freedom. I'd never been trapped for so long.

Andrei wasn't wrong about teaching me. At least, if he called what he did most mornings a teaching. There was no lesson. He told me that Ivan was a Pakhan, the boss, and I had to show him respect. That was lesson one. Great, as if I didn't know that. Lesson two, I got to know the main brigadiers. I knew him and Slavik. Then there was Ivan—but we referred to him as Ive—Yahontov, Victor Abdulov, Peter Orlov, and Oleg Pavlov. I couldn't remember meeting them.

Each lesson was pointless. They didn't give me the rules and he was doing it on purpose.

Ivan's words came back to haunt me: *"That is not a man who hates you, Adelaide. I am going to give you a piece of advice. He has probably already told you what he needs for you to have more freedom. Andrei doesn't trust easily."*

I shouldn't care about him.

Andrei could handle himself, but even as I

thought it, I couldn't help but wonder about the man I'd married. What had made him this way? Why didn't he trust easily? Who had hurt him in the past? Why did it bother me? It's not like he was a good person. This was the man he wanted to be. Who he chose to be.

But that didn't mean I couldn't wonder about him.

He always got in late. The last couple of nights, I heard him arrive home, but I chickened out of kissing him, pretending to be asleep, until I finally drifted off before he even made it to bed.

Tonight, I'd drunk coffee—a lot of it. I enjoyed coffee but usually I gave myself a cut-off time so that I wasn't wired all the time.

He didn't come to the bedroom. For a good twenty minutes I lay in bed listening, waiting for him to arrive, but nothing.

Pushing the blankets off, I slid my feet into my slippers and went to find him. I wore a pair of pajama shorts and a tank, quite modest compared to the negligees neatly folded in the drawers. Stepping out of the bedroom, I waited a moment, unable to hear him. He wasn't in the kitchen or the living room. The dining room was clear, which left the small library, study, his office, or the spare bedroom.

I decided to check his office, and sure enough, that's where I found him, standing at the floor-to-ceiling window, enjoying a glass of liquor, staring out across the city.

The moment I entered, he pulled out a gun and pointed it directly at me. I froze into place. This was the first time a gun had been pointed at me. I held my hands out in front of me.

"You shouldn't be sneaking around," he said.

"I wasn't."

"Why are you awake?"

"I … er … I heard you come in." This wasn't going according to plan. I had hoped he'd come into the bedroom, get ready for bed, and I could kiss him quickly and swiftly in the hope of getting out of the penthouse tomorrow.

This was confrontation. This required me to look at him.

"Do you know what today is?"

"No?" I asked. He didn't need me to be smart with him and tell him the date, month, and year.

"This is the anniversary of my father's death," he said.

"Oh, I'm so sorry."

He burst out laughing. "Oh, sweetheart, you don't have to be sorry for that. I was the one who killed him."

I'd never been privy to his past. I'd never heard of him doing anything wrong, at least not before tonight. There was always the hint in the news, across the media, and amongst the circles my parents were part of. This was … I didn't know what to say.

"The bastard had it coming," Andrei said.

How the fuck should I respond to that?

"You do know the Bratva isn't some childish gang where we share secrets with one another. It's a blood loyalty." He put his glass on the edge of the desk and moved toward me. I stayed perfectly still, watching, waiting.

Button by button, he started to open his shirt, revealing his muscular and heavily inked chest. The only time I'd seen him up close was out of the corner of my eye in the shower, but I'd not faced him. Not as he washed himself. I'd kept my back to him, trying to keep my body covered, from my husband. It wasn't how I imagined a marriage to be.

The shirt fell to the floor.

"You can't see it, but you can still feel." He reached for my hand, pulled me close, and put my hand on his arm. "This is where he slashed me for breaking his fucking vodka bottle. I nearly died because of it." Next, my hand went to his stomach. "He beat me so hard, I was pissing blood. Here is where the buckle of his belt slashed me."

He ran my hands over his body, which was covered in scars, most of them from his father. Tears filled my eyes as I imagined Andrei as a scared little boy.

"So, when the opportunity came to kill him, I took it." He held his arms open wide. "I am the only surviving Belov, Adelaide. The only one of my line and I'm loyal to Ivan Volkov. The bastard son of the previous Pakhan. You want the rules to survive. You're loyal to him. You swear your life to him, and to me. You don't see or hear anything. You see me covered in blood, you help wash it off. You bear my children. You belong to me, and in return, you will have a life you only ever dreamed of." He dropped his hands. "That is what your father wanted. To have our wealth and power, and to do it, he gave us you. Betray us, and you will long for death before I grant it."

I'd never seen him like this. "Is this to scare me?"

"Not to scare, to make you aware. I've got many enemies. Ivan has many enemies. There are plenty of people in this world who will want us dead, and they would have no qualms about using you to get what they want."

This was the reality. He was giving me exactly what I wanted to know and yet right at that moment, I wasn't sure if I could handle it. My husband was warning me. Telling me that if I didn't learn to accept this life, then I was dead. There was no way out. I was to stay by his side, be loyal to him and to Ivan, until I either died or was killed. There were no cops to save me.

Andrei would kill me if I betrayed them.

My parents had done this because they couldn't stand to be penniless. They handed me over without a bat of the eye. None of them thought I could handle this. Anger filled me.

"Do you keep your word?" I asked.

"What?"

"When you make deals or promises, do you keep them?"

"Yes." There was no hesitation.

"Then I promise you, Andrei Belov, that I will never turn my back on you. I will never seek out anyone to hurt you or to hurt Ivan Volkov." I take a step toward him, knowing that my words don't matter, not really. Andrei doesn't trust. Loyalty to him must be shown and earned.

Even as every single sense within my body repelled and told me to run, to get as far away from this man and this life as physically possible, a part of me, a small, tiny sliver, didn't want to.

Andrei intrigued me.

He terrified me in equal measure, but there was no doubt in my mind that I also liked him. This was stupid of me to even think that. He'd shown no inclination to like me or care for me. I was not the woman for him.

And yet, sleeping beside him, night after night, feeling his arms wrapped around me, was comforting. Even down to the fact he locked me up in this penthouse suite to protect me, I wasn't sure. There was a lot I didn't know or understand.

I was within touching distance now. All I had to do was reach up, put my hands on his chest, and feel him, but I didn't do that. I simply held myself completely still.

His naked chest was so tempting. Why did I hold myself back?

I lifted my hands and moved to touch him, but he grabbed my wrists and stopped me.

"What are you doing?" he asked.

To tell him I was going to kiss him seemed a little lame to me, and totally out of place. Nibbling my lip, I glance over his shoulder, trying to think of the right thing to say. Instead, I step toward him so he has no choice but to move our hands, or have them against his skin. Did he hate me touching him, or just touch in general?

"I'm here to give you payment," I said.

We were going to be in a constant vicious cycle if one of us didn't give in, and I was not ashamed to need my space. Kissing Andrei would mean something to him, but I imagined he'd been with plenty of women whose kisses didn't matter. Just a physical action to him he'd done thousands of times, if not more. I had to learn to keep my emotions in check. This kiss wouldn't mean a thing. I hoped.

"You're not a whore," he said.

I flinched. I couldn't help it. "You were the one who said I had to kiss you to get out of this damn apartment. I don't have to be insulted by you. I'm not a whore. How dare you!" If he didn't hold my wrists, I'd have slapped him right across his smug, arrogant face. As it was, he had my wrists and as I tried to tug them free, it was pointless. He was the one who held all the power.

Growling, I was about to raise my knee when suddenly my hands were released, but I didn't have time to react because within the next seconds, his lips were on mine. The kiss started out soft, a simple brush of our lips, and I expected it to be over. It certainly would have been a lot easier if it had, but Andrei had other ideas.

His hands sank into my hair, holding me close, gripping me tightly as his tongue traced across my bottom lip. A whimper escaped me and that was all he needed to gain entry. He plunged inside, making me moan as he deepened the kiss.

This was a real kiss.

Not sweet or gentle, but an all-consuming passion that stole my breath and made me hate and crave him just a little bit more.

Who was this man, this husband of mine? I had no idea, but with kisses like that, I knew I would happily follow him into hell.

****

Andrei

Cinnamon buns, purchased at a fucking vegan deli, no less. Strong coffee with plant milk, at the same place, and before me lay Adelaide's cell phone, laptop, and the credit card I'd acquired with my name.

All I waited for was Adelaide to make an appearance.

I'd already told Leo that he wasn't needed today. Terrance was on guard duty, where he needed to be. There would always be guards nearby waiting to protect.

I sat enjoying my coffee, and sure enough, I didn't have to wait long before Adelaide stumbled out of our bedroom, still dressed in shorts and a tank top. Her long brown hair was a mess. She looked like she'd been fucked long and hard into the night. All I'd done was kiss her and send her to bed. By the time I joined her, she'd been fast asleep.

Keeping Adelaide in the dark wasn't bright. I knew that. Last night, the anniversary of my father's death, I always went to dark places. There was no controlling it. That day was the best of my life—where I could finally release the chains he had on me and become my own man.

I was a man who prided myself that I feared nothing, and yet, when it came to my father, my biggest fear of all was that I'd turn out to be exactly like him. It's why I wasn't in a rush to father children. Like always, I'd make sure to do my duty for Ivan, but that didn't mean I was in a rush.

I had two years. Two years of having Adelaide all to myself. I was a selfish man, and if that was all I had, I would enjoy every single moment.

"You're still here?" she asked.

"Sit," I said. "A vegan cinnamon bun and a coffee."

"You're amazing." She pulled out her chair, took a chunk of the bun, and shoved it in her mouth. She chewed for a few seconds before she moaned. The sound was deep and went straight to my cock. Next she had a sip of her coffee.

"I've gone to Heaven."

Good for her, because I was in Hell.

She licked her lips, lifted the cinnamon bun to her mouth, and then her gaze was back on me. "Is everything okay?"

"As you can see, I've got your cell phone, your laptop, and your credit card in front of me."

"You had these with you the whole time?" Adelaide asked.

"Today you've earned the chance to leave this penthouse. I will take you wherever you want to go."

"Wait? You're coming with me?" she asked.

I nod.

"How can that be freedom?"

"It's nonnegotiable." It was either me or one of my men and I didn't appreciate anyone else being near my wife.

She put the bun down. "You knew this even before the kiss. You changed the rules."

"I was the one who kissed you last night. I'm being nice to you. The least you can do is not be a brat."

"Oh, my … you think I'm being a brat."

"You will not be leaving this penthouse alone. I'll be by your side."

"Ugh, you know what? Fine." She slammed her coffee down on the table and marched away, only she didn't go far. I watched her ass that was far too covered in the shorts she wore. She stopped and turned back toward me, and this time her hands went to my face. I grabbed her wrists, but she slammed her lips down on mine, and I held her there, enjoying the soft feel of her mouth on mine.

To test how far she was willing to go, I stick my tongue out and trace across her lip, waiting for her to either tell me to leave her alone, or jerk back. She did neither, and kissed me a little harder. Running my thumb across the pulse at her inner palm, I waited to see what she was going to do, but it wasn't long before she jerked back. "I earned that!" She went for the cell phone, but I picked it up before she could. "What are you doing?"

"You'll get this when I find out why you want it so bad."

"Seriously?"

"Yes."

"It's my cell phone. I had a whole life before I was married to you. I had friends," she said.

"Get rid of them."

"No!"

I pocketed her cell phone. "I suggest you go and get dressed before my good mood disappears."

"You're an asshole."

I smiled to which she glared. Her hand turned

into a fist, and I expected her to hit me, but instead she rounded on her heel and marched away. Her ass was a temptation. I couldn't wait to get my hands on it, to explore her beautiful body. I'd have Adelaide come apart within seconds if she gave me the chance.

My dick ached. I wanted her so badly. So, so bad.

I craved her.

Hungered for her.

Was desperate for her.

But, I controlled myself, and waited. Adelaide wasn't ready for me.

I expected her to take a long time, but she surprised me again by being ready within a matter of ten minutes. Her long brown locks were pinned atop her head in a messy bun. She wore a shirt that had seen better days, looked heavily washed, and torn jeans.

This made Adelaide different from other women. No one else would have allowed me to see her looking anything but perfect. Adelaide had no makeup and no jewelry other than the garish wedding ring that was a statement to the world and to her family. She wore clothes that didn't even have a designer label. She looked perfect to me—the complete opposite of the women I normally went for.

"Ready?" she asked.

"You're sure you want to go out like that?"

"Yep."

"Okay." I wondered if she would take me shopping and force me to sit through hours of her trying on new clothes. She had an entire closet I'd chosen for her. This had to be one of her old outfits that she'd brought along with her. Her parents had gotten rid of most of her stuff, but it would seem Adelaide knew what to do.

We left my penthouse. I nodded at Terrance.

He'd be following behind us in the second car. So that Adelaide didn't feel so aware of her position, I was driving us wherever she wanted to go. I still had her cell phone in my pocket. I'd not switched it on, but I knew her whole life was there. She wasn't on social media of any kind. Her cell phone was just used for calls, texts, and very rarely for emails. She kept to herself mostly.

"Where would you like to go?" I asked, expecting her to tell me the name of a mall.

She tells me the location but not the name. I've never heard of it before and have no choice but to type it into the navigator to be pointed in the general direction.

"I could have told you where to go," she said.

"It's fine."

"Aren't all guys against getting directions?"

"This is not getting directions. I've never had to talk to anyone to get what I want."

She chuckled and I chanced a glance at her.

"Is this some exclusive boutique?" I asked.

"Please, I hate shopping."

"I find that hard to believe…"

"Why? Because that was all my sister told you to do?" She snorted. "Bethany and I are nothing alike. If you wanted a wife who liked to shop, then you should have married her."

I gripped the steering wheel, annoyed with her.

Bethany bored me. She always tried too hard. I know she made everyone believe we were fucking, and we weren't. She never aroused me. Her voice always had that edge of whining to it. I hated hearing her talk. To be honest, the only reason I took her with me on business trips, apart from the fact she was supposed to be with me, was the distraction she provided. I knew she slept with everything that had a dick. She tried to get a rise out of me, but I just didn't care. Her pussy was already well-used before I came along.

"You owe me my cell phone."

After last night, I expected her to be scared, or at the very least worried about being in the same room as me. This woman made no sense. Rather than act scared, she seemed to be talking back. When had Adelaide grown a spine? The shaken, panic-stricken woman of our wedding was long gone. In her place sat a very beautiful and determined female.

She reached for the window and pressed the button, letting in the fresh air. Adelaide tilted her head toward it. This was the first time during the day she'd been outside. The only other time I'd taken her out was during our dinner with Ivan and Slavik.

"I don't owe you anything."

"That means you're not a man of your word, and you lied."

Irritated, I reached into my pants pocket and handed her the cell phone she was so anxious about.

"What are you doing?"

"I'm a man of my word. That means I tell you the truth, and I expect the same in return."

"I have no reason to lie to you."

"There is always a reason to lie."

Out of the corner of my eye, I watched her press the power button. "It's dead."

It would be. I didn't waste time charging it. That was the other reason I hadn't given her the cell phone. She would need time to charge it, even when we made it home. She pulled down the glove box, shoved her phone inside, and closed it. I expected her to be angry.

She stared out the window. Her hand was cruising out of the window, sliding up and down.

"We're nearly there," she said, suddenly sitting forward.

I slowed down as she started to point to where she wanted to go. When we arrived at an animal shelter, I couldn't have been more shocked. When she lived with her parents, she'd volunteered at a shelter, but I figured that was to look good to the press.

She clapped her hands, looking excited. I had no choice but to follow her as she'd climbed out of the car and rushed toward the main reception. I wasn't dressed to be at a shelter.

I watched as my wife talked to an elderly woman behind the counter. The two shook hands, and then Adelaide saw I'd arrived.

"Er, this is my husband, Andrei. Would you mind if I showed him around?" Adelaide asked.

"No, of course not, dear. You go right ahead."

Adelaide turned toward me, her hands clasped together. "Would you like a tour?"

I noticed she didn't introduce me to the woman on the counter, whom she clearly knew.

"Yes," I said, surprising her.

"Right, let's go then." Adelaide took a step toward a set of double doors, leading toward the back of the shelter.

I grabbed her hand, locking our fingers together. I wasn't going to let her out of my sight. This was a surprise. I guess Adelaide hadn't been using the experience to look good to the press, and I was now even more intrigued.

Chapter Six

Adelaide

I love all animals—dogs, cats, rabbits, hamsters, guinea pigs, cows, horses, the list goes on and on. I adore them. I had always wanted one, but growing up, Bethany couldn't stand them. None of the animals liked her and I used to think it was because they were known for sensing evil. Lame, I know, but I had to get my kicks out of it somehow.

So, no pets. Even my parents hated them.

After the basement episode where I tried to build my own shelter, my mother decided it was best for me to invest my time elsewhere. That's when she got me to volunteer at the local animal shelter. She thought it was a phase I was going through. Much like my veganism. When she realized I wasn't going to change my mind, she didn't bother to try and change it for me. She let me run with it.

I wasn't allowed pets, but at the shelter, I took care of and loved them all. There were no limits. It was the first time my mother had done anything selfless. At the time I didn't realize it also made her look good to the press. I should have known she wasn't doing it to help her daughter, it was all for herself.

As I walked with Andrei by my side and saw the animals that had been rescued or given to the shelter, I felt like I finally had a purpose.

During my tour, I'm surprised to see Andrei from time to time going toward the cages and putting his hand inside, stroking the dogs. I thought they would attack him. Some of the shelter dogs have only known abuse, as well as the cats, but none of them attacked. They sniff his hand and he greets them, petting them gently. I'm shocked. There's no other word for it. I'd never expected him to be so … kind.

He'd admitted to me he killed his own father, and I wasn't a fool. I knew that meant he took lives on a daily basis. That was who he was—the Bratva man. But right now, as I watched him pet a German shepherd, I had to wonder about him, about the boy he'd told me about.

Andrei wasn't a bad man. He'd been made into who he was by the people around him. He couldn't trust anyone. Was that why Ivan had warned me that Andrei didn't trust easily? The people who should have loved him, taken care of him, nurtured him, had abused him. It didn't take a genius to understand the kind of pain he experienced as a boy left a mark.

There was so much about Andrei I didn't know.

Until this moment, I'd not been too interested in finding out, but looking at him now and seeing the dogs react, I had to wonder. They were good at sensing evil, after all, and they didn't react to Andrei the same way they did to my parents or to Bethany.

The tour came to an end when he got a phone call. From the look on his face, I wasn't exactly sure what had happened, but his face was a mask—a dark one.

He made his excuses and didn't allow me to say goodbye to the lady at the desk. I'd not gotten her name. I'd known of this shelter because I'd taken the time before marrying Andrei, to learn about my location. My father had told me I'd be living with Andrei, and I hated going to new places without learning every single detail, so I'd spent hours studying this place.

This was the biggest animal shelter near the city. When I'd been thinking of volunteering here, I had not considered my husband locking me up in his penthouse suite. I was just thankful I'd not made any arrangements ahead of time, as I'd have looked like a fool.

Andrei didn't let go of my hand until we were at the car, where he helped me into the passenger seat. He surprised me even more, leaning in and fastening my seat belt. I could do it, but with how close his face was to mine, I got a little distracted. The sight of his lips so close. The two kisses I'd now shared with him had completely ruined me. I wanted to hate him, to put him in a neatly organized box of a monster. He wasn't that.

But a few kisses didn't make him a good person. He was messing with my head, but I had a feeling he wasn't doing it on purpose.

He slammed the door closed and rounded the vehicle, climbed behind the wheel, turned over the ignition, and pulled out of the shelter.

"Are you okay?" I asked.

He didn't say a word. His focus was on the main road. I noticed his guards had followed us to the animal shelter. Another hit of harsh reality—that we couldn't go for a simple visit without someone there to guard us.

Was his life in danger every single moment of every single day? I'd read about the fictional side of the Bratva life in books, but I figured they were overdramatized versions. With how fast he drove, I had to wonder just how true they were.

Gripping the edge of my seat, I was sure he was going to crash into something. I closed my eyes at certain points, not wanting to see the danger ahead. I'd already considered the best way to die, and as far as I could tell, it was to not be conscious for it. Lame, I know, but I hated pain. Physical pain. I'd do anything to avoid it.

"Andrei, what's going on?" I asked.

He still didn't talk to me.

I hated this.

Squeezing my eyes closed, I hoped a cop was close by just so he'd stop us or do anything that would slow him down. I didn't want him arrested. The cop thought was a bad one. Andrei or his men would probably kill him. A cop wasn't a good idea. It was a very bad one. No cops. Just get us home in time.

The odd thought made me pause. *Home.* I'd never considered the penthouse suite a home before. It wasn't my home. It was Andrei's, but I felt like I was going home. Was this all part of the Stockholm syndrome thing? I wasn't sure what qualified Andrei as a captor. I nearly burst out laughing when I thought of Andrei as my kidnapper. He was my husband, but he might as well have been the villain in my story.

We arrived back at the penthouse suite's underground parking lot, alive, in one piece. When I climbed out of the car, I nearly sank to my knees and kissed the cold cement floor, but alas, I didn't have that luxury.

Andrei acted like a crazy person. He grabbed my arms, snapped his fingers at his men, and marched me toward the elevator doors. His grip was bruising, but he didn't let me go.

What had I done wrong? What had happened? I'd been a good girl my whole life. All I did was take him to the animal shelter. One by one, I tried to find the reason for his sudden change of behavior, and nothing came to mind. I drew a complete blank.

Did he hate the dogs? Was that his issue?

I hated this.

His guards travelled in the elevator with us. This was a first as far as I knew. He'd kept a lot of the guards away from me. Just the guy on the door, who was a pain in the ass. We got to Andrei's penthouse suite, and it had become his, seeing as he was now hurting me.

"Andrei, what's going on? Please talk to me," I said.

"Shut up and go to your room."

He spoke to me like I was a child. What happened to the man who wanted me to kiss him in order to earn rewards?

"Why won't you talk to me?"

"I don't have time for your childish behavior, get the fuck to your room, now."

There was something in his eyes and the fact his men were so close, that I knew if I disobeyed him, he'd hurt me. I was not entirely sure if that was accurate, but holding the cell phone I was able to grab from his glove box before he became … this, I walked away and did not give him a second look.

I closed the door quietly and rushed toward the closet where I'd seen several chargers in a drawer. Rifling through them, I tried to find the perfect fit for the phone I had. It took me three attempts to find the right charger. Sliding the cable into the wall, I fired up my cell phone. I was amazed it still worked.

Tears blurred my vision and I batted them away. I wasn't going to cry. It had gone from a perfectly good day to a shitty one. Story of my life, but I wasn't going to let it get me down. I'd look at the positives instead. I got to go out, see a bunch of animals I already loved, and I had my cell phone.

I stayed in the closet, and even when one of the guards came to the room to drop off some food, I didn't leave the sanctuary of this room.

With my cell phone charging, when it had enough battery life, I began to go through my texts, missed calls, and emails. My main contact was Nathan, the only guy who'd not been wowed by Bethany. He'd seen right through her and had not been impressed.

I looked at all the texts from him.

Nathan: **What the hell is happening?**

Seriously, you're giving me the silent treatment.

Adelaide, I don't like this silence.

Come on, girl, you know I want to talk.

I go away for three months and the next thing I know, you're living in a different city, married to the guy who was supposed to be seeing your sister.

Adelaide, please talk to me.

I had to stop looking at them. They were constantly asking me to text back. The emails were from him as well. Each one sounded even more sad than the last. There were missed calls from him and from Bethany, but I ignored them all. There was no point in listening to the voice messages, so I deleted them.

Next, I hovered over Nathan's name. Should I call him? Andrei had said I wasn't to have any contact with my previous life, but he didn't get to tell me what to do when he was yelling at me like that. I clicked on the button and made the decision. Some might think it was a stupid one. Putting the cell to my ear, I had no choice but to move onto the floor on my stomach as the cable wasn't long enough for me to sit.

I waited.

"Adelaide?" Nathan asked.

"Hey, Nathan," I said.

"Oh, fuck me, thank God you're okay. I had no idea what the hell was going on, and I was freaking out. I even had to go and talk to Bethany, and you know I can't stand that fucking viper. What is going on? Is what Bethany said true?"

I smiled. It was nice to hear from a voice I knew cared about me, and he did. He cared about me a whole lot.

Taking a deep breath, I tried not to let the tears spill over, but I knew it wasn't from hearing Nathan. No, it was the sudden realization that my husband didn't love me. I mean, it wasn't stupid of me to finally realize it. I knew it. Our marriage wasn't some crazy whirlwind love match. We were business, nothing more, nothing less. But I also realized he didn't care about me at all.

I was probably nothing more than a game to him.

That was what hurt.

"Er, I can't talk about it now, but how about we make plans to meet up? Would that work?" I asked.

I had no way of knowing if I would ever get the chance to meet up with Nathan again. Trying to get my cell phone and some freedom was hard enough, but having dinner with an old friend … I'd try.

"Yes, I'd like that."

We made arrangements to meet in two weeks. Nathan was going to be here anyway, for some kind of contract that I wasn't sure of. His work was a bit hazy, he rarely talked about it, and often changed the subject.

I swiped at my cheeks as the tears fell. They were wasted and completely useless. This was my life.

"Are you going to stay in the closet forever?" Andrei asked.

I tensed up, not saying a word.

"You're angry with me."

Pulling my knees up to my chest, I wrapped my arms around my legs, tried to make a shield, or anything that would ward him off.

Andrei had hurt me and what was more, he had no idea how or why. He didn't make promises he couldn't keep. There had been no conversation about how to make this marriage work.

"Adelaide?"

My name sounded so good on his lips.

Getting to my feet, I clench my hands into fists, and move toward the door, looking into the bedroom.

He's sitting on the edge of the bed, looking defeated. It's not a good look for him.

I instantly want to go to him, but I hold myself back, not wanting him to see my feelings as a weakness. I have no feelings for this man.

Neither of us talk.

His gaze is on me and I wait.

"I shouldn't have spoken to you like that."

If that was the apology I was going to get, then I wanted to sink right on back to the closet.

"Something has happened, and I—"

"In two weeks' time I want to go out to dinner," I said. "With an old friend."

"That's not happening."

"I will find a way out, Andrei. If I have to kiss you, fine. If you want sex, fine, I'll do that, but I will be going out with my friend." My heart is racing. I don't know why I'm making these demands. I'm in no position to do so.

He gets up off the bed and I stand firm. I'm not afraid of him. I'm not going to back down. His hand goes to my cheek, his thumb grazing the bottom of my chin, and tilting my head back so I had no choice but to look into his eyes.

"You think you can make demands on me?" he asked.

"I've been a good wife to you, Andrei. You've been a shitty husband to me," I said. "I'm not asking you for anything other than a day where I can go and meet my friend."

He stared into my eyes, and I had to wonder what was going on in his mind.

"No," he said, and without another word, he walked right out of the room.

I would find a way to see Nathan.

A SENSE OF DUTY

****

Andrei

The news of Ivan's death startled me.

The man who was the head of the Volkov Bratva was a pain in the ass, but he was worth fighting for. He was worth being loyal to, and to hear he was dead angered me.

There was a pain inside my chest, and it didn't ease, not for a long time. All that kept me going were Ivan's words to me. He told me something was going to happen, and he needed me to keep fighting.

The news of his death had spread like wildfire, and it shouldn't have, however, it brought repercussions. When Ivan originally took over from the Bratva, he forged deals, pushed other players out. My city was once owned by part of the Italian mafia, but he'd pushed them back until they had a small state to call their own, as well as Evil Savages MC. For the longest time, I'd been dealing with them, and now I had news of them entering one of my nightclubs and burning it to the ground.

That was where I stood right now, on the outskirts of one of my best nightclubs. The firefighters had been too late to the blaze, and I knew it was because of the Evil Savages Prez, Demon.

"Sir?" Leo asked.

I had already handled the police. They had wanted a report of my whereabouts. The fire marshal had also given him an assessment. To rebuild was going to cost me a small fortune.

"Round up the men," I said. "We're going hunting."

This was an outright attack. I also had my men piling up, and it was time I ended this.

Ivan Volkov might be dead, but my city wasn't going to burn without a fucking fight. I turn away from the smoking embers, pulling out my cell phone to see Ive Yahontov calling me.

"What?" I asked, not in the mood to make small talk.

"The Cartel have taken the product," Ive said.

I cursed.

Ive's territory held a port that was once known for smuggling drugs and women into the country. With Ivan's death, the Cartel were now attempting to take their turf back.

"This is a war. You have no choice but to play fire with fire. Destroy them. Do not take any prisoners. They think the Volkov Bratva has fallen, you make them aware that it will never fall." I hang up my cell phone.

So far, the only one who had been able to keep order within his state was Oleg, which I didn't like. It meant something wasn't quite right. He'd also handled the news of Ivan's death, easily. I would have to talk to Slavik and arrange a visit to Oleg's territory.

My cell phone rang and I saw it was from an unknown number. It wasn't unusual for me to get calls from people I didn't know. I hovered over the red symbol to end the noise. Instead, I pressed the button to accept.

"Hello, Belov."

I wasn't a fool. It was the MC Prez, Demon.

"Do you like your present?"

I don't respond, keeping my thoughts and opinions to myself. He's known for wanting to rile people up. He wants me angry so I'll do something stupid and attack him without thought. He doesn't have the first clue who he's dealing with.

Laughter rang down the line. "This is only the beginning, Belov. I'm going to burn your city down to a fucking crisp and bask in the bloodshed."

His threats bored me.

I hung up my cell phone and walked toward my car. Leo was already waiting for me. As I climbed in, I told him to head to my penthouse. I'd not taken Adelaide out since that day. I'd also not left unless it was to attend to important business like today.

She hated my presence. I sensed her anger and disappointment. Her day at the shelter had gone so well. I'd surprised her with how much I loved dogs. It had been too long since I had a dog of my own. In fact, after my father's dogs had died of old age, one by one, I hadn't replaced them. Their passing had been the worst kind of feeling I'd ever experienced in my life. I missed them so much, but as with all passing, time had helped. I'd not gotten another dog.

Love and emotion were weakness. I didn't have time for weakness.

My cell phone rings again. Glancing down, I see it's an unknown number. Gritting my teeth, I end the call. This happens, two, three, four, and five more times, until I finally accept the call.

"What the fuck do you want?" I asked.

"To say *surprise*."

I tensed up.

"Ivan?"

"The one and only, back from the dead."

"But … you're supposed to be dead." I sound so fucking stupid.

"I know, and hopefully, you're very happy to hear from me."

"I … yes, of course." I was happy. Fuck me, I was.

"Tell me what's going on."

I explain everything. How my territory has the MC back, trying to fight for turf as well as the mafia. My section of mafia is not the same as Slavik's. Aurora was the daughter of one of their head guys. The whole arrangement had been organized by Ivan. As it happened, the guys from my territory were enemies of Slavik's guys. They fought amongst themselves rather than band together. That's how Ivan had brought about his power. He'd made sure to bind us, to make us stronger.

I told him about Ive's Cartel issue. How Victor had an uprising amongst the soldiers, Peter's issue with the law, and then Oleg's perfectly organized territory.

"I fucking knew it," Ivan said.

"Are you going to tell me what is going on?"

"One day, but for now, my sudden rise from the dead will be a secret. What are your plans for Demon?"

"He has a daughter," I said. "I think it's only fair that we take from him what he considers the most precious."

Ivan laughed. "I like this. Make the arrangements. I'll call you soon."

I hung up my cell phone and smiled. I have no idea what is going on, but Ivan would tell me what I needed. This was his job as the boss. I could only imagine he was sniffing out a snake. Was Oleg his target? I had no idea.

Leo followed me up to my penthouse suite when we arrived in the building. Opening my front door, I paused at the sound of music playing way too loud. This was new. Adelaide rarely made any sound.

Reaching for my gun, I saw Leo do the same, out of the corner of my eye. We close the door quietly, and move through the penthouse, and I come to a stop when I catch sight of Adelaide. She's not under attack from anything other than liquor.

She'd never been in my office before, but it would seem since I left, she had decided to go and sneak inside. There was nothing there for her to find.

The music blasted too loud, and she held the whiskey bottle in her fist. Her eyes were closed as she swung her head, left to right, jumping up and down like a crazy person.

Looking back at Leo, I nod for him to leave.

Adelaide still hadn't seen me so I reach for the remote, and press "pause" on the music, sending the whole room into silence.

"What the fuck?" Adelaide asked.

She whirled around to look at me, and she was a little unsteady on her feet.

"Liquor does that." I nodded at the bottle.

"Oh, please, this is the best feeling I've ever had. The taste is so damn nasty. I don't know why anyone drinks it but then I got to thinking, maybe that's what can keep me locked up in here. Drinking and partying." She stumbled toward me and reached for the remote. I hold it out of her reach. "Stop being a stupid party pooper. It's not like you care about what I'm doing, or who with." She giggled like a little schoolgirl. "That is so funny to think of you even caring. No, you leave that to Bethany. She got to have whatever she wanted. I bet she didn't have to kiss you for it." She tilted her head to the side. "Nah, she probably did a whole lot more than that, and was even good to you in bed." She wrinkled her nose. "Gross. I have to have sex with a man who put his dick in my sister first."

I had no idea Adelaide could be so free with speech. The drink was having the effect. She'd spent a great deal of time ignoring me. Rather than find her outburst annoying, I thought it rather refreshing and cute. She swayed to whatever music played inside her head.

"We don't have to have sex. We didn't on our wedding night. We're not having a honeymoon. You have to come up with some lame excuse to force yourself to kiss me." She laughed a little more. "This is so ridiculous." She covered her mouth with her hand, as if she understood the joke. "I'm married to one of the scariest men alive and I've got to have sex with you. I bet you don't want to have sex with me at all." She put her hand on her waist. "I've been told enough times I'm not as good as Bethany." She dropped the bottle to the floor and I watched as it smashed.

Adelaide bent forward laughing.

Anyone else, I'd have found this outburst annoying, but watching her, listening to her, I found her utterly enchanting. She snatched at the too-large shirt, ripping it over her head.

The only issue I had was the broken glass and her tender feet.

"Adelaide," I said.

"No, no, no, you don't get to come near me unless it's to grant me a divorce." She threw her shirt to the floor. I watched as she stumbled, stepping on broken glass. Adelaide cried out each time she did, and I went toward her, but she would only move away. As we did this dance, she removed her clothes until she stood before me in a pair of sexy white lingerie. All silk and lace, and so fucking sexy against her pale skin.

If I wasn't so worried about her hurting herself, I'd give into the pleasure of being aroused, but watching those tender feet of hers, I felt fear. Her feet were already bleeding and I had to wonder about the amount of alcohol she'd consumed. She giggled again.

"You see, I'm nothing like Bethany. I am everything she hates. I don't mind. I love my body," she said. "But this is not what you want."

She had no idea what she was talking about.

"Divorce me," she said.

"Not going to happen."

"You hate me! You can't stand me. This is what you want, isn't it? To find a reason to get rid of me so you don't have to be near me. It's why we haven't consummated this marriage." She lifted her hands into the air to give air quotes.

She stumbled, and this time I couldn't stand to see her fall. Capturing her in my arms, I cradle her head against my chest, wanting to hold onto her. I breathed in her strawberry cream scent that was soon replaced as she bent forward and vomited all over my trousers and shoes. I should have expected that. Adelaide wasn't a drinker.

Lifting her up into my arms, I realized she was a lot bigger than Bethany, but I didn't care. I loved the feel of her in my arms. This, to me, felt right. She was perfect. She attempted to wriggle in my grasp, but I refused to let her go.

I went straight to the shower, where I dumped her on the floor and turned the shower on. I let the cold jets hit my back, covering her body so she wasn't cold. Kicking off my sodden shoes and tearing my clothes away, I stood before her in a pair of boxers.

I lifted Adelaide up into my arms. "What do I have to do to get you to like me?"

I didn't answer. Silence was the best.

The drink was making her weak, so I started washing her, taking my time, soaping her body, and then her hair. When she was clean, I held her in my arms. She still had on the bra and panties, and I wasn't ready to take them off. She looked so good in them.

With a towel wrapped around her, the last of her energy was zapped away. I quickly dried her, and then took her through to our bedroom where I settled her into bed.

"My feet hurt," she said.

Her eyes were already drooping. This is why I

loved whiskey. The good stuff had a way of numbing any kind of pain. When I was sure she was out cold, the soft snores coming from her lips made me smile.

Returning to the bathroom, I cleaned up the blood from her feet, grabbed the first aid kit, and got to work at removing the shards of broken glass. Piece by piece. I didn't need a doctor to look at my handiwork. Adelaide had been lucky as she'd only stepped on a couple of pieces. Her feet would sting, but there would be no lasting damage. Gripping her ankle, I lay a kiss to each one of her feet, and wondered if she would one day know the complete truth.

Chapter Seven

Adelaide

I had a very bad headache. Jerking up in bed, I covered my face with my hands as the pain exploded.

"There are painkillers by the water," Andrei said.

His voice sounded way too smug.

Dropping my hands, I looked into the smirking face of my husband. I didn't care. Glancing to my left, I saw the tall glass of water and the white pills. They looked like the kind for migraines and for now, I was willing to take them. Would Andrei kill his wife after having a party?

His liquor had been so gross but once I started, it was like the monster just wouldn't stop. One sip had been two, then three, then four, then five, and well, half the bottle had gone. I wasn't a drinker. I hated wine and beer. At dinners I drank it, and by drank, I meant sipped, and often asked the waiter to change it for water.

I don't know what happened yesterday. One moment I'd been lonely, trying to figure out how to meet up with Nathan. I missed my best friend and wanted to see him so desperately, but Andrei had been colder and more aloof than ever before. Something was going on in his life. I got it, and to a point, I understood it. He was an important person in the Volkov Bratva. He had a lot of important things to deal with. I wasn't important. I'm the wife, the annoying person he didn't want in his life.

I swigged back the painkillers, one after the other. I hated taking pills. For some reason I felt like they were three times larger than they were. I knew I swallowed more in a mouthful of pasta than I did in a single pill, but that was beside the point. After the pills went down, I finished the glass of water, needing something to take the taste away.

I winced and looked at Andrei. "Did I vomit?"

"Yeah, you did, and even though I took care of your feet, I didn't think you'd appreciate me attempting to brush your teeth."

I pulled the blanket off, hoping to go and clean my mouth, but I was in a pair of panties and bra. Gasping, I grab the blanket, trying to hide my nakedness, but that didn't help.

He chuckled. "I've seen it all yesterday."

Vague, hazy memories filtered through, and I knew I'd made a fool of myself. Odd conversational pieces of where I compare myself to Bethany come to mind.

I drop my head into my hands. "Oh, God, I was … did I come on to you?"

"Unless you count demanding a divorce as a come-on?" Andrei asked.

This made me lift my head. "I … asked for a divorce?"

Andrei moved from the chair to the bed, toward the edge.

I moved my legs out of the way to make room for him. Licking my dry lips and hating the taste in my mouth.

"Adelaide, you're not getting a divorce. The only way out of this marriage is by death, or old age."

I nod, pressing my lips together. "I know you wanted Bethany. You were supposed to marry her."

"Bethany was a piece of shit and a slut. I didn't want her. I was doing what Ivan wanted me to."

"You don't get to call my sister a slut."

"She's a piece of shit and that's acceptable?" he asked.

"You didn't live a celibate life. You don't get to call her anything."

"Your issue here is the double standard?" He tilted his head to one side.

I frowned, running fingers through my hair, and groaned. "It's a lot of things. Just ignore me. Bethany and my feelings about her are complicated. She is still my sister."

"Yeah, and she hates your guts, Adelaide. You don't have to pretend for me."

"I don't..."

"She was the one who made sure your dress was too small at the wedding," Andrei said. "On the night before the wedding, she took your room away from you when she realized I was the one who arranged for you to be waited on."

"What?"

Andrei pursed his lips. This was news to me.

"Bethany and your parents knew what they were getting themselves into. You did not. Binding you to me, I can imagine would be difficult for any woman, and I figured if you had ... the night before you were due to marry me, I'd arranged an all-spa treatment for you, to help you to relax. Bethany found out, and she took it."

"I had no idea." I nibble my lip. That was kind of sweet, and now I'm pissed off that once again, Bethany was there to take something that didn't belong to her, as usual. Taking a deep breath, I exhaled slowly.

"I was hoping to avoid the panic attack you inevitably had at the wedding."

"That was ... I was able to marry you but it was what Bethany said afterward." I looked down at the blanket.

"What did she say?"

When he asked me this on our wedding day, I'd avoided talking about it. Pushing some of my hair, which had to look a mess right now, out of my face, I looked over his shoulder. My stomach was not happy right now.

"She told me that you liked … that you … this is … you enjoy pain. You enjoy making a woman bleed, and you relish hitting women. It was a whole big explanation about how in order for you to get off, you beat a woman to death, and that was what you would do to me. That my virgin status would only make you more thirsty for my blood."

With Bethany, she'd used more descriptive words and vulgar language.

"She was trying to scare you, Adelaide."

"I know. If you were so awful, you wouldn't have left me alone on our wedding night, and other nights since we've been married." I shrugged. I didn't know for sure if I was happy that he left me alone. Was it a good thing? "I guess, looking at it like that, we could get an annulment. No need for death or divorce."

"Not happening."

"Andrei, you can't be happy."

"Happy or not, Adelaide, you're my wife and you're staying that way."

It was like talking to a brick wall.

"I don't want to be miserable," I said, feeling the tears fill my eyes. He went blurry as I tried to fight them, but I couldn't. "I don't want to live like this anymore, Andrei. The way you talked to me, treating me like a child." I glanced around the penthouse suite. "I'm not used to this. I need my freedom." Running a hand down my face, I didn't want to give up. "Don't you want to have a marriage you can … enjoy?"

He looked at me.

Silent.

Pressing my lips together, I was ready to give up. There was no point in trying to find an amicable solution, but then, I couldn't do it.

Weeks, months, and years of living like this—the very thought made me miserable. I didn't even want to imagine the time spent actually living it.

"Can't we be friends?" I asked. "Don't you want that at least? I … you didn't want to be married to me, but don't you want to at least find some peace where you're happy to come home, or to see me?"

"Is that what you want?" he asked.

"I want it for both of us." I reached for his hand, and was surprised he didn't fight me. "I know a lot of women as girls planned their marriage. They even thought about what their husband would be like. I never did. Not for a single second did I waste time looking through magazines, admiring dresses. I've always been a … I guess a loner, really. I like my own company, but if I were going to marry, I'd hoped it would be for love and with a man who could love me. I don't expect you to love me, Andrei. I know you can't, but I want to care about you, and I hope you can one day care about me."

Was I talking trash? I don't know.

Andrei looked at our hands and he gave my hand a squeeze. "What do you suggest?"

"You … you mean that?" I asked.

"I'm listening, Adelaide, but you only have this one time to sell it," he said.

I laughed and couldn't help but cup his face and kiss his lips quickly. "You've got to let me go out on my own, maybe even volunteer at the shelter."

"No to both."

My smile fell.

"I will compromise. You cannot volunteer, but you can donate and visit the shelter to walk the dogs or whatever it is you do, so long as you have a man of my choosing by your side."

That didn't sound like the greatest idea, but it was

better than nothing at all. A compromise. "Deal."

"Anything else?"

"I want to be able to have use of my cell phone and laptop whenever I want," I said.

He tutted.

"I swear I will not do anything you regret."

"You're to make this place your home," he said.

"What?"

"If you have your laptop and cell phone, you're to put your mark on this penthouse suite."

"You mean that?"

"I don't say anything I don't mean."

I smiled. "Okay, and how about you try to make it home so we can enjoy dinner together?"

"I'm not going vegan," he said.

This did make me laugh. "I'm not going to ask you to."

"Deal."

I felt so much happier than before. This was new. This was hope that we could finally make it work.

"I'm sorry about last night."

"Don't be, even though you did ruin a perfectly good scotch and an amazing decanter."

I groaned at the guilt.

"I'm sorry."

He waved his hand in the air.

I was about to say something else, but the sound of our doorbell rang through the penthouse.

"I'll be back," he said.

The moment he left the bedroom, I rushed to the bathroom, used the toilet, washed my hands, and then quickly brushed my teeth.

Staring at my reflection, I winced. My hair was a mess. At least I didn't have puffy eyes or anything like that. I'd not cried myself to sleep. I grabbed a brush and ran it through my hair a few times, trying to bring some order to the wayward color.

I gave up. Each time the brush touched it, it seemed to go even more unruly.

At least my mouth was a lot fresher. Returning to the bedroom, I found Andrei waiting. He'd gotten a tray with coffee and a cinnamon bun on the plate.

"Breakfast?" I asked.

"I know you like them."

Cinnamon buns were my favorite. I couldn't get enough of them.

I still wore the white lingerie that was far too revealing. For a few seconds I hesitated, feeling the need to hide my nakedness, but Andrei didn't seem to notice.

Sliding back into the bed, I pulled the covers up to my chin and took a sip of coffee. I didn't care that I still had the full taste of peppermint from my toothpaste. The coffee was exactly what I needed. After a few scalding sips, I reached for the bun and marveled at how warm it still felt. One bite and I was lost. Cinnamon was one of my favorite spices. I loved anything that contained it. I even enjoyed cinnamon-scented candles.

Every now and then, I looked toward Andrei, but he finished off his own cinnamon bun and coffee.

"I need to leave for work soon. Get dressed, I have your guard outside and I want to introduce you."

"So soon?"

"Yes."

"Okay." I swallowed the last of my coffee, and Andrei took the empty cup from my hand.

He turned away and left the room.

Climbing out of bed, I rush to the closet, and rather than pick one of the outfits I'd managed to steal away from my parents before they threw them out, I look through the clothes Andrei had chosen. I settled on a black pencil skirt and white cowl-neck blouse. Wrapping my hair into a bun, I glanced in the mirror, happy with how I looked.

My feet were hurting but the pain was bearable. If I showed any signs of pain, he might not let me leave.

Checking my cell phone, I see Nathan is in the city, and he wanted to meet up early. Typing a response, I promise to meet him at lunch. He sends me a link to a restaurant I'd never heard of, and I agree to meet him. I don't want to keep Andrei waiting another moment, and rush out to see him.

When he catches sight of me, he doesn't look pleased. I had dressed for him, in the hope of making him happy. It's all part of the compromise. This was the first day our marriage had seemed hopeful. How could he not be happy with the clothes he'd chosen for me to wear?

"Adelaide, this is Leo," he said. "He will be your guard, escorting you wherever you need to go."

I recognized Leo as his driver. Was he the only guy he trusted? Who was going to take care of him? I didn't complain. Forcing a smile to my lips, I held out my hand but Andrei took it.

"Er, it's nice to meet you," I said.

Leo nodded, but he didn't smile.

This didn't seem at all like it was going to be a good fit.

****

Andrei

The only man in my employ I trusted with Adelaide's life was Leo. The man was married with three children. He worked hard to keep his life away from his family. I helped to a point, but there was only so much I could do. There was no way he'd fall for my wife, nor would he put her in danger.

Running a hand down my face, I glanced over the

endless list of files that had mounted on my desk. I'd gone back to the casino, which was my main base for work. I had plenty of offices around the city and across my territory, but this was the place I settled into most. This was where I had access to everything I needed.

My thoughts kept returning to Adelaide. To the hug she'd given me that very morning. Women hugged me all the time. She was right, I didn't have a celibate life. I'd enjoyed plenty of women but none of them had been my wife.

Adelaide was different. She'd dressed this morning, and wore the clothes I'd picked for her, but I did not like it. They were not her at all.

I know I just need to get laid. Since the wedding and the shit with Ivan, I haven't had the chance to take care of my own needs. There's no other woman that appeals to me. No one I want, other than to feel Adelaide's virgin cunt sliding down my dick. That's what I wanted, but I wasn't going to get it.

I had to focus. To get my thoughts away from my fucking wife and to think about the business at hand.

My spies at the Evil Savages MC compound had told me exactly what Demon was going to do. He planned to attack six of my warehouses. Three of them contained cocaine, two had guns, and the other two were empty. The plan was to transfer all the drugs to one location ready to distribute. The guns could go. We didn't need them, and they were excess storage. I planned to catch them off guard and strike as they raid our base.

The target was his oldest daughter, considered the princess of the club. I glanced at the picture of Cassie. She was a stunner, no doubt about it. Endless lengths of blonde hair, shocking blue eyes, with a face that made men take notice. She had an attitude. The picture alone showcased that. From the details I'd been given, she had a temper as well. She wasn't a nice woman. Spoiled since birth with an entire club at her beck and call, all because of her father. She would be in for a rude awakening by the time I got done with her. I smiled, thinking about it.

I closed the file, opened my bottom drawer, used the key to access the spare panel, and slid the file inside.

Patience was a gift, and when the time was right, I'd take care of my enemies. I'd not heard from Ivan yet, but I had heard the rumors of his reappearance. The man always wanted to make an entrance.

The door to my office opened.

"You can't go in there."

I looked up to see Bethany striding across the room toward me, with a wicked glint shining in her eye as if she had some kind of special secret she couldn't wait to tell me about. Glancing at the guard, I dismissed him with a nod of my head. I'd deal with him later. For now, I had to handle this fucking bitch. I hadn't seen her since the wedding.

"What do you want?"

"Is that any way to greet an old fiancée?" she asked, flicking her hair over her shoulder. The blonde wasn't her natural hair color. There wasn't a whole lot of Bethany that was real.

Fake tits, cheeks, ass, and lips. All of it came from a plastic surgeon. Her mother was the same way. Both women were addicted to surgery.

Locking my fingers together, I waited.

She giggled. The same fake sound she used on men when she tried to get what she wanted. Bethany had never liked me. Her feelings never mattered to me, because I couldn't stand her either. I played the part, pretended the whole role, even allowed her to make up lies about it. It was all easy. The marriage was the final goal and Ivan always got what he wanted.

I don't know the exact details of what Bethany did to piss him off, but either way, her ass had been kicked out, and Adelaide's was next. I had an inkling it had to do with the way she treated Slavik's woman, Aurora. I'd scolded her at the time, cut off her funds, but Ivan went to the next level.

Aurora clearly had a way about her. I think I might have referred to her pussy being golden or something along those lines. Slavik was certainly smitten. I'd never known him to be so pissed off with me talking about a woman like I had.

I chuckled and Bethany stopped. "I find it funny you would call yourself *old*, but that is very true. You didn't have what it took to be my wife."

Bethany pouted. "You say such cruel things."

"You're a bitch and a whore, Bethany. You and I both know you've got a problem. It's one of the reasons your parents worked so fucking hard to keep the money flowing. How does it feel to need your little sister to help pay the bills?"

Her hands clenched at her sides and the lips she tried so hard to keep plump had gone into a weird shape, I was guessing a sneer. What was the draw? Bethany was beautiful. No doubt about it. She could snap her fingers and people would come running, but I wasn't just anyone.

There was a whole world full of Bethanys—spiteful, nasty pieces of work. They were not ashamed or afraid to use others to get what they wanted.

I know it's absurd to be offended by her, but I was the one who used people, not her. I wanted her out of my office. Instead, Bethany moved further in, coming toward me, perching on the end of my desk, crossing her legs. The skirt she wore was small and I could tell she didn't have any panties on.

"You know, I can make every single fantasy come true," she said, spreading her thighs wide. "I can rock your world, Andrei. I know you need a real woman to handle your needs." She spread her thighs again. "I can take it all. You can have whatever you want. My pussy, my ass, my mouth. One after the other. You can flood me with your spunk, and I'd lick it right up off the floor."

She reached toward me and I grabbed her wrist, stopping her. Her lips did that weird thing again.

"You want money."

"Adelaide doesn't want you. She's too good. Too squeaky clean to want you near her. I'm dirty, Andrei. I can give you it all. Ride my cunt, fuck me raw, baby. I know you want to."

I'd never touched this woman. I twisted her hand and she cried out and grabbed the back of her neck. I slammed her across my desk and tugged hard on her hair until she was pressed flush against my desk as I dug into her back.

"If you ever speak about my wife like that again, I will cut your disgusting throat. I never wanted your nasty cunt, Bethany. I had no plans to be with you at all. Now, I suggest you get the fuck out of my office before I change my mind. I'm in the mood to see this neck dripping with blood."

I move from behind the desk, tossing her away from me, where she crumbles to the floor.

"Please, I need money, Andrei. He told me he would kill me if I don't get him the money first."

I shake my head knowing it's not my problem.

"Where?" I asked.

"What?"

"Where did you find him?"

She told me the location and that pissed me off even more. If Bethany hadn't been in my territory, I could send her right back to her parents without a care in the world. She purchased drugs from one of my clubs, by a guy who didn't work for me, and someone I'd never heard of before. It pissed me off.

"Get the fuck out," I said.

"Please, Andrei, I'll do anything you want."

"Then get the hell out of my sight before I kill you myself. Tell me where you're staying. I'll deal with your problem, then you get the hell out of my city."

Ivan didn't want me to kill Bethany yet. When he did, I was more than happy to deal with it.

Once Bethany was out of my office, I was done. I needed to get her stench off me.

I left the building, found my car, and slid behind the driver's seat. With Leo taking care of Adelaide, I hadn't chosen another driver. There was Terrance who I could give a shot to, but I didn't trust easily.

The drive through the city toward my penthouse didn't relax me. Bethany's appearance pissed me off. I knew she was up to something, and with the Evil Savages MC causing me trouble as well as the mafia, I didn't have time for her to be a problem. She hated her sister. With her begging for money and help, that had to mean something.

I parked my car and headed to my elevator. I had to use a special code to get inside, which I typed in. This was added protection for myself and my wife. As I stood in the elevator, I checked my cell phone to see several texts from Leo. Opening them up, I froze as I saw my wife eating lunch with a man I didn't recognize. The images were clear. She hugged this man, kissed his cheek, and they sat, sharing looks with one another.

Jealousy wasn't an emotion I was used to. Adelaide was my wife. Her smiles and kisses were all mine, and I didn't know who this man was.

My elevator doors opened, and Terrance was standing guard. I dismissed him as I entered. Leo stood near the living room and I nodded at him to leave as well. Adelaide was on the floor, legs crossed, with several pictures in front of her.

"Andrei," she said, getting to her feet.

The skirt and blouse she wore this morning were gone, replaced with a pair of sweatpants and an oversized shirt. Her hair was still in the bun but several strands had escaped.

"Who was the man you had lunch with?" I asked.

The smile dropped from her face. "What?"

"You heard me."

She glanced down at the pictures she'd been holding. "He's a friend. That's all."

"And I told you not to have anything to do with someone from your former life."

"He's the only friend I've got."

"And I'm not allowing my wife to have lunch with another man."

"Andrei, you're blowing this completely out of proportion."

I took a step toward her, staring down at her beautiful, plump mouth. I had missed her all fucking day and she went and had lunch with another man. I didn't accept it.

Sinking my fingers into her hair, I tug her close, and kiss her hard, almost bruising. I needed to wipe the memory of the man she'd been with from her mind.

Chapter Eight

Adelaide

Nathan had been worried about me.

How could he not? I all but vanished while he was away. There was no time to explain to him I was getting married to a man he'd never met before. If our roles were reversed, I'd be worried too.

He'd wanted to know every single detail about Andrei—how we met, how I ended up marrying my sister's fiancé. There was a whole list of questions and I hadn't been able to answer all of them. He wanted to know if I was in love with him, and that had been a hard one to get past. Nathan knew I avoided most of the questions and I hated lying to him so much.

As Andrei's lips possessed mine, all anger fled my body. I dropped the picture I'd been holding, and against my own will, I wrapped my arm around his neck, pressing my body flush against his. I enjoyed Andrei's kisses.

While I'd been looking through our wedding photos, I'd thought of his lips against mine. Seeing him back home, I'd wanted to kiss him, but his stony face had stopped me. Was this our destiny?

Leo had to have told on me. The moment we got to the restaurant he'd been against me seeing my friend, but I'd insisted. I wanted to see Nathan. To finally be around someone who cared about me.

I broke away from the kiss, gasping as Andrei lifted me up and carried me across the penthouse toward his bedroom. I noticed he avoided being close to any windows and for that I was grateful.

"What are you doing?" I asked.

My heart pounded inside my chest, threatening to explode as he lowered me to the bed. I cupped his face, kissed his lips one final time, but Andrei took my hands and removed them. He didn't like when I touched him. Gripping the edge of the bed, I watched fascinated as he pushed me back.

"Wait," I said.

Sex was going to happen between us. I knew that. Was I ready? Did it matter if I was? Would Andrei take what he wanted without a care to what I wanted? So many questions.

"Don't you think we should talk first?" I asked.

"I'm not going to fuck you, Adelaide," he said.

"You're not."

He smirked. "Not today, but I am going to do something else, if you'd let me."

This came out of the blue. Did I want to know what he was doing? Was it going to be good or painful? Nibbling my lip, I threw caution to the wind. We were compromising and I had to learn to trust Andrei, which wasn't easy. I'd deal with the Nathan problem once he finished doing whatever it was he wanted to.

He sank to his knees before me. His hands went to my waist, and he grabbed the waistband of my leggings. They were not skintight but comfortable.

"Lift your ass."

I pressed down on my hands, lifting my body up long enough for him to pull the leggings right off my thighs. This was … new. I still wore my panties. I enjoyed large, comfortable clothes, but when it came to my lingerie, it had to be sexy and lacy. It was what I liked.

Staring at Andrei, I didn't know why he was doing this. What had changed during the kiss? Our relationship wasn't normal. There was fire and ice, and it shocked me how readily my body responded to him.

His hands went to my knees, and he opened them,

slowly. "How much have you done with a man?" he asked.

"Nothing."

Should I lie and tell him I'd done something? There were no boys. No men. The moment I met someone, my sister had been there to stake her claim. I'd immersed myself into my studies and volunteering. Finding a life away from them.

He groaned. "You have no idea how much that pleases me. Lie down."

"Will it hurt?" I asked.

"Why do you assume everything I do is going to hurt you?"

I wasn't about to point out to him that he was a Bratva man with a reputation for killing things and causing pain. That would spoil the moment, right?

"Trust me."

I hesitated for a split second and then I lay back. Compromise. That's what we'd agreed to. Or at least I'd agreed to it, but I'm not sure what Andrei's compromise was. So far, other than placing Leo as my guard, he'd not sacrificed anything. He wanted to keep me apart from my friend. To cut off my life. Nathan was a good guy. If he gave him the time of day, he'd see that, but as usual, nope, not him, not my husband.

All thought left as the tips of his fingers traced up across my thighs, moving closer toward my pussy. Sinking my teeth into my lip, I held onto the blanket beneath me, trying to find focus, and struggling as I did. I'd never been touched like this, or kissed. This was nice.

He paused, the tips of his fingers so close to the edge of my panties at the front. What would it feel like to have his hand flush against my core? To stroke me? I was not a stranger to arousal. There had been no men in my life, but I had touched myself, finding my own pleasure.

He groaned. "I love these panties, but they have to go." He gripped them in his hand and tore them in half.

With the panties gone, there was nothing to protect me from his gaze. I stared up at the ceiling, feeling a little unsure. What should I do?

He moved his hands down, going to my feet, which still ached from the glass cuts. The anticipation of what was going to happen next stopped all care of the pain. His hands on my body were better than any shot of liquor.

Andrei lifted my feet, resting them on the edge of the bed, and as he did this, he moved to my inner thighs, opening them.

I was exposed. The lips of my sex opened just a little. There was no hiding. Not from him and certainly not from this.

"So pretty." His hands slid up my thighs, moving toward my pussy. The tips of his fingers grazed across my lips, and then tugged them open. He wasn't rough. This was gentle. An exploration. Allowing me to get used to the feel of him between my thighs.

I wanted so much more, but he wouldn't give it to me. His touch was almost feather-light as he stroked and caressed, never quite touching me the way I wanted. Sinking my teeth into my lip, I tried to contain my moans, but when he finally did slide his thumb through my slit, the instant hit of pleasure was like a lightening bolt that went off.

My cries filled the room, echoing off the walls. I tightened my grip on the blanket beneath me, hoping for anything to hold onto, in order to contain my sanity, but there was nothing.

Andrei leaned in close, his breath brushing across

my heated flesh. Was he going to? Anticipation rolled down my back as I waited to see exactly what he would do next. The tip of his tongue danced across my clit, heightening my senses, flooding me with need, making me scream for more, not wanting him to stop.

At first, he just rocked his tongue back and forth across my sensitive nerves, but then he began to move, going down to my entrance, circling my pussy, before making his way back up, making me hungry for more.

He growled against my flesh. "You taste so fucking good."

I had no idea what I tasted like but his hands moved from my sex, going to my ass, where he gripped me tighter than ever before, and then his mouth ravished me. He sucked my clit into his mouth.

I moaned his name, not wanting him to stop, thrusting against his mouth, craving my orgasm. With how good it felt to have his mouth on me, I couldn't think of a single reason why we'd stop doing this with each other.

This wasn't sex. This was different. Foreplay?

I don't know what has come over Andrei, all I know is that I don't want it to stop. His mouth moves back to my clit, and then he's drawing circles, focusing on that tight little bundle of nerves, and I feel my orgasm start to build. Slowly and then quickly turning into a fever pitch of need as I explode, calling out his name.

He captured my hands, pushing them to the bed, keeping me in place as my orgasm took over, sending me to the rooftops and higher still. Andrei stopped when I was a shuddering mess, begging him to because I couldn't take another moment.

I'm not sure what I expected to happen after he'd licked my pussy, but I watched, mesmerized, as he stood, his hands going to his pants. I hadn't even realized he was still completely dressed, whereas I was nearly naked. All that remained was a bra, but it didn't offer me anything in the way of protection.

Andrei shoved his pants and boxer briefs down, and I saw his hardness for the very first time. His cock was long and thick. He wrapped his fingers around the length, starting from the tip, working down to the base, and back again.

I wanted to touch him. He looked hard and soft at the same time. I'd already moved to sit up, and I reached out, wanting to give him the same kind of pleasure he'd given me.

"Don't fucking touch me," he said.

I jerked my hand away as if I'd been scalded. Why couldn't I touch him? I'd noticed Andrei avoided my touch. He kept this distance from us. He could touch me any time he wanted, I had no choice in the matter.

"Take your bra off," he said.

I wanted to tell him to go fuck himself, but I think I was working on autopilot as I reached behind my back and flicked the catch of my bra, removing it, so he could get his fill.

He groaned, worked his cock, and when he found his orgasm, he spilled his cum right across my breasts. I didn't want to look at him. Not after how he'd made me feel. The orgasm had been great, but I wasn't even given the chance to make him come.

Once he finished, he put his dick away and left to the bathroom. He came back seconds later with a cloth, intent on cleaning me up, but I took it from him.

"Adelaide," he said.

Ignoring him. I got off the bed, and with as much dignity as I could muster, I left him standing in his bedroom, without another word.

He didn't want my touch. He wouldn't get my

words either.

****

Andrei

"This is rather small," Ivan said.

This was his first visit to me since his supposed death and rebirth. He'd already briefed me on what caused the charade. I had only met Cara briefly. The woman had been one of Slavik's brothel women, or something like that. She hadn't seemed important to me.

I'm aware there was some kind of history between the three, but again, all of that was just rumors, and I'd never paid much attention to it.

"You didn't seem to mind it when you visited my wife last," I said.

Adelaide was out, again.

Since our episode, she'd been distant with me. Not that I could blame her. I expected her to cave soon, but she'd already tested me this past week. Other than dinner, which was a silent affair, she didn't talk to me. Breakfasts were silent, as were the nights I made it home.

There was a distance now that hadn't existed before.

"I know, but with you here, it does look small." Ivan pursed his lips. "Do you think this is a good place to raise a family?" He shook his head. "I don't know what it is with my men. You always seem to go for the penthouse option. Kind of boring."

I wasn't going to point out that he lived in a penthouse suite as well.

"Speaking of family, is Adelaide pregnant yet?" Ivan asked.

"No."

I got to my feet. "Can I interest you in a drink?"

"You can, but you do know I'm not an idiot, don't you?" Ivan asked.

I paused on my way to our drinks and turned toward him.

Ivan smiled. "Get me that drink." He winked at me, and I poured us both a generous helping of whiskey. Adelaide had replaced the decanter on one of her many journeys out of the house. Ever since Leo had been given as her bodyguard, and I'd allowed her to leave, she was never home. I didn't agree with this compromising bullshit. Adelaide was nowhere to be found.

Handing Ivan a glass, I took a seat, sipping at the dark amber liquid. It was the strong stuff, burning as it went down.

"Do you hate Adelaide?" Ivan asked.

"No. She's my wife."

"Ah, but you see, to have a true wife, you need to fuck her. Not drive her crazy until she's happy with pathetic visits out. We both know you've not given her much of a life. At least Slavik did his duty."

He'd never compared us before.

"Are you questioning my loyalty?" I asked.

"No, I'm not. I'm simply stating a fact. He got the job done. Aurora is very much pregnant, and you've not even taken your wife. Your marriage could be annulled like that." He clicked his fingers. "Speaking of the charming woman, where is she?"

"Out," I snapped the word, taking a large drink of my whiskey.

He chuckled. "I thought you were supposed to be good with women."

I was amazing with women. The kind that wanted money for a good time. They were easy to handle.

Ivan sighed. "You know, I'm thinking that you and Adelaide might not be quite the good fit."

"I will get her pregnant soon," I said.

"I'm more than happy to take her off your hands.

She's more than a handful. I'm sure she'll keep me entertained for plenty of months to come."

My grip on the glass got too tight and it smashed within my hand. A couple of shards slid into my flesh, but I didn't mind. The welcoming bite of pain doused me in a harsh reality check. I couldn't kill Ivan. He was my boss. I was loyal to him.

Ivan smiled as if he knew what I was thinking.

"Those feelings rushing through you right now, I don't know if you know this, Andrei, but they come in handy with women. It helps to bring them closer."

"I know how to handle my woman."

"Do you? Because from where I'm sitting, you seem to have a state of blue balls."

My mind went back to the other night. Adelaide, naked, her eyes looking crushed as she watched me. I didn't want her to look at me with anything other than pure heat. Spilling my release onto her chest had been a fucking waste, but I didn't want to hurt her. She deserved more than that from me.

"You came here to talk about business," I said, hoping to change the subject.

When it came to Adelaide, I kept fucking up, and I didn't know how to stop it. Nothing I did was ever right.

"Ah, yes, I did. I want an update on everything."

So I gave him a brief on everything that had happened. Since Ivan's reappearance, my mafia problem had settled down. They had even handed me over three of their soldiers who they claimed had started the revolt against Ivan Volkov. It was all bullshit. I knew that and they knew that. They had played their true cards, and now I had to be on guard. It wasn't like I ever dropped it. I was always cautious, always waiting for someone to strike.

Now, when it came to the Evil Savages MC, they were another problem. They had gone quiet immediately after Ivan's rebirth, but they still plotted to take out my warehouses. My informant was more than happy to give me the details, but I had to be cautious.

My guy on the inside had never been so free with information. Demon would never allow it, and now as I sat with Ivan, I gave him every detail.

He sat back, running a finger across his lip, his gaze straight ahead. "Interesting."

There is a long silence and rather than interrupt his thoughts, I finish my drink, get to my feet, and pour myself another one.

It was good having Ivan back. He pissed me off constantly, but he was a good man, a good boss. He took care of all of us, and he helped bring us peace, even if for a short time.

"Do you have any update on Oleg?" I asked.

"He claims to have known about the situation, which is highly doubtful," Ivan said. "To make this work, I had to keep everyone in the dark. Cara needed to be assured of my death, and the only way to do that was for people to believe it."

"I would have been by your side," I said.

He waved his hand in the air.

"When I give an order, I expect people to follow it."

The only person who'd been allowed to go was Slavik. I don't know what the other brigadiers' instructions were, but mine were clear. With the mafia and MC problem near my borders, I had to remain in place. Without my presence, they would have the ability to take over.

It would take them some time, but I knew those fuckers would do it, especially now that they had tried, and that was still with me here. This was one of the many things that made Ivan stronger. He was always one step ahead of the game, while the rest of us constantly played catch-up.

"How could he have known?" I asked.

"That's the point, he couldn't have." Ivan frowned. "There's something not right about that. A few of my men have gone missing from his territory. It's what alerted me to the possibility of Oleg's deception."

"We need someone on the inside," I said. "Someone he doesn't know is working for us."

"I know, but Oleg is smart, he's aware of people on our payroll."

I sat back, trying to think of someone who'd be able to get inside without any trouble, and no one came to mind.

I looked at Ivan as my front door opened and closed. The sound of Adelaide's heels could be heard through my office door, which I'd kept open.

"Ah, we've had way too much business. I think it's time to move on to other pressing matters."

I wanted to stop him. He looked way too happy with himself getting close to my wife, and I didn't want to share her. Leaving my glass on the coffee table, I followed him out to see Adelaide removing her shoes, wincing.

She'd started to wear the clothes I had picked out for her. They made her look too serious. Her long, beautiful hair had been pulled back into a tight bun. She'd not seen us yet, and I watched as she tugged out the pins, allowing the long length to flow freely. It had a natural curl to it. I imagined those locks wrapped around my fist as I took her hard and fast.

After the way I treated her the other night, I doubted she would have any time for me, and I couldn't help but be a little pissed off about that fact. I didn't say anything, though, admiring her instead.

"Aren't you a charming sight?" Ivan said.

Adelaide spun toward us, shock on her face.

Leo nodded at me.

She'd gone to see this Nathan person again. I didn't like him. I had tried to look for details on him, but his entire life read like a fucking saint, and I just didn't believe it. There was something off about him. I wanted to kill him, but doing that wouldn't win me any points with Adelaide. Not that I needed any.

Leo shared with me pictures of her with Nathan. This was the third time she'd seen him this week, and I didn't like how close they were getting. She was my wife. She should be close to me, no one else.

"Ivan," she said. The smile on her lips was forced. "It is so good to see you."

I'd not told her the news of Ivan's supposed death. She didn't need to know every single detail. I clenched my hands into fists as the two shared a quick embrace.

"And you, as always. You're looking so beautiful." He pouted. "But I had hoped to hear some good baby news."

Adelaide's cheeks went bright red. "Will you be staying for dinner?"

"Only if I get the pleasure of your company?"

"Of course." She kept smiling even as her face was flushed. "Please excuse me, I have to change."

"I'll order dinner," I said.

She didn't look at me. Gritting my teeth, I waited for her to leave before excusing myself, and going to Adelaide. She was at the doorway of our closet, looking in.

I grabbed her waist, spun her around, and pressed

her up against the wall. "Your little silent game ends tonight," I said.

She glared at me.

"Oh, I understand. You want me to play the doting wife, right? The one that can't touch her husband." She suddenly shoved her hands up above her head. "Don't worry, I won't give the game away that there's no chance of us ever having kids, since that would require you to actually want my touch, but we know that's not what you want. All you want to do is get your rocks off."

She took a deep breath, and I hated to admit it, her fire turned me on.

We'd not broken Adelaide yet. This life wasn't for weak women. It destroyed weak women, but as I stared at Adelaide, I wondered if I'd misjudged her.

"Are you done?" I asked.

"Yes. I'll be out to entertain our guest soon."

Her lips looked too good to deny myself, and so I didn't. I slammed my lips down on hers, capturing her wrists, which were still above her head, and taking complete advantage of the situation, kissing her hard. At first, she protested, wriggling against me as if to ward me off, but it didn't take long for her to give in and start kissing me back.

I broke the kiss first, stepping back, giving us some space.

"Don't be late."

I was being a dick, and I didn't care. When it came to Adelaide, I'd take whatever I got.

Chapter Nine

Adelaide

"You're quiet today," Nathan said.

Leo stood a few feet away looking every part the disapproving guard. He wouldn't allow me to be alone with Nathan, even though I knew he was a good guy. My one and only best friend.

"I'm sorry. I've got a lot of things on my mind."

"You can share them, you know." Nathan glanced back at Leo and frowned. "Does he have to come to every single one of our meet-ups?"

"My husband is a little bit paranoid. This makes him feel safer."

"I'm surprised he'd allow you to come and see me."

I pressed my lips together.

"Ah, I take it he doesn't like it?"

"I … I don't have to do everything he wants."

Nathan laughed. It was a deep, throaty laugh as he sat back.

I felt a little cold. The summer was ending fast and fall was approaching. I normally loved this time of year, heading into winter. I loved the seasons—Halloween, Thanksgiving, Christmas, New Year. There was so much to enjoy and celebrate during this incredibly dark period, and yet, nothing felt right. My marriage was a complete disaster.

Andrei and I were simply existing together. In the past few weeks, he'd been so busy with work. He rarely came home for dinner, and when we were in the same room for longer than five minutes, we ended up yelling at each other.

Some people would think I was a fool to anger my husband in such a way. He was Bratva, but I just couldn't help it. He drove me crazy. I was so angry at him, but also, he made me feel so alone.

Wrapping my arms around myself, I tried to ward off the cold.

Nathan tutted. "I don't know who you're trying to please with these outfits you wear, but it's not me. You're going to catch your death in this."

I smiled as he removed his jacket and placed it over my shoulders. "What about you?"

He shrugged. "I run hot. I'm not cold at all."

"I can't take your coat."

"You can, Adelaide. It's the least I can do."

I sighed. He always seemed to be taking care of me. "So, how long will you be staying?" Nathan had only meant to be here for a couple of weeks, but his plans had changed, and he'd been staying at some hotel. I couldn't remember the name of it.

"A couple more weeks. Business is going great. Also, I can't just leave, not yet." He nudged my shoulder. "I've got my bestie most days. You know how selfish I can be."

I laughed and rolled my eyes. "You're not selfish at all."

"When am I going to meet this husband of yours?" he asked. "You won't even allow me to come and visit you at your place. You do know how secretive you're being?"

"My husband is not for everyone." She shrugged. "Trust me, you're not missing a whole lot."

Nathan was interrupted by the ring of his cell phone. "I've got to take this." He stepped away from me and I leaned forward, staring down at the ground. His jacket was nice and warm, but the chill I suffered was from the inside and there was no getting away from that.

My life had taken a dramatic turn. I don't know

what was worse—my current stalemate with Andrei now, or when I was bored out of my brains.

Nathan returned seconds later. "I hate to do this, but I've got to head off. I've got a meeting to attend. Can we do this another time?" he asked.

"Yeah, of course. Sure. Work is far more important. Here," I said, removing the jacket, "take it back."

"No, you keep that on. I don't want you to catch a cold." Nathan wrapped his arms around me, pulling me close. "I don't know what's going on with you, babe, but please, you have to learn to trust me. I can make it all better for you."

I wanted to tell him that I felt better already, but I just embraced the hug. He felt good, warm, and comfortable.

Pulling away, he dropped a kiss onto my forehead. "See you soon."

I waved at him, watched him leave, and then turned toward an ever-disapproving Leo.

"Andrei wouldn't like this," he said.

"You sent him pictures. If he had any issue, he'd be here, rather than allowing you to guard me."

"Do you have any idea what this is potentially doing to his reputation?"

"What?"

"You're visiting a man often. Word of this gets out, Andrei becomes a laughingstock."

This made me laugh. "You're kidding, right?"

He raised a brow. I didn't know how he was able to look so disapproving with one glance. I didn't like it, but rather than tell him, I just offered him a glare. "I don't mean anything … he's a friend, okay? The only person I know and trust."

My cell phone rang, and I answered it without

looking at who called.

"Hello," I said.

"Hello, dear sister, long time no chat."

"Bethany?"

"You don't have any other sisters hiding. It's just me."

I felt myself tense. "What do you want?" I asked.

Leo looked at me intently. To him, I was just one giant fuck-up. Nathan was no threat to me, to Andrei, to anyone. He was my best friend.

"I was thinking, it's time for us to have a talk, don't you agree? As sisters."

"Why?" We'd never been close. Growing up, Bethany had despised me, and there was no love lost between us.

"Come on, darling, we're sisters. There doesn't have to be any bad blood between us. I'm insulted that you seem to think so."

I didn't think so. I knew so.

"There is much we can talk about. Come on, Adelaide. You always wanted a big sister, didn't you?" she asked. "This is our chance to finally be close."

I had no idea what she was up to, but I also didn't want to head back home. "Where?" I asked.

She told me the restaurant. "I'll meet you there in twenty minutes," I said and hung up the phone.

"I don't think that's a good idea," Leo said.

"Then call Andrei and tell him to go meet her and deal with this. It's my sister, Leo."

Even though I said those words, I knew it was a lie. My sister was a viper. Her only course of action was to attack. That was what she did. She hated me for what had happened, but that was all on her. I hadn't done anything to take her husband away.

Leo held the door of the car open, and I thanked

him.

Sitting in the car didn't help to make me feel better. In fact, all I felt was a whole lot worse about everything. This wasn't what I wanted. Covering my face with my hands, I leaned back and took several deep breaths, attempting to find some peace and calm, but nothing helped.

"Andrei cares about you," Leo said.

Dropping my hands, I look at my guard. "You don't know that."

"I have been driving him around for years, Adelaide. I've built up his trust, and yet, to help you, he put me in charge of your protection. He told me nothing could ever happen to you, and I will protect you with my life."

"I don't want that, Leo," I said. "I don't want you to do that."

He snorted. "I will gladly do it."

Tears filled my eyes as I thought of Andrei. "He's difficult to get to know." I had promised myself I wouldn't get too close to Leo. He was doing a job and I wouldn't pretend he was my friend.

"Andrei cares in his own way. Having his own territory is not easy and he's under a lot of stress right now."

"What kind of stress?" I asked.

"You will have to ask your husband." He slowed the car down to park and I glanced over at the restaurant.

"Will you come in with me?" I asked. The thought of seeing Bethany without any kind of backup scared me.

"Yes." Leo pulled the car away, going toward the parking lot. I climbed out of the car, and Leo moved toward my side, one hand at my back, the other at the base of his, and I knew he held his gun.

This was my new reality. Gone were the days of walking around nonchalantly.

We headed into the restaurant and I saw Bethany was already seated. She looked even more slender than usual. Leo let me go toward my sister, who stood when I got close, and air-kissed each of my cheeks.

"You look stunning, sweetheart," Bethany said.

"You do as well." She looked ... ill, but I wasn't going to tell her that. I could also tell with the way her lips were pursed, she'd gotten more work done.

There were times I felt like it was a competition between Bethany and our mother, about who could get the most work done. I hated hospitals, needles, anything like that, and so I was happy to keep my face and my body as it came to me.

"I'm so pleased you decided to see me. I was worried you wouldn't."

I frowned but didn't get a chance to question her as the waiter came with a bottle of wine, pouring us both large glasses. He promised to return with the menus.

"Why wouldn't I want to see you?" I asked.

"There's a lot of history with us." Bethany glanced down at the ring. "I guess Andrei decided that I could grace his bed, but I wasn't the woman he wanted to mother his children."

I froze. "You've not seen Andrei yet?"

Bethany pouted. "Do you still believe in monogamous relationships?" She tutted. "Honey, you of all people should know by now, that men don't want that." She held her hand out and pointed at her. "I've had to tell you this again and again. They want people like me, and I'm sure you can tell Andrei is getting his needs met. He leaves me very satisfied."

These had to be lies. Andrei was moody. He wasn't a happy man. Was that because he had to come home to her? Did he want to be with Bethany?

"Man, his tongue, it can do wonders on your pussy, can't it?"

I hated this and felt sick to my stomach.

"This is why you wanted to meet with me?" I asked. "To tell me you're having an affair with my husband?"

"Yeah, and I felt so bad about it. I was thinking we could come to some arrangement with him."

The waiter returned to offer us the menus, but Bethany smiled. "I don't think we'll be needing these." She handed over her card. "I'm sorry to have wasted your time."

I shouldn't have come here. I was an idiot to have thought for even a moment that Bethany wanted to have any kind of relationship. Staring at her now, I never thought I could hate a human being as much as I hated this woman. My sister—the woman I should be more than happy to die for, but I couldn't stand. She had a cruel edge about her that knew no bounds. This woman was vile.

My marriage … there was no marriage, and knowing Andrei was having an affair, well, there was no way it was going to work. Not now. Not ever.

"Are you going to cry?" Bethany asked.

"I have no reason to cry."

Bethany chuckled. "You don't have to be big and brave for me."

I shook my head and smiled. "You see, Bethany, you think this matters to me. Do you think I care what you and Andrei are up to? You're a perfect match for each other, but me, I was the one good enough to be married to."

The waiter came back. "I'm sorry, Miss, but your card has been declined."

I snorted. "That's okay, Leo will pay the bill. After all, you may have Andrei's dick, but at least I've got his money."

I didn't care about his money or his position, but I knew it would piss Bethany off, and I had to get out of there with my head held high. Even though all I wanted to do was collapse into a ball and sob.

****

Andrei

Leo had given me the update. He'd told me about the meeting with Nathan, and then the lunch Adelaide had with her sister. I should have known Bethany would be on some kind of warpath and Adelaide would be her target.

Standing in the penthouse suite, I waited for her to return. Rubbing my thumb and fingers together, I didn't know what I expected, but as Leo and Adelaide entered, she looked calm and collected. Her eyes gave her away, though. They were full of so much emotion. The moment she caught sight of me, I knew she felt pain. Bethany had hurt her.

"Leave us," I said.

Leo didn't say a word, just opened the door and left.

Adelaide looked at the closed door before turning her gaze back on me.

"I should have known you'd be here. Was this to get a kick out of seeing what she's done?" she asked.

"I have no idea what Bethany has done, but I can guarantee I don't find any of this amusing."

"I want a divorce," Adelaide said.

"Not happening."

Once you were part of the Bratva, you were there for life. There was no easy escape. Signing a piece of paper didn't beak away from the Volkov Bratva. Only

Ivan could grant such a motion and as far as I knew, he'd never allowed a divorce to go through. No one had gotten away. Unless it was six feet under.

"Fine. Then we'll go for an annulment. How about that?" she asked. "We don't have to get a divorce. Sex has to have happened between two people for there to be a need for divorce. I *know*!" She screamed at me and I watched her eyes fill with tears, and I hated them.

"What do you know?"

"About you and Bethany. I know you're sleeping with her. I know it's why you don't need to be with me. Is that it, huh?" she asked. "Is that why you don't want me to touch you because you can't stand the thought of these hands on your body? You've got Bethany, and I don't compare?"

So that was what Bethany was trying to do. To drive a wedge between us. I was still having to deal with her drug dealer, but I had my men on the bastard's tail. Now that Bethany had meddled like this, I wasn't going to help her. That nasty fucking bitch was going to get what came to her.

"You know what, I don't need to hear you say it. Do you think I don't know that I'm nothing like Bethany? I've been told that all my life. She has taken everything from me. Anytime I had friends, she stole them away, turning them against me. I had no boyfriends because Bethany made sure to always be around. The only person I ever had was Nathan, and you keep trying to take him away from me too. What is your game? Is it to make me miserable?"

"I have never touched Bethany," I said.

She shook her head. "Liar."

I moved toward her, and Adelaide shocked me as she took a step toward me too.

"You don't scare me."

"You're lying."

"I want out of your life. I want to be as far away from you and this fucked-up life as possible. I hate it here and I hate you, and I want out."

She went to hit me, but I captured her hands, holding them behind her back, causing her to be flush against me. She wriggled within my grasp, and this close, her body felt so good against mine. I didn't want to let her go.

"Listen to me," I said. "I have never been near Bethany. Even when we were engaged, I never fucked her. My dick has never been near her. I don't like her. I can't stand her. She's a nasty fucking bitch."

She shook her head. "I don't believe you."

"I know. The only woman I've been with in a long time is you. Just you. No one else."

"You're not with me."

"What we shared the other night, that's what I have had. Not Bethany."

Tears spilled down her cheeks. "I still want a divorce. I can't live like this. I don't want to live like this."

I let go of her hands and wrap them around her instead, trying to offer her comfort, even though I'm the last man she wants any of this from. She was not getting a divorce or an annulment. Cupping her face, I tilted her head back so she had no choice but to look at me. I swiped the tears off her face. She was too beautiful to cry.

Kissing each eyelid, I took possession of her mouth and started to move her through the penthouse suite, toward our bedroom. I would deal with Bethany very soon, but for now, I had my wife to handle.

Once inside our bedroom, I didn't bother to close the door. I tugged my wife's hair out of the bun, watching it fall freely. Next, I tore the clothes I had so carefully picked out for her, but hated. They were not her. I loved seeing her in sweatpants and shirts, jeans, the clothes that made her, her.

Running my hands over her body, I flicked the catch of her bra, and those luscious tits spilled out, and I cupped them in my hand.

"No," Adelaide said.

"You want me to stop?" I asked.

"I don't … Bethany…"

"Is nothing. She's trying to get inside your head to ruin this, Adelaide. You're my wife, and I have not been with another woman. I will never be with another woman." I took her hand and laid her palm against my heart, letting her feel it beating. "I don't trust easily. I've been hurt way too many times."

No woman was allowed to touch me. Adelaide didn't seem to understand that she was the only woman I craved. The only woman I had ever *wanted* to fucking touch me.

Ivan, the son of a bitch, knew this. He knew how hard I fought against this pull that Adelaide had over me. That bastard probably found it amusing. I didn't.

Women were weakness. They made men fucking stupid, and many years ago, I had vowed to never allow one to make me weak, but Adelaide was different from the start. She didn't even remember our first meeting all those years ago, but I remembered, and that was all that mattered.

Adelaide's touch was light at first. I let go of her wrist to stroke down her body, following the indent of her waist, to spread out to the curve of her hip. She wasn't leaving this bedroom a virgin. I wanted her virgin cunt on my dick. There was no way she was getting away from me.

Grabbing my shirt, I tore it open, not caring as the buttons flung left and right. I allowed her to place her palm directly over my heart, to feel it beating. This is what I wanted.

Adelaide stared at her hand.

My body was covered in ink, to hide the scars from my body. For me to know that I had been the one to win. Not my father. Not anyone.

I was strong. Others were weak.

I gripped the back of her neck, tilting her head back, and stared into her eyes. "Don't ever let Bethany come between us. She is not you. She will never be you." And before she had a chance to respond, I took possession of her lips, drawing her close until her breasts touched my chest. Her hand was between us, but I ravished her mouth.

Letting go of her neck, I slid my hand down her back, gripping the cheek of her ass, giving the plump flesh a soft little tap. She had such a ripe ass. Using both hands, I kneaded the flesh, and it made my dick so hard.

Moving her toward the bed, I laid her down.

"Wait?" She held her palm up. "I want to see you."

She could have anything she wanted. All she had to do was say the word. I removed my clothes easily.

Ink decorated my legs and parts of my thighs. I'd gotten them when I was younger. Crawling onto the bed, I moved Adelaide until she was against the pillows. Dropping a kiss to her lips, I trailed my mouth down, sucking each of her hard nipples into my mouth. She arched up. My name spilled from her lips as I used my teeth to arouse her.

Her grip on the blanket tightened, and I kissed down her body, going toward her pussy. Spreading open her thighs, I stared down at her pretty virgin cunt. No other man had been inside her before. She was all mine, and I fucking loved that. No other man was ever going to know how tight she got, how wet.

To take her tonight, I was going to have to make her dripping. She was going to feel pain. Woman always did on their first time. She'd be my first and only virgin.

I sucked her clit into my mouth, sliding my tongue back and forth across the sensitive bud. I loved hearing my name echoing off the walls. I was doing everything right. The urge to fuck her with my tongue was strong, but I held off. The only way I was breaking that hymen was with my stiff cock. Focusing all my attention on the swollen bud, I stroked her clit, bringing her closer to orgasm.

One day soon, she was going to come with my dick deep inside her, so I could feel her milking every single drop.

I didn't have to wear a condom, and Adelaide came, screaming my name. Her body was overcome by the pleasure, and I didn't draw out the pain.

Moving between her thighs, I stopped stroking her pussy, grabbed my cock, aligned the tip to her entrance, and slammed balls-deep inside her, tearing through the thin piece of flesh that made her a virgin. In doing so, I consummated our marriage, finally, stopped any chance of annulment, and made Adelaide mine in every single way that counted.

She screamed, and her body tensed. I captured her hands, holding them against the bed so she wouldn't hurt me. Not that her fists could fight me off. She was no match for me.

Tears filled her eyes and spilled down her cheeks. Her cunt was so tight. I knew it would be. There was no easy way to claim a virgin. I waited, being patient, allowing her to become accustomed to my sheer size before I started to thrust within her. Going deep, making her take all of me.

I hated that I hurt her, but now, there was no chance Bethany would come between us again. I was going to fill my wife with my cum, and have her completely dripping with it. She would be pregnant in no time.

Chapter Ten

Adelaide

I was no longer a virgin.

Laying in the bath as my sore muscles attempted to relax, I knew it was part of Andrei's plan. Now I couldn't get an annulment. Is that why he had sex with me now? The tears wouldn't stop. They kept falling from my eyes, even as I batted them away.

He said there was nothing going on between Bethany and him, but there was this … doubt. Why wouldn't he want to be with her? They had been engaged before.

I was a fool to have let this happen. Having sex with Andrei didn't prove anything to me. We weren't a love match. This was business.

I covered my face, gritted my teeth, and prayed the tears would stop. I didn't want to be one of those women who sobbed all the time.

If Andrei spoke the truth—and I saw no reason why he didn't—then what did Bethany get out of it? What game did she play? Was it just to torment me? I wouldn't put it past her. She lived for making me miserable, or at least whenever she thought I was happy, she went out of her way to make me the opposite.

Could she lure Andrei away? Did I want her to? Would it be easier if he cheated on me?

Our marriage was a farce. Nothing more than a business negotiation between my parents and Ivan. I wasn't an important piece to any puzzle. I was the stand-in. The second choice.

Dipping my hands beneath the water, I lifted them up and pressed them against my face. The last thing I wanted Andrei to see was my tears. I'd always imagined my first time being with someone who loved me and whom I loved. Did I love Andrei? The simple answer was no. I didn't know him.

I splashed more water onto my face, hoping to wipe the evidence of my tears away before he came back. This was not a time to be emotional, even though I'd lost my virginity. It had been painful.

Andrei's eyes had stared into mine, and for a brief time, I thought we had a connection, but that couldn't be the case. I was going crazy right now.

"I've cleaned the bed," Andrei said, entering the bathroom.

Glancing over my shoulder, I'm aware of his nakedness even more now. I couldn't help but see the evidence of my virginity against his … dick.

I turned away to stare back in the water, expecting him to leave me alone. He surprised me by moving past me and climbing right into the tub. Everything Andrei owned was of the best quality and high luxury, including his bathtub, which could have easily held an orgy.

"Talk to me, Adelaide." His voice was deep, demanding.

"There's nothing to talk about."

"This was your first time. You don't have any girlfriends to talk to."

I couldn't help but flinch at his assessment. He wasn't wrong.

Wrapping my arms around myself, I tried to sink beneath the water and the bubbles. He'd put in some bath salts, I assumed to help with the aches and pains.

"Don't hide."

"I'm not hiding."

"I'm not fucking your sister."

I lifted my gaze to his and he cursed, closing the distance between us and pulling me into his arms. I started to fight him, wriggling against him, hoping to get free, but he was much stronger than me, and water kept sloshing over the sides, which annoyed me. I didn't want to make a mess, but I also didn't want him to hold me.

"Let me go."

"I'm not doing this with you," he said. "Bethany is fucking toxic. She's only interested in ruining lives. She hates that you're my wife. That you get all the luxury, not her. Why can't you see that?"

He moved us so that I was beneath him, and all it would take was for him to dunk me under the water and hold me in place. Would he do it? Drown me? Had my life come to this?

"Please don't kill me," I said. My voice broke with every word I spoke and I hated how desperate I sounded.

Andrei tightened. His hands still held me in place and the water covered most of my body from the neck down. I'd surprised him.

"I'm not going to kill you."

I couldn't help but be doubtful. This was a man whose life was devoted to killing—I thought.

"Adelaide, you will always be safe."

"Then why do I need a bodyguard?"

"I'll never kill you."

"Unless I betray Ivan Volkov?"

I saw his jaw clench.

"You're not going to do that."

"What if I want to?" I asked. "What if I want to put an end to this life, and just be done with it? To be at peace. I never asked for this. I never asked for any of this." He pressed one of his hands against my mouth, silencing me.

"Do not ever fucking threaten that. You don't want to die, Adelaide. You're trying to cope with the shit your sister is trying to fill your head with. I'll get to the bottom of what Bethany wants, but until then, do not throw out useless threats. You don't deserve to die, and I won't allow you to sign our death warrants."

I frowned. "Ours?"

Andrei smiled. "Don't you get it? You go down, I go with you."

"No." I shook my head, denying it. That couldn't be.

"You'd never do anything to harm him. You're his … man."

"And do you think Ivan would trust me if my wife so blatantly betrayed him? It would kill him."

"You're in charge."

"Only for as long as I can be trusted."

This had to be a trick. The thought of Andrei dead twisted my stomach. He couldn't die because of me. My threats were idle. I'd never betray Ivan, even if I hated being married.

Today had reminded me of what Ivan and Andrei had gotten me away from, and that was my family. My parents and sister were horrible. Being near them could poison the best of people.

"I won't do it," I said. "I didn't mean it."

Andrei searched my gaze and nodded his head. "I know."

He lifted up, and helped me to sit up as well. Andrei moved in behind me. The warmth of his body surrounded me. I watched as he reached past my shoulder, grabbing a bar of soap and lathering up his hands.

No words were spoken.

His hands went to my body, and I held my breath as he started to wash me. I expected pain. After the way I'd just spoken and treated him, I should have gotten it.

Other men would have beaten me.

"I've spoken with Slavik," Andrei said. "We're going to visit them soon. You can spend some time with Aurora."

"Thank you."

"I know you've not seen much of each other, but you seemed to hit it off at the wedding."

Anyone would have been a welcome relief at our wedding, other than Bethany and my mother. Aurora had been a breath of fresh air. She looked so out of place next to her husband. Sweet and innocent. I felt like she didn't deserve to be part of this Bratva world.

"Do you like Slavik?" I asked.

"He's got good business sense."

"That's not what I asked."

"I never like anyone, Adelaide."

He used his hands soaked in water to rinse my body. Andrei reached for the soap and I didn't deny him as he washed my hair, taking care as he used shampoo then conditioner.

I wanted to do the same for him, but I shouldn't have been surprised. He wouldn't want me touching him, and I understood why. After my outburst, why would he want me to touch him?

Andrei got out of the bath first and wrapped a towel around his waist. I couldn't help but admire the tattoos covering his body. I'd not gotten the chance to properly look, but they were sexy. Heat filled my cheeks.

Andrei helped me out of the bath, wrapping me in a towel. We walked into the bedroom together and I looked toward the bed, to see clean, crisp sheets were already on. I wanted to know what happened to the other sheets, but to speak of what happened made me a little uncomfortable. There had been blood and his release combined. When I'd walked into the bathroom, I'd felt it spilling down my leg with each step I took. I was grateful none ended up on the carpet. There was only so much embarrassment I could deal with.

Andrei wasn't finished with his caring routine. He had a second towel within his grip, and he used it across my shoulders. He gave me the towel to dry my hair, but he wasn't finished drying the rest of my body. I was about to head into the closet after he took the towels back to the bathroom, but he grabbed my arm and moved me toward the bed.

It was warm in the room.

Both of us still completely naked. He moved me so I sat in front of him.

I waited.

He slowly ran the brush through my hair, and the kind gesture surprised me. I wasn't expecting it. Andrei was a cold man, why was he being so nice to me? It made no sense.

I didn't say a word as he continued brushing my hair. Whenever he got to a knot, he held my hair and worked it out so that it didn't hurt. Was he treating me like a child? I felt not. This was something new, intimate. I pressed my lips together not wishing to spoil the moment as I enjoyed his hands on me. They were so tender.

Once he finished, he helped me into bed, and I lay down. At first, I faced away from him, sensing him at my back. It was late and I'd not eaten anything all day. Rolling back over, I looked at him. Andrei stared at me. Neither of us spoke.

I didn't want to break this … whatever the hell this was. He kept looking at me. What did he see? What did he feel? I had so many questions I wanted to ask him, but I stayed silent.

Finally, after what felt like an eternity, he reached

out, putting his hand against my cheek, leaning in close, and kissing my head. I waited with bated breath as his arms surrounded me, and then his warmth flooded my body. I wrapped my arms around him, afraid I would make a wrong move or completely mess this up.

He kissed my head again and hummed against me. This was nice. I liked how he smelled and I loved how comfortable I felt in his arms. I never wanted this to end. I smiled against his chest and closed my eyes.

Of course, my body had other ideas. The lack of food made itself known as my stomach chose that moment to growl. I didn't know what embarrassed me more—the evidence of my virginity, my jealous outburst, or my crazy hungry stomach.

Andrei chuckled. "I knew we'd forgotten to do something." He kissed her head. "I'll feed you."

The moment was lost, all because my stomach couldn't stay quiet. Stupid hunger.

****

Andrei

I don't know what Bethany's agenda is, and I don't like it.

Adelaide was staying by my side so I got Leo following Bethany around. If she hoped upsetting her sister would have me reacting, she was very much mistaken. I didn't play the games of that woman. Adelaide was my number one priority, and now that she was my wife completely, there was no going back. Divorce and annulment were off the table.

"You don't have to stay in because of me," Adelaide said. She came toward the dining room table where I'd just read the text from my informant in the Evil Savages MC, that the plans had changed.

I was still waiting for more details on this Nathan person who'd made a sudden appearance in her life.

Adelaide was an amazing person, far too trusting for her own good. A man like Nathan, who'd appeared out of the blue some time ago, and just befriended her ... I didn't believe it and I was going to get to the bottom of it. Especially because I couldn't find any details about the man. No records. It was like he didn't exist. That raised alarm bells, which was why I'd also traded places with Leo. There was no way my wife would go to see this Nathan without me.

Closing my phone, I looked up. Adelaide wouldn't meet my gaze. Was she still sore? It had been two days since I'd taken her virginity and I wasn't going to wait too long. Seeing her virgin blood on my dick had given me deep pleasure. No other man would ever know just how fucking perfect she was.

"Work can wait." I pointed out the cinnamon bun and coffee I'd had Terrance get for her.

Her eyes went wide. "Why do I feel you buy me these to shut me up?"

"I buy them because you love them." I happened to enjoy the sweet treat as well.

I watched her take a bite, relishing the pleasure that crossed her face. There was going to be a lot more pleasure. For too long now, I'd denied myself the pleasure of my wife, and that was going to change. I figured a couple of days was more than enough time for her to recover from her first time.

"I didn't know you had a sweet tooth," she said.

"I don't, but there's something about a cinnamon bun that just tempts me."

Adelaide's mouth closed and some of the dark sugar coated her lips.

I got to my feet and her eyes opened. Leaning against the table, I reached out, putting my thumb against her lip, and swiping it off. Showing her my bounty, I pressed it to my lips and sucked it into my mouth with a moan.

She gasped and her mouth fell open.

"What are you doing?" she asked.

"What does it look like I'm doing?"

She shook her head. "I have no idea."

I chuckle and stroke the curve of her neck. "I'm attempting to seduce my wife."

"Why?"

I pull her chair out and move between her spread thighs. Running a finger across her chin, I force her to look at me.

"Because I loved the feel of her pussy wrapped around my cock, and you made a point the other day."

"I did?"

"Yeah, this marriage is forever. We're not getting away from each other, so why don't we just enjoy one another?" I stroke her breast, fingering the edge of her shirt.

She wasn't wearing the clothes I'd picked out for her, and now I found her even more attractive. I'd have to take her shopping for the clothes she wanted. My wife didn't need to fit any kind of model. I didn't give two fucks what people thought of me, and anyone who said anything about my wife would answer to me. I'd relish the bloodshed.

"This is what you want?" she asked.

"Do you want to enjoy us?" I asked.

She nibbled her lip, her gaze looking past mine. I wanted to know what was going on in that head of hers, to find out how she ticked.

"Yes."

Her answer was so soft I had to wonder if I heard it.

I grabbed her arms, lifting her up, shoving the

coffee and cinnamon bun out of the way. I pressed her against the table, and she let out a gasp.

"Andrei?"

"You can say no at any time," I said. "I'll stop." I'm hoping she won't.

Kissing the spot right over her pulse, I heard her gasp. I knew where to touch her. Adelaide was a body of beauty, and I loved feeling her against me. She wasn't trained in deception. Running my hands down to her ass, I push them into the waistband of her sweatpants and grip the supple flesh.

Our moans fill the air, and I nudge her back against the table. Moving my hands to the front of her pants, I give them a tug, pulling them off her body. My wife was wearing panties, and it's another pair I had shredded in no time. They were a hindrance and getting in my way. Cupping her naked pussy, I slid a finger between her slit, stroking across her clit, before gliding down to feel how soft she was. I no longer had to wait to break this pussy. She was all mine.

I rocked my finger in and out of her. Adelaide held onto the dining room table, eyes closed, and I took the time to simply admire her. I saw her face flooded with pleasure. Moving a second finger inside her, I saw it was a tight fit as she winced, but I pushed my thumb against her clit, playing with her, taking away the bite of pain by tormenting her. She tilted her head back, filling the air with the sweet sound of her moan.

I wanted it.

Kissing her hard, I swallowed her cries, keeping them all to myself. Rocking my palm against her cunt, I filled her pussy, wanting it to be my cock. With each stroke, she grew wetter, and that was what I needed. I didn't intend to hurt her. All I wanted was for her to be mindless from pleasure.

"Andrei," she said.

"Do you like what I'm doing to you?" I asked.

"Yes."

"Do you wish it was my cock?"

A whimper.

Pulling my fingers from her pussy, I ran my hands up to her stomach. Within seconds, I removed the rest of her clothing, wanting her bare. There was no room for hiding when she was with me.

I marveled at her body. There was not a single flaw about her as far as I could tell. I craved her. My dick was so fucking hard it hurt. One taste wasn't enough. Adelaide had to be mine to be able to quench this desire I had for her.

I saw her heart racing, but she didn't attempt to cover herself up. Sitting down in the chair before her, I moved it close and put my hands on her knees.

"What are you doing?"

"Taking my time."

I lifted her feet onto my knees, and then I spread her legs wide, so she was open to me. "This pussy is mine, Adelaide," I said.

I didn't expect her to say yes to my cock. She is so new to her own body, and I can't wait to explore every inch of her. To awaken her desire. My hope is one day she comes to me when her body needs loving.

Reaching between her thighs, I move my fingers toward the lips of her pussy and spread them open, staring at her hole. Was she pregnant already? I had to wonder if my baby was already growing inside of her. I take two fingers and ease them into her pussy, watching her take them. With my thumb, I press it against her clit and stroke back and forth. Each time I do this, she releases a little whimper and I see her body shake a little under the onslaught. My dick is so hard.

I want to just fuck her. First, I'm going to taste her. Pulling my hands from her cunt, I move my chair forward, grasp her hips, and then press my face against her pussy, licking her sweet clit. Sliding my tongue back and forth across her nub, I glide down to circle her hole before pushing forward, fucking into her.

Adelaide's moans fill the air, and it is the sweetest fucking sound I've ever head. I'm heady with excitement. My cock is so hard, it's nearly punched through the fabric of my pants. Letting go of Adelaide's hips, I don't stop loving her pussy, as I ease down the zipper that contains my raging erection. Wrapping my fingers around the length, I work them up and down, making myself ache with need for her. She is all I want.

Pre-cum leaked out of the tip, and I smear it all over my dick. With some of it still on my fingers, I press it inside her, wanting every single reason for her to get pregnant. There was no time to hold back.

Drawing my tongue back up to her clit, I focus on that tiny nub, sliding my hands beneath her ass and licking her, tasting her, sucking her, bringing her closer to the peak, and when I feel her orgasm starting to build, I stop, because I'm a selfish bastard and I want to feel her release wrapped around my dick.

Adelaide whimpered.

I guide the tip of my dick to her entrance, and then staring into her sweet brown eyes, I slowly, inch by inch, feel her surround me. She's so fucking tight. So hot. All mine.

I'd never been a man to care about any woman's previous lovers, but there's something primal about knowing I'm the only man Adelaide will ever have. Just the thought of it has me grabbing her hips and slamming all the way to the hilt inside her.

Her pussy is so soft, and she's so close. Tiny little

ripples wrap around my dick, sucking at me.

I let go of her hips and stroke across her nub, and I watch, feeling her body as she gets closer to that peak once again, and this time, as she's close, she hurtles toward it, on fire, need pulsing through her. I held her, wanting to pound inside her, to mark her, to claim her.

She's all mine. All fucking mine.

I don't give her chance to come down from that peak. Grabbing her hips once again, I pound inside her.

The table is more than a hindrance as it moves with the power of my thrusts. I have no choice but to pick her up and carry her through to the bedroom. I drop her onto the bed, and this time she has nowhere to go. Holding her down and in place, I slake my desire, fucking her harder than I ever have before, shoving my cock as deep as I can. I'm not myself. I need to come inside her, to flood that pretty pussy with my cum, and to see it filling her.

I growl her name, feeling how close I am, and as my orgasm starts to build, I grab her hands, locking our fingers together. When my release comes, I stare into her eyes, not wanting to let her go, feeling the aftershocks of her own climax, as I'm close to mine, and as I fill her, I wonder if this will be the one to get her pregnant. I went from not being in a rush to get her pregnant, to wanting it so damn much.

Every single pulse fills her cunt, and only when it's over do I pull out, my cock dripping with my spunk, and I open her thighs, watching her pussy. Some of my creamy cum drizzles out, and I use my fingers, trying to push it back inside her, wanting it to take.

What the fuck has happened to me?

Chapter Eleven

Adelaide

"How does it feel to be pregnant?" I asked, looking over at Aurora.

She looks so happy and it's a surprise to me. The man she's married to doesn't strike me as a kind man, or one that would be easy to love. He's cold and cruel, and Aurora is the complete opposite.

"It's surreal at times," Aurora said, smiling at me. "Do you think you will be pregnant?"

I put a hand on my stomach and wonder. We were not using any kind of protection. My parents took away my birth control pills when Bethany was removed as Andrei's fiancée. They said I couldn't take anything that would stop me from having a baby.

The pills helped to control my menstrual cycle, nothing else. I'd never had a boyfriend or anyone I could have gotten pregnant by.

"I ... I don't know," I said.

This wasn't the first time we'd visited Aurora. Andrei and I were celebrating six months of marriage.

Six very long months. I was in a bit of a shock myself. We'd not been on a honeymoon and Andrei spent a great deal of time at work.

Ivan had come to visit us last week and told us both that we needed a vacation. Wrapping my arms around myself, I hadn't seen my husband much during this trip. Ivan was also present, and at least one other brigadier as well. They called him Ive, even though his name was Ivan. Andrei had told me it was so there was no confusion. I didn't tell him that I was already confused about the things they did. It wasn't my place to tell them how to run things.

"Adelaide, are you okay?" Aurora asked,

reaching out toward me.

"Of course. I'm fine."

"You're not happy."

"I am. I am ... happy." I press my lips together. "I'm so happy for you."

Aurora shook her head. "That's not what I meant and you know it."

Pressing my lips together, I reach into my jeans pocket and pull out my cell phone. Andrei hadn't taken it off me, even as we were on the plane heading here.

"Bethany sent me this," I said.

My sister hadn't stopped trying to drive a wedge between me and Andrei. I believed him, at least I think I did, that he wasn't having an affair, but now I see this. It's a picture of them, and I don't know when it was taken, it looks like they're in a nightclub of some kind. Either way, they are looking way too cozy.

Andrei hasn't taken me to any clubs, and certainly no fancy restaurants. We don't ... date. I can leave his penthouse apartment and go to the shelter. He won't allow me to see Nathan. That he has banned, and then of course, there are the few times I can have dinner with Aurora. There's no real life for me, though. I'm constantly going through the motions until Andrei arrives home. That's it.

That is the extent of my life—reading books, cooking, and just waiting. I'm bored, I'm lonely, and I had thought things would change, but Andrei is cold. He's not mine.

"Bethany is a spiteful woman," Aurora said. "I know she's your sister and I'm sorry about that."

I shrugged. "Bethany has always been this way. Trust me, I'm used to it." I reach for the coffee mug, and bring it to my lips.

"Adelaide, talk to me."

"Andrei told me he is not having an affair." I don't tell her that was weeks ago. "I trust him."

"But?"

"Even if he's not having an affair, and this was taken some time ago, it means that he was at least happy with her. Didn't you see that?"

Is that what bothers me more? Andrei being happier with my sister? I'm the second choice. That's who I am. It's all I've ever been.

Aurora shook her head. "Stop it. No, I don't believe that for a second."

"Pictures don't lie," I said.

My words have Aurora laughing so hard. "You're kidding, right?"

"They don't."

"Adelaide, I know you're young."

I'm twenty-one years old. Bethany is nearly thirty. My mother was quite surprised when she had me. I've always been a lot older than my years, though.

"What does my age have to do with anything?"

"Some photos are designed to be deceptive. You have no idea when this was taken or why it was taken. It looks like a professional shot. It could have done the rounds for all those media papers and stuff. Trust me when I say this, Andrei never looked as happy as he does with you."

"You saw them together as a couple?"

Aurora nodded.

"Did Andrei smile?"

"From time to time."

"Did he listen to Bethany?"

"Adelaide, you've got to stop."

I put my coffee down and stood up. "I'm sorry, but I need some air." I smiled at her. It was forced and I felt my eyes fill with tears, but I bat them down, refusing

149

to allow them to leave. I'm not going to cry over him or this situation again.

Bethany was doing exactly what she set out to do and I knew that. She wanted to drive a wedge between me and Andrei. The sex was good. I enjoyed being with him, but I always felt like he was bored … I duck my head as I ignore one of the soldiers. I don't know how Aurora lives with guns constantly on display. They still terrify me.

I find a door leading onto the back porch that overlooks the garden, and as I step outside, I take a deep breath. Leaning against the door, I suck in more oxygen, even as I feel my chest tighten. Anxiety threatens to claw its way up my body, but I fight it, using my breathing to ground me, to keep me from going over the edge that can suck me down too hard.

Opening my eyes, I look out over the garden. Aurora and Slavik's home is beautiful. They have a special connection. What I've noticed in visiting them is that they don't show it. Not in public, but I've seen them when they don't realize anyone is watching, and I've heard them. Slavik is completely in love with Aurora. He would die for her. They are a love match. Even if they didn't start that way, it's what their marriage has become.

Andrei and I are not a love match. We're a business contract. That's why I know Andrei doesn't really want me. The sex is good because he's obligated to have sex with me. I overheard Ivan talking to Andrei one night a few weeks ago. He asked if I was pregnant yet, and Andrei said he expected it would happen soon.

What kind of man does that? He doesn't want me. His touch isn't filled with passion for me. I'm a duty.

Wrapping my arms around my body, I step toward the grass. Aurora and Slavik's home is so big, anyone could get lost. Removing my sneakers, I take a step onto the cold, wet ground.

There had been a storm last night. I'd lain awake in Andrei's arms, listening to the ferocious sound. As a child I'd always hated storms, and that hadn't changed as I aged. I always feared that the wind would be so strong it would tear the roof right off whatever place I was at. I'd lie awake for hours, listening, terrified of what could happen. Oftentimes I'd fall asleep, and the next morning I'd see the devastation.

It was like Mother Nature was too afraid to befall the Volkov Bratva's wrath, as there was no damage to his property. Even the trees didn't dare shed any branches.

"Hello, Adelaide."

I've already stepped into the wet grass when I look up to see Ivan approaching. His gaze seems entertained when he sees me standing on the cold wet ground. I'm freezing, but I'd rather feel the chill than the icy knowledge my husband doesn't want me. It was easier to live with him when he ignored me. I'd rather be invisible than go through this.

I thought I could handle it, but seeing Aurora and Slavik hurt more than ever. Bethany's constant taunts and pictures were eating away at me.

"Mr. Volkov," I said, bowing my head and showing respect.

Ivan clapped his hands together. "Adelaide, you are forever a delight."

I doubted that.

"Did you conclude your business?" I asked. Andrei never talked to me about what he and the others did. I wasn't expected to know, and for the most part, I kept my nose out.

Understanding his business wasn't part of my job description, at least that's what I'm always told. My job is to have babies. To shut up. To not make waves.

In that moment, I think about my parents. Not once did they make an effort to see me. When I'm alone, I'll turn the television on and go check out their channel, but other than seeing all the boring shows every single day, nothing has changed for them. I sometimes checked them on the Internet as well. Random pictures would appear—my mother shopping, my parents out together or with Bethany. No news about the daughter they were happy to give up for that pleasure.

"In a sense." Ivan stared at me. "Are you okay?"

"Yes, I'm fine."

It was a perfect and easy mantra to keep saying. No one wanted the truth. They were happy with careful lies.

"You're lying."

I tilt my head back and look up at the sky. It's dull. Not a single speck of brightness to be had, which was how I felt. Rubbing my hands up and down my arms, I know I need to escape this.

"I'm tired," I said, making my excuses.

"You know you can talk to him, don't you?" Ivan asked.

I glance at Ivan who is still staring. I wonder at times what is going on in his head. He's always plotting. Always keeping one step ahead of the game.

Talking to Andrei was out of the question. It has always been out of the question. He has his own life.

"I'll see you at dinner," I said.

Ivan doesn't stop me from leaving. I pass so many guards as I make my way to Andrei's and my sleeping quarters. He's not here and I'm glad about that.

Sitting down on the edge of the bed, I rest my palms flat on my knees and take a deep breath, then another, and then another. I'm still taking them, trying to calm my nerves, when my cell phone beeps. Pulling it out of my pocket, I'm almost hesitant to look. The last thing I want to see is another picture from Bethany. I promised myself I wouldn't let anything she said bother me, but how could I be so foolish to think I would get over it? This is my sister we're talking about. She takes great pleasure in hurting me.

It's not from Bethany.

Nathan has texted me. I've not seen him in quite some time, and I miss my friend with his easy smile and heartwarming words.

Nathan: **I need to see you.**

Andrei asked me not to have any contact with him. So I haven't. Leo didn't approve of me seeing Nathan. I don't have feelings for my friend. I'm not attracted to him in any way.

Nathan: **I have to tell you something. I know what is going on, Adelaide. I can help you.**

I doubt very much he can help me. Can he stop me from feeling this way? Can he stop my sister from hurting me?

Adelaide: **I can't talk right now. I'm away with friends. I'll let you know when I'm back.**

I'll meet him one final time to let him know that I can't see him. Pushing Andrei's buttons is not sensible. He might not kill me, but I bet he wouldn't have any qualms about killing Nathan.

****

Andrei

I'd never known such a big fuck-up in my entire life as I stared down at the bruised woman that was not Demon's daughter, Cassie. The plan was simple. While Demon thought he was hurting me and taking out some of the Volkov main warehouses, my men had gone on a mission to extract his precious daughter, Cassie—the Evil Savages MC princess.

What did I get? Lottie, the bastard daughter, the one known to be his, but he never fucking claimed. The one who was constantly left out in the cold because her mother had been a club whore who'd become a rat, so Lottie became known as the Rat's daughter. She was all but useless to me. Ivan was on his way to me as I watched this young woman. Eighteen fucking years old.

I'd already killed the men responsible for getting me the wrong woman. Lottie looked nothing like her sister Cassie.

Running fingers through my hair, I glance at Terrance who's been quiet since I killed the two men who were lying in a puddle of their own blood. My thirst to kill was strong. Rage consumed me.

I had no choice but to wait for Ivan, and I don't even know why he was in town without my knowledge. Ivan always did whatever the fuck he wanted. The usual rules of the Bratva structure didn't apply to him. He always had a plan in motion, and there was always a reason why he did what he did.

Hands on my hips, I waited. My cell phone beeps, and I see my other little problem is also being taken care of as we speak. I'd deal with that problem after I handle this one.

Of course, Ivan arrives within twenty fucking minutes. I have no idea how he's able to get to and from wherever he is within such a short amount of time, but he arrives looking collected and calm. I bring him up-to-date.

Lottie is still out completely cold. The tranquilizer we gave her would see her dead to the world until tonight.

"Now this is an interesting turn of events," Ivan said.

"Do you want me to kill her and dispose of the

body?" I asked.

"Why would we do that when we have a far more interesting player?" Ivan moved toward Lottie and crouched down. "Now, my sweet, I didn't think of you, but this is going to go very nicely indeed."

I frowned. "She's not Cassie."

"You're right, and that bitch would be difficult to handle. This one … this one is perfect, and don't you think she will look interesting on Ive's arm?" Ivan asked.

"What?"

Ivan chuckled. "Move her to secure location. I'll handle the rest, and I don't want to see her harmed in any other way, do you understand me?"

There was no point in arguing with him. What Ivan wants, he will get and I'm more than happy to grant it. I nod my head, and he smiles. It's not nice at all.

Ivan's the first to leave after I've made the necessary arrangements to transport Lottie. I'm not sure she will suit Ive, but I'm not going to criticize that decision. Ivan's in charge of who we marry. There's no chance of us making that choice. I'd tried to deal with Bethany, to accept my future with her, and then he handed me Adelaide, and well, I was learning to accept this life with her.

I tell Terrance where to take me, and I sit back, pulling out my cell phone and seeing a text from Leo, telling me that Adelaide is fine. She decided to stay in the apartment. I opened the app and glanced through the cameras, but I don't find her. I spot Leo in the sitting room, and I don't have time to question it, as Terrance pulls into the warehouse.

Three men are stationed outside the door, and I climb out of the car, making my way inside to the man currently tied to a chair, bleeding. It's the best look that son of a bitch has had. He was quite a hard man to track down.

Dragging a chair toward him, I take a seat and stare at him. His face is swollen, but one of his eyes is open.

"I see my men have kept you busy," I said.

"Fuck you."

"Let us both save all of our troubles and tell me what a fucking hit man is doing playing friends with my wife?"

Nathan is not his real name. The life he claimed to be living is not real. The man is good, there's no doubt about that. He knows how to blend into a crowd and manipulate those around him, but I'm not most people. From the moment I saw his picture, I knew there was something off about him, and not just because he was near my wife. There was something about him that I couldn't quite put my finger on, and then it had all fallen into place.

He's a hit man with many aliases.

Over forty years old, multiple passports, and so many kills under his belt. I'd met him once, nearly twenty years ago on the streets. He'd been a cold dead killer then, and staring at him now, he hadn't changed. Age marked his face, but I recognized him.

Nathan burst out laughing. "Do you think I pose a threat to Adelaide?"

I wrap my fingers around his throat, cutting off his air. "You don't get to say her fucking name."

It's pointless. This man has been trained to withstand all kinds of torture.

"If you had questions about my friendship with her, why didn't you just ask?"

"I did."

Nathan coughed, spitting up blood. I'd told my men that he didn't need to arrive at the warehouse in one piece. He just had to be alive. That was my only requirement.

Now I'm wondering if he had to be alive. I'd gladly have him dead.

Adelaide hadn't seen him in a while. They'd texted but not met. It would be so easy to cut him out of her life, and that's what I wanted to do. First, I wanted to know what brought him to Adelaide.

"Have you been hired?" I asked.

Nathan sighed. "I'm not here to kill her."

I frowned. "Why are you friends with her?"

"Because she's so sweet, don't you think?" Nathan asked. I wanted to kill him, but he spit out some more blood, and it looked like a tooth had come loose as well, as that was mixed with the blood. "Bethany is the person I was hired to kill. She pissed off the wrong people several years ago. Adelaide was unexpected. She was selling some nasty-ass lemonade, helping some kids. Bethany was supposed to be volunteering, but as always, she put Adelaide to the task. That's where I met her, and that's where Nathan was born."

"The charming gay friend with a job she doesn't understand."

He chuckled. "Exactly."

"You're not here to kill her?"

"I'm here to protect her," Nathan said.

This made me pause. "Why?"

"Do you really think her sister is going to allow her to play 'happy family' at your side? Bethany got out of the contract on her head. I don't know how, but I got paid and she's still breathing. I follow the money, but Adelaide always needed someone in her corner. Do you think Ivan Volkov is the only person Bethany pissed off?"

This made me pause.

Just as I was about to answer more questions, I heard the commotion outside, and then my men stepped forward as Adelaide entered the warehouse. Without Leo. On her own. Her gaze went to Nathan and then to me. What the fuck was she doing here?

I see the red dot on her chest and I know it's not from my men. Someone lured her here. Someone who knew I would be here, and before I can stop it. I watch Adelaide's body jerk as someone shoots her. One to the chest and the other to her stomach.

I charge forward as she starts to fall. "Fucking kill them!" I scream, pulling Adelaide into my arms.

Blood has soaked through her white shirt. Two gunshot wounds.

"I … I…"

"Shut the fuck up, Adelaide. Conserve your strength. You're not dying on me." Her face has already gone pale.

"I … I'm so cold."

My hands are covered in blood as I cup her face. "Look at me."

I don't know how Nathan got loose, but in the commotion, he's on the other side of her.

"*Adelaide*!" I scream her name, shaking her.

Fuck.

No.

Fuck.

This is not supposed to happen. Adelaide was meant to be at home. Safe. Away from danger.

"We need to get her to the hospital," Nathan said, reaching for her.

I punch him hard, staining his cheek with Adelaide's blood, but I don't care. "You stay the fuck away from her."

I don't have time to tie him up, and while my

men deal with whoever fired at my wife, I pick Adelaide up.

Terrance is there, but I ignore him, climb into the car, and hold my wife close to me as I pull out of the warehouse and head to the first hospital. I'm not thinking straight but I don't give a fuck. This is my wife. Adelaide—the nicest person I've ever had the pleasure of meeting, who didn't deserve me as a husband, and who should have never come near me. Who I stayed away from even though I craved her, and she became mine. Ivan knew what he was doing the moment he replaced Bethany.

Adelaide was mine. She *is* mine.

I pulled up outside of the hospital. I don't park the car, I abandon it and carry my bleeding wife into the hospital. Doctors and nurses surround me. They keep bombarding me with questions and in the end, I warn them. I tell them who I am, and that I will end all the fucking lot of them if they don't fix my wife.

One of the doctors comes forward, and he takes charge. Adelaide is put on a gurney and carried away from me. A nurse puts her hands on my chest and tells me that I can't follow.

I need to know Adelaide is alive. She has to live. I cannot accept any other outcome.

With my hands clenched into fists, I stay in that one spot, staring at the door. I don't know when my men arrive, but Terrance is the first.

"Sir."

"Sir."

"Sir."

He keeps repeating my title, and I finally turn toward him. "This is Adelaide's phone. There's a text. It tells her that if she wants to see you, she has to go to this location. It's sent from an anonymous number."

I don't care.

Nathan has arrived with my men. His face is still bruised, but he's cleaned away some of the blood.

"He helped to detain the men responsible," Terrance said.

We're in a public place. I can't kill him right now. I don't have to worry because over his shoulder I see Ivan appear, and I know he's come to deal with the shit that just went down, because for the first time in my life, all I can feel is grief.

Chapter Twelve

Andrei

They didn't know if Adelaide was going to make it. The bullet missed her heart, but there was too much blood.

She had also lost our baby. I had no idea she was pregnant and I guessed she didn't either. The doctor told me there was no way to save the baby. That shouldn't hurt. I was not like this. I had no bastard feelings, but I was struggling to hold it together. Ivan, my Pakhan, my boss, the one I served, handled everything, donating a large sum of money, and apologizing on my behalf as he made sure my wife was given the utmost care.

I was standing at the foot of my wife's hospital bed, looking at her attached to tubes and wires as machines monitor her.

They told me to have hope. Seeing my wife fighting for her life, I had no choice but to feel hope.

****

Adelaide. My precious, sweet Adelaide, who didn't even remember we had met before. It was some time ago, she had only been about eighteen, and for some reason, she ended up volunteering along with a few nurses. I think she must have been doing some basic medical training, but again, I'm not sure.

A deal had gone bad, I'd managed to get Ivan out of the place without a single scratch on him, but I'd ended up cut up really bad. You should have seen the other guy, he was unrecognizable. He'd been one of my men, and he'd turned on me, and that was what had caused the fuck-up in the first place.

Which is why I don't trust anyone.

Anyway, Adelaide had been in the alleyway where I'd taken a moment to rest. A bunch of nurses and do-gooders were helping the homeless, trying to make a difference and all that crap, when Adelaide stumbled upon me.

I'd been cut bad. A slash right across the stomach. It wouldn't kill me, but it sure did sting like a son of a bitch. The Volkov Bratva had been in full power at the time, and after killing the men who'd turned on me, I'd been alone and stumbled through my city, which is why I'd ended up in the alleyway.

Adelaide hadn't questioned me about the cut. She'd tended to my wounds. Even when I yelled at her. Even when nurses recognized my brand and were terrified to come near me, Adelaide had treated me herself. What my precious wife didn't know at that time was that she did something to me. I'm not exactly sure what it was, but I kept a close eye on her ever since.

It wasn't like she'd done anything special. I figured she didn't understand the ink decorating my knuckles, but then I realized, even if she did know what it all meant, she would have still cared for me. My wife has a kind heart. She is a kind soul, and in comparison, I'm a monster.

She doesn't know when to leave well enough alone.

****

The door to Adelaide's room opens, and I turn to see Ivan, carrying a cup of coffee. "I figured you needed something to drink."

"Ivan, you shouldn't be here," I said. There was not enough protection for him, and I'm not going to lie, I'm not exactly in a state of mind right now to protect him. My focus is my wife.

"I'm where I need to be." Ivan held out the coffee and I took it, taking a sip, thinking, oddly, about cinnamon rolls.

The coffee was rank, some of the worst I'd ever tasted, but I wished Adelaide was awake. She'd wrinkle her nose in that cute way she did and still drink it, because she was nice.

"I shouldn't have married her," I said.

"Don't start," Ivan said.

I turned toward the man who I once thought I would give my life to, the only person I'd die for, but Adelaide had proven that wasn't the case. I would give anything to be in that bed rather than her.

"Bethany was the one cut out for this life."

"And you think I was going to allow that little whore to be wife to one of my men?" Ivan asked. He tutted. "You should know me better than that."

"Adelaide is too good for this world."

"Adelaide can handle this. She's not some delicate flower, Andrei. You're just too stubborn to see it."

"She doesn't deserve to be in that bed. Fighting for her life. She should have a husband who is not going to get her killed."

Ivan looked away from Adelaide. His gaze focused on me. "And you think you'd have been able to handle that? You think I don't know the hours you spent, keeping an eye on her. Giving yourself little rewards just to make sure she was safe, happy?"

No one should have known about that. No one. I'd been so fucking careful. Always lurking in the shadows when it came to Adelaide's life, and I shouldn't have been surprised that Ivan knew. The man knew everything.

Sipping at the coffee, I grimace. It really is bad.

I take a seat beside Adelaide. The tubes are hideous and distracting.

"She is going to wake up," Ivan said.

I stay quiet.

"The man responsible is waiting for you to deal with him."

I nod. I have every intention of dealing with that fucker.

"I can stay here," Ivan said.

This made me turn my head to look at him. "Don't you want to deal with him first?"

"This is for you, and I imagine with Adelaide like this, there's no one else you could trust with her safety." Ivan released a yawn. "Don't worry, I'll take care of her."

I highly doubted it, but I got to my feet.

"I've also given permission for Nathan to be taken care of as well, and no, I don't mean killed. The nurses are fixing him up. Did you have to break the face of one of the best hitmen?" Ivan asked.

"He lied."

"For good reason. You don't want everyone to find out you're a hit man. It would be bad for your reputation."

I wasn't in the mood for jokes. I stepped toward the bed and stared down at my wife's current unconscious body, and I begged for her to live. She couldn't die. Life was unfair and cruel, but it didn't have to be—not with her.

"I'll be right back," I said.

I don't know if she can hear me. I hope so. Touching her cheek, I feel a slight warmth, but there's no animation there. Just stillness, and it's breaking my fucking heart.

I vowed to protect her, to keep her safe. What did I do? I all but killed her.

Gritting my teeth, I stand up, turn to Ivan, nod in his direction, and then leave the room. With Ivan offering to take care of my wife, I don't have a choice. This means he wants me to handle business first, and I'm a good soldier.

Terrance and Leo are waiting for me.

I'm angry at Leo, but I also knew what happened. Adelaide drugged him with some sleeping pills she found in our penthouse. I don't recall ever having them, and I know for a fact Adelaide never had, but they were there. She'd used them to spike Leo's drink so she could leave without being questioned.

He looked down. I saw the shame on his face, and this was why I couldn't punish him. Neither of us expected my wife to do something like that. She'd been desperate. All her life, she'd been alone. There had been a guard from time to time, but she'd been able to wander freely.

I want to kill Leo. I do. He shouldn't have drunk the coffee, but then, I'd have asked him to do anything to make my wife happy. Those were my instructions today. She'd been miserable for some odd reason.

"Let's go," I said.

Leo looked up.

"Sir?"

I held my hand up. "I get what happened and I understand why, but don't try to test my patience. Take me to the shooter, now."

My voice is firm as I say that final word.

Terrance had gotten him into a secure place, organized my soldiers to keep guard, and then come to the hospital. Leo had done the same. The two men are my constant. I still don't trust them, but they were the best of the best. They had so far proven their loyalty to me and to Volkov.

Leaving the hospital was fucking hard. One look up at the building, and I want to go back to see Adelaide.

To kiss her lips, touch her face, beg her not to leave me.

I can't stand the stillness.

"How is Adelaide?" Leo asked.

That was too much.

Slamming my fist into his stomach, he immediately bent forward. I grab a fistful of his hair and lift him up. "Let's be clear right now, you are only alive right now because I know she will be upset if she thought for a second her actions got you killed. You should have known better, and my patience has already been tested today. Do not test it again. I'm not in the mood." This is an understatement.

I let Leo go, and he has no choice but to pull himself together.

Terrance and Leo get in the car, knowing not to question me as I climb behind the wheel.

My hands are no longer covered in Adelaide's blood, but as I put them on the ignition, I remember the sight of it. I'd stood in the bathroom while Ivan supervised as I scrubbed at my hands. The pristine white sink, soaking red as I cleaned the mess off my hands.

"I ... I'm so cold." The fear on her face. She'd gripped my shirt, as if she was begging me to warm her up.

Pulling out of the hospital, I get on the road, navigating the traffic. Nothing distracts me. All I see is Adelaide jerking. The scene plays over and over in my head, on replay. The red dot. The indication that she's a marked target. The speed with which everything happened. Feeling her in my arms, shaking, in pain, so cold.

When I arrive at the abandoned warehouse where the shooter is kept, my anger has reached a whole other level. I want one thing, and that is for my hands to be soaked in his blood. Without waiting for Leo or

Terrance, I ignore the men waiting at the door, keeping guard.

The moment I step inside, I see him. The weapon he used is laying on a table, along with several other implements of torture. Rage consumes me. I don't think straight.

The moment he looks at me, I see Adelaide, her smiling face flashing through my mind, mixing with the stillness of her body. The doctor's voice telling me the baby we'd made together didn't make it.

I step toward him, and the smug look on his face is too much. I slammed my fist against his face, hit him five times, and I think I took him by surprise.

At one point, he gasps as I step away. My knuckles have cracked, but I don't care. I force myself to step away.

"Who do you work for?" I asked.

"I … I…"

He's taking too long, so I do no more than grab the nearest weapon, which happens to be a screwdriver, and slam it into his leg. His screams fill the warehouse. I'm not done. Pulling it out, I plunge it into the second leg.

My patience is not the best, especially as I have Adelaide's voice going around my head like a constant record on repeat.

"I … I'm so cold."

"I … I'm so cold."

I can't stand it. Those cannot be the last words I hear from her.

I pull the screwdriver out, even as he's cursing and screaming. This is not my first torture. I'd perfected the art many years ago. I had taken training from a corrupt doctor, in order to find the best way to keep men and woman alive, while I brought them as much pain as humanly possible.

My years on this earth had taught me many things, but the most important was to never be shocked by the utter cruelty of humankind. I should know. I'm taking great pleasure in his screams as I plunge the screwdriver in his shoulder.

"Hurts, doesn't it?" I asked.

"I ... I'm so cold."

Pulling the screwdriver out of his chest, I drop it to the floor and reach for his gun. "Who sent you?" I asked, seeing the safety off and the gun loaded for more rounds.

I press for the red dot to appear, and it's there, right on his chest.

Adelaide's chest flitters through my mind. Her smile. I see her naked beneath me, taking my cock, and then the fear in her eyes, along with the pain. So much fucking pain.

Dropping the red dot to his crotch, I fire, and take out his dick. One shot, and he's screaming in pain. It's not like he's ever going to use it again. He won't be leaving this warehouse alive. All I want is a name.

I'm expecting Demon, or Oleg. That fucker might know we're onto him. The mafia has been quiet. Could it be them? Who would go after my wife?

The hit man is good, I'll give him that, but he's not as good as me, and I'm just getting started. Pliers are next, and Leo, being the suck-up he currently is, holds my hit man in place while I manage to remove three teeth, pretty solid as well, but that must be the final straw for this man, because he gives me a name I wasn't expecting.

"Bethany. My contact is Bethany." He pants. "My target is Adelaide Belov. The wife of Andrei Belov. I was to kill her today."

I drop the pliers.

Pulling out the knife I always have on my person, I slide it across his neck, watching as the life slowly leaves his eyes, and I step back.

I'd made a mess. If Adelaide hadn't come when she had, I had every intention of doing that to Nathan, killing him.

Bethany had sent a man to kill my wife, and it wasn't Nathan.

Anger consumed me.

I stepped back.

The warehouse was silent.

I'm covered in blood.

I reach for the cleanest part of the man's clothing and wipe my blade before moving away.

"Sir?" Terrance asked.

"Get his body disposed of. I'm going to the hospital."

"You need to change," Leo said.

I look down at my shirt, covered in more blood, and I'm ashamed of it mingling with my wife's. This piece of shit didn't even deserve to be in the same room as her, but now his blood was mixed with hers, and I hated it. I removed my shirt and threw it on top of him, to be disposed of. Leo, like so many times before, removed his shirt.

My hands were covered with blood, and there was a small bucket on the floor, as there always is because my men know what is required. I wash the blood off my hands, and even as it turns the bucket red, it doesn't bother me. Not compared to Adelaide's blood on my hands. With clean hands, I take Leo's shirt and slide it on over my body. Without another word, I turn away and head back to the car.

Leo follows me, shirtless. Neither of us talk as I

climb behind the wheel. Words are completely unnecessary.

All I want to do is kill. Bethany is responsible for the hit taken out on my wife. I'm a little disappointed in the hit man. He'd cut my fun early. When it came to Bethany, though, I had no choice but to go to Ivan.

Gripping the steering wheel tightly, I drive through the streets heading straight back to the hospital. Leo remains silent, which is exactly how he should fucking be. My thirst isn't quenched yet.

Arriving at the hospital, I leave the parking to Leo, then I head inside and go straight to Adelaide's room.

I'm aware of the nurses and doctors, all stepping out of my way, clearly afraid to do something that would make them a target. I couldn't give a fuck what they're afraid of. To survive, they better stay away from my wife, and to keep this hospital running smoothly, my wife better not die.

Ivan's sitting in the chair I had been in when I arrive back at the room. There was no change in Adelaide. I step toward the bed, hoping to see some sign of life. Anything. There's nothing.

The machines are making their sterile noises and it pisses me off. All of this pisses me off. Adelaide is hooked up to a machine, and Bethany is…

"It's Bethany," I said, cutting through the silence that was starting to make me angry.

Ivan's brows go up. "You're sure?"

"It's her. I'm clear. After what I put him through, I believe it's her."

"You were gone for an hour and a half."

"I didn't waste any time."

I touch Adelaide's hand. There's no response.

"Interesting," Ivan said.

"There is nothing interesting about it."

"Not to you, but I've been keeping an eye on her. She doesn't have the means to hire a hit man, or even know how to contact one." Ivan runs a finger over his lips.

"Do you think someone is playing her?" I asked. I didn't care either way. I was going to kill her.

"We could pretend Adelaide is dead," Ivan said.

"No. You did the whole dead thing and rising up, and look what shit that gave us. Not happening."

I wasn't going to allow Adelaide to die. She would wake up soon, and I wasn't going to live with her being somewhere else. Not happening. I would fight Ivan on this.

He chuckled. "And you were pissed at me for making her marry you. Please, you should be thanking me."

"She could have died," I said, losing myself. "Fuck, shit, I'm sorry."

Ivan held his hand up. "It's fine. I always find it refreshing being spoken back to. Kind of a turn-on."

I roll my eyes, knowing he's doing it to get yet another rise out of me. This is what Ivan did. He was a master at manipulation.

"I expected him to name Demon or Oleg," I said. "It was Bethany."

"She has the jealousy, Andrei, just not the means, and certainly not the funds to pay for someone."

"I can find out."

I tense and look toward the door to see Nathan. One of his eyes is swollen shut, and his mouth looks too big for his face, but he's standing there as if I'd not put him through the fucking ringer.

Reaching for my gun, I keep my hand wrapped around it, ready to kill him. I want to kill him. This man had gotten way too many smiles and laughs from my wife. He'd gotten to see her happy and relaxed.

"Ah, our true hit man," Ivan said. "You do intrigue me."

This isn't good. I want to kill Nathan. If Ivan likes him and sees a use for him, then his death wasn't going to happen.

"You're right. Bethany has no means or power to gain access to a hit man. Someone had to have helped her, and I can find out who that is for you," he said.

"I don't trust you," I said.

"You have every reason not to trust me. I'm friends with your wife and you're jealous of that. I care about Adelaide. She's a special person. Sweet, kind, it's why I've been keeping an eye on her all these years. A sister like Bethany brings nothing but death to those around her."

I want to kill him.

"Word on the street is there's a potential hit out on you," Nathan said, looking at Ivan.

"This isn't news to me. I've always got a hit on my head. It's the fun part of being the boss."

"From one of your own men," Nathan said. "The biggest problem right now is finding anyone stupid enough to take you on."

Ivan winked and I didn't have time for jokes.

"It's him," I said.

I'm not sure how much Nathan had heard, but I wasn't going to say the fucker's name. I wanted to launch a full-scale attack on Oleg. To bring him in and strip him of his title. That piece of shit wasn't going to last, not when I got my hands on him.

"You're going to need to get the information out of Bethany," Nathan said.

"Consider it done," I said, happy to end the little

slut's life.

Nathan sighed. "You won't be able to kill her. You have an MC issue, correct?"

I don't like how much this son of a bitch knows.

"What are you suggesting?" Ivan asked.

"Diversion. If they believe you're onto them, they'll cover their tracks. You want to know without a shadow of a doubt what's going on, right? Well, use me. Send me into Oleg's territory. I can win his trust, bring him down from within."

"You lied to my wife. I don't trust you."

"I lied to protect her. Do you think she'd have remained friends with me if I told her I killed people for a living? I did it for her."

Regardless of his reasoning. I still didn't trust him.

"Are you gay?" I asked.

"Yes."

Ivan looked from me to Nathan. "Now I'm curious. Your biggest concern is him finding your wife attractive?"

"She is attractive," Nathan said. "Just not my type."

"Enough!" I turn to Ivan, and from the look on his face, I just knew he was considering this. "Please tell me you're not thinking about this?" I asked.

"It makes complete sense. Oleg would expect an attack by now. We go to Bethany, she names them, and he will run. If we don't act, they can assume we killed the hit man without finding out who sent him. Nathan can gather the information we need, and eventually we can exact justice. It's long and futile. Do you think you can garner his trust? Get close?"

"I can, but even if I can't, I have the means to make sure I get the answers."

I don't believe this. It sounded so fucking logical. I'm pissed off.

I look to Adelaide, stare at her, and then I see it— her hand moved. It was subtle, just the tips of her fingers, but they fucking moved. Looking at Ivan and Nathan, I don't want Nathan here when Adelaide finally opens her eyes.

"You can't be serious. You don't know if you can trust him."

"He's been in your territory for months and hasn't killed you or Adelaide. If we couldn't trust him, then your wife would already be dead, and you wouldn't have been able to find him. His identity was secure long enough for him to get in and out. This is a good plan, and I suggest you get onboard, Andrei. Your wife is waking up."

I had no choice. There was more to consider than just killing Bethany. We had to find out the truth about Oleg, but we also needed to find out how deep his betrayal went. I didn't like it, but I had no choice.

Killing Bethany wouldn't help matters right now, but when the time came, I was going to make sure she longed for death, and I wasn't going to show her any fucking mercy.

Chapter Thirteen

Adelaide

Waking up in the hospital was strange.

Staring up at the white ceiling, hearing voices was also new to me. I struggled to comprehend what they were saying, but the image was suddenly Andrei. I remembered marrying him and the months of marriage to him, but getting to the hospital was all a blur.

The doctors came in to help with the feeding tube, which was an experience I never wanted to repeat. They told me what had happened, asked if I had any memory, and the truth was, I didn't.

I'd been shot once in the chest, but it had missed all major organs and blood vessels. I'd been lucky. The second shot had been to my stomach. They didn't say anything about the stomach shot.

The morphine, or whatever drugs they had me on, helped to numb the pain. I felt ... okay. Like I'd been run over by a truck, repeatedly, but I was alive. I was breathing.

Every now and then, I'd see flashes of Andrei, his arms wrapped around me, yelling. None of it made sense.

Rubbing at my temple, I realized that the doctors left the room, and I wasn't sure exactly what had happened or been said. Focusing on words seemed so hard right now.

Ivan and Andrei remained in the room.

"Am I in trouble?" I asked. I licked my dry lips and Andrei reached for the water, holding the straw toward me.

My stomach hadn't actually been hit, just my abdomen, but the doctor hadn't said anything more, other than I was on the mend.

"Why would you be in trouble?" Andrei asked.

"I got shot."

"And you naturally assume you did something wrong?"

I look from Andrei and Ivan. They're Bratva. They make people pay for their wrongdoings.

"I … I…"

"Tell me exactly what you remember?" Andrei asked, putting the cup down again.

I frowned. "I remember … last night? How long have I been in the hospital?"

"Two days," Ivan said.

"Oh, then I guess I remember the night before I got shot. I think. Everything else is fuzzy." I felt the start of a headache.

Andrei took my hand and sat beside me on the bed. "Then don't overthink it. There's no need to."

"I got shot. Twice."

"And you're in the hospital."

Ivan put a hand on my other hand. "And you're going to make a full recovery. You will be fine. I will leave you two alone for now. I'll be back to check on you tomorrow. See me out."

Andrei gave my hand a squeeze and I watched as my husband walked his boss out. I was trying to understand what was going on. They know something I don't.

Glancing around the room, I try to find clues. Anything that would tell me what happened the other day. Why did I get shot? Where was I? None of this made sense to me.

"Stop overthinking everything," Andrei said, returning to the room.

Ivan was nowhere to be seen.

"You try being in a hospital bed with two wounds that you don't have any recollection of getting. Then you tell me not to be confused."

"I'm going to take care of you, Adelaide. You're not going to get…"

"Shot anymore?"

He nods.

Sitting back, I release a sigh. "How are you?" I asked.

His brows go up. "You're the one in the hospital but you're asking me how I am."

I can't help but smile at that. The pain medication is making me feel lightheaded.

"Can I tell you a secret?" I asked.

"You can tell me anything."

I doubted that. "I hate hospitals. I always have."

"Seriously?"

I nod. "People die here."

"And people get saved here."

"I know about the saving, and don't get me wrong, I have a whole lot of respect for doctors and nurses and all that. Trust me, I do, but I just … I don't know. I think they scare me." I hate feeling alone.

The visiting times always bothered me.

"Have you called my parents?" I asked.

Andrei shook his head. "No."

"Oh."

"Do you want me to?"

"No, there's no point, right?"

"Adelaide, if you want them here, just say the word."

Did I want them? Would I want my mother here in this room, bored out of her mind, blaming me for yet more wrinkles? She wouldn't be loving or caring. I was a burden to her. A child she ended up having but didn't want.

I ruined her figure.

"No, I don't want them."

My dad hadn't called me in the past six months. The only person to have any contact with me was Bethany and that was to be spiteful.

Tears filled my eyes, and I quickly averted my gaze, not wanting him to see.

"Don't cry."

Too late. They fell down my cheeks and I hated them. I try to rub them away, but clearly my emotions from getting shot are all over the place.

"I'm sorry," I said.

"Don't be sorry."

Andrei takes my hand and presses a kiss to the knuckles. "Stop. You can cry."

"I don't even know why I'm crying."

"It doesn't matter why you're crying. Sometimes you just need to cry."

This makes me snort, but the pain in my stomach is a little too great, so it sounds like more of a pain grunt.

"Have you ever cried?" I asked.

"When I was little, I cried a lot."

"I highly doubt that."

"My father would beat me to within an inch of my life, Adelaide. He would find any means to hurt me. Even my tears offended him. Trust me, a little boy with no true understanding of hiding his emotions will cry."

"Oh, Andrei," I said, once again feeling for the little boy he'd been.

He shrugged.

"Why did your father hate you?"

"I wasn't his real son."

"Oh?"

"My mother had an affair with one of the soldiers and the Pakhan decided my father needed an heir, and his decision was for him to raise me as his. He didn't like it.

So, he made sure to hurt me and attempted to kill me at every possible term."

This didn't stop my tears. It made me cry even harder.

"Do you want to be a father?" I asked.

Andrei froze and looked toward me. "Why do you ask?"

"I just … we never discussed a family. I know…" I lick my lips, and he reached for the cup, presenting it to me, and I thank him. I'm so thirsty. I feel like I could drink for days. "I heard you and Ivan talking. About us needing to start a family."

"You heard that?"

I'm not at all comfortable with this conversation but I know it's one that I do need to have with him.

"I figured that's why you've not been using condoms. I was a virgin with you, Andrei, but I took sex ed. I know how making babies works. My parents took away my birth control when I was … you know … picked for you." Glancing down at the bed, I force myself to look up. "Do you think I should get myself tested?"

"Why?"

"It's been six months and we're still not pregnant."

"Give it time, Adelaide."

"What happens after two years?" I asked.

"Nothing happens. Ivan would like us to have a baby within two years. Don't worry yourself. We'll get pregnant on our own time."

"I'm going to have to recover from … this." I point at my stomach as best I can. Too many movements hurt the wound near my chest.

I still couldn't believe I'd been shot. I imagine that comes down to the morphine.

"We never had a honeymoon," Andrei said.

This surprises me.

"Our marriage didn't need one," I said.

"Our marriage is the same as every other one, Adelaide. As soon as you're healed, that is exactly what we're doing. We're going on our honeymoon."

I smiled. I couldn't help it and when I looked at Andrei, I saw him smile at me. What was going on? He rarely showed me any happiness, and it did make me a little nervous.

"You should smile a lot more," I said. "You look very handsome."

The morphine must be making me a little loopy.

"You're the only one I get to smile for." He winked at me, and my heart nearly exploded.

"What's going on?" I asked. "You're not like this with me. You do know I'm not Bethany, right?" I feel tired.

"Don't say her name."

My eyes feel so heavy.

"Everyone loves her, you know. Everyone. They love her beauty and her smile. I'm always considered the ugly one. The lame one. I'm boring."

"Adelaide?"

"I don't know why you married me. You must have been so disappointed in me."

I opened my eyes and smiled at him. "I'm going to go to sleep, okay?"

"Where would you like to go on our honeymoon?" he asked.

"You don't have to take me away. I'm fine. I don't need any special treats." I closed my eyes and welcomed the darkness swirling up to get me. I'm way too tired, and all I want to do is sleep.

Sleep would make everything better.

A SENSE OF DUTY

****

Andrei

Lottie made a lot of noise. She banged against the doors, cursing everyone out, and I have to say, I didn't know the woman at all, but it even sounded like she wasn't used to using those big words.

Ive shook his head. "You want me to take her?"

Ivan nodded. "Yes. It will keep things interesting."

Ive looked ready to throw up. No one would believe he'd kept people prisoner before, torturing them.

All of Ivan's brigadiers had a reputation. Ive was a deadly son of a bitch. I'm not sure where Ivan found him. There were always so many rumors surrounding our lives. There was rarely ever truth about us.

One of the rumors about my initiation was that Ivan found me on the street, bleeding, nearly at death, and I begged him to save me, to do anything to end my miserable existence. Then of course was the rumor that I went hunting for Ivan and turned on my father, to finally take over the family. All of it was bullshit. We all had our own stories to tell.

Ivan saw my potential as a brigadier, and I saw his as a Pakhan. The rest is history. There were a few more details, but they were pointless.

"What is it with you and keeping things interesting?" Ive asked. "You do know she's the bastard daughter?"

"Yep," Ivan said.

"And you want me to what? Kill her?"

"Not kill her. Keep her company until I give you other instructions." Ivan smiled. "Trust me, you're going to want her."

Ivan was up to something and I had a feeling I would be glad I was already married.

The steel cage contained Lottie. The small window that had bars across it helped us to hear her, but the cell she was in was way too big. It was narrow but tall.

Ivan nodded at his men to open the door, and this time, Ive stepped forward. The food we had sent her the past couple of days had gone uneaten.

With the door pulled open, Lottie tried to make her escape, charging out of the room, but we all saw that coming, so Ive captured her in his arms. She struggled against him, but he easily had her arms pinned behind her, with a fistful of her hair, as he shoved her back into the room. He threw her onto the bed and she spun around, glaring at us.

"What the hell do you want?" she asked.

"Well, my dear, I have to say, we want *you*," Ivan said.

She looked at all of us, and I noticed how her breathing deepened. "I don't know what this is about, and I swear whatever is going on here, I can't help you. If it has anything to do with my dad, then you're looking at the wrong person. He will never help me."

Fear sparked in her eyes, and it looked good on her. Her lip quivered. With every second that passed, she seemed to withdraw into herself, terrified.

Scaring young women did nothing for me. I had always been the kind of guy who went after men bigger than me. That was where the real pleasure came in.

Ivan took a step toward her and I watched as she visibly flinched, but I also noticed something else as well. She seemed to freeze. Her chest stopped moving. Her gaze was on Ivan, and her body looked rock solid, as if she was nothing more than a statue.

"Ivan?"

"Lottie?" He reached out and she merely closed

her eyes, tensing up, as if expecting pain.

I didn't like this.

Ivan pulled back and stared at her.

"Do you have anyone?" Ivan asked. "Anyone at your clubhouse we can call?"

"Please, just let me go."

"Not happening, Princess."

I looked toward Ive who merely shook his head. He'd not wanted to make the journey as he was still dealing with the Cartel issue. Ivan was well and truly alive, but there had been a ripple effect everywhere. We were still dealing with the repercussions. Just like I was handling the Evil Savages MC. It was a long process, but I was the one who held the power, and it wouldn't be long until they fell in line. They wouldn't have a choice.

"I'm not a princess," she said, opening her eyes. "I'm nothing more than a piece of trash."

"A piece of trash who is taken care of," Ivan said. "Name of who I can call. It might save your life."

Seconds passed.

"Rage."

"Good."

I didn't see the syringe until he plunged it into her leg. She tried to fight him off, but it was no good. She was out before she had the chance to fight back.

"Fuck me," Ive said. "What the fuck was that?"

"We're moving her to your territory," Ivan said.

He turned his gaze toward me.

"Do you know Rage?"

"He's the current VP," I said. "I haven't talked to him but my informant told me he's reasonable. He's the only one that didn't agree to strike out against you."

"I like this," Ivan said.

"That girl has already been through a lot," I said.

"I know, which means she will be more than

adequate to deal with what I have planned."

There were times I thought Ivan was soft. Maybe a little too soft for being a Pakhan, but watching him now, I knew he was up to something, and he wasn't going to allow Lottie's reaction to hinder his plans.

I look toward Ive. He didn't care either. If it hadn't been for Adelaide, I doubted I would have cared. She was back at the penthouse with Terrance on the door, and Leo, well, he was by my side. I'd hired one of the women from the casino to take care of Adelaide. It was a fucked-up decision to do, but she had been a nurse at one point. She liked the money she got working for us. After her husband had left her with three kids to feed, she turned out to be more loyal than her husband. Anna was a sweet woman. The moment I approached her, she had been more than happy to help with Adelaide.

"Arrange a meeting with Rage," Ivan said.

I nodded.

"Transport her tonight to your territory. No hiccups. I don't want her dead, and you make sure she's taken care of," Ivan said, looking toward Ive.

"Consider it done."

"Good." Ivan snapped his fingers, bringing an end to the conversation, and then he walked away.

Ive looked back into the cell and I moved closer to him.

"What do you think?" I asked.

"I think she's going to be a handful." He ran a hand over his face. "How is married life treating you?"

"Fine."

Ive looked at me with a raised brow. "Just fine?"

"Yeah, just fine." It wasn't just fine but I'm not the kind of guy who talks about his feelings with every person I meet. "Good luck."

I have my suspicions about Ivan's plans. I think

he's going to make Ive and Lottie marry. I don't think he's going to kill her, but then this is Ivan, he could change his mind at a moment's notice.

Leaving the cell, I make my way outside where Leo is standing by the car. He hasn't fucked up at all. I know he feels ashamed for being manipulated by my wife. Ignoring him, I climb into the back of the car and pull out my cell phone.

Clicking on the security app, I check in on my wife and find her sitting on the sofa, arms folded, looking a little pissed off. She didn't like me hiring someone to take care of her. She also didn't like that Leo wasn't playing guard to her either. The moment the doctors had said she could go home, I'd made the necessary arrangements, but she didn't understand why I wouldn't allow Leo to take care of her.

I type a message to her.

Me: **Cheer up.**

I wait to hear back from her and I don't have to wait long.

Adelaide: **I'm bored. There's a big surprise.**

I can't help but smile.

Me: **I'm on my way home. What do you want for dinner?**

Adelaide: **Nothing.**

Me: **Attempting to starve yourself?**

Adelaide: **I just don't feel very hungry.**

Taking a deep breath, I don't know what to say to that, so I pull up the image on the app and watch her.

Anna moved toward Adelaide, taking a seat on the coffee table. I didn't turn up the volume, but I see my wife's stiffness. Anna's smiling, her usual sweet self. That's why men kept returning to the tables. Not just to gamble away their money, but to be near her. I had to wonder if Anna would have made better money in one of my many brothels, but she had a knack for distracting customers and was damn good at math. I know she could have easily been married off multiple times, but she refused each offer, not wanting to be tied down to a man. Her husband had sure done a number on her.

I closed the app, sat back, and watched the city go by.

Bethany was still out there, not suffering. She hadn't reached out yet, but this is all part of the plan. Nathan is already in Oleg's territory, working the fighting circuit, gaining a reputation. He sent me regular updates of his progress. I still didn't like him but Ivan was convinced we could use him. No good would come from him, I could guarantee it.

I tell Leo to head straight for the penthouse suite. I'm looking at houses to move Adelaide into. When she is fully recovered, I have every intention of getting her pregnant again. I'd not considered myself father material before, but thinking of having a child with her filled me with something close to yearning.

Rubbing at my eyes, I try to clear my mind, but the truth is, I need to kill. Taking out the shooter hadn't quenched my thirst, and every day I'm with Adelaide makes me want to murder her sister even more. Whenever she asks about her parents, I get this sick feeling in the pit of my stomach that won't go away, and it pisses me off more than anything.

All I want to do is protect her. With our enemies constantly looking for a weakness, the risk to her life is ever increasing.

Leo arrived at the parking lot, and I climb out of the car and head toward the private elevator. We still don't speak as we ride up to my floor. Terrance is there, holding himself firm. I nod in his direction, relieving him. Leo would take over now.

I hear Anna's laughter as I enter the apartment. This is why she's so popular within the casino. She is pure seduction. She has this way about her that puts everyone at ease.

Entering the main sitting room, I can see Adelaide is not at ease. This is a surprise to me. My wife is so nice, she is so calm and collected, and yet here she was, showing no signs of easing up on Anna, who was just trying to be a friend to her.

"Mr. Belov," Anna said. "Are you here to stay?"

"Yes."

"I will get going then. Same time tomorrow, Adelaide."

In response, she simply smiles, but it's not an actual smile. Just a small widening of her lips.

I leave Adelaide and head toward the door to let Anna out. She's pulling on a jacket.

"How is she?" I asked.

"Sad, mostly. She's having a hard time, I think."

"She will warm up to you."

Anna put her hand on my arm. "She might not. Some wives don't like it when men bring in other women to care for them. There's a competition and jealousy, even when there's no need to be."

I stare at Anna and wonder if that's how she sees herself, as competition. Her mask is in place, and I have to wonder if she still enjoys her job.

"Anna, do you have a problem?" I asked.

"Not at all. I'll be back tomorrow." She gives me a smile and I watch her leave.

Heading back into the main sitting room, Adelaide is sitting with her back to the main windows, and this is another reason I'm searching for a house. She hates heights.

"You're being very rude to Anna," I said. I came

into the room and sat down beside her.

"I don't need a babysitter."

"I need someone to take care of you so I know you're not overdoing it."

"So, you pick someone from your casino, or is it really a brothel? Yeah, I know who she is." She shook her head and shoved the blanket off her lap. "I can take care of myself."

"You're more than capable of taking care of yourself. I like having someone here when I'm not, and I can assure you, Anna doesn't work in any of our brothels. She does work in the casino, and saves us quite a bit of money, I might add."

"Then what about Leo?"

"No, not happening."

"Why? What did he do?"

Her memory of the day still hadn't returned, and for that, I was glad.

"Anna will continue to take care of you."

"Are you fucking her?"

This made me pause. "What?"

"You're determined to have her take care of me. You're both clearly close and I see the way she smiles at you. With her working in one of your casinos, I guess she's close to you all the time. Knows what you like … intimately, huh?"

Her face was red and I saw the tears glinting in her eyes. I don't know what caused this, but I had no attraction to Anna.

"I'm not having sex with Anna."

"I don't care if you are or aren't. It's none of my business." She stood up and I noticed the small action made her wince.

The doctor had said her recovery would be based on her ability to rest and, well, Adelaide was proving to be a very difficult patient.

"You're jealous," I said.

"I'm not jealous at all."

She tried to brush past me, but I capture her arms and stop her. I have no idea why I'm so happy, but I have a feeling it's because Adelaide is feeling jealous, and that makes me very fucking glad.

"I need to use the bathroom."

There's more to be said, but for now, I simply drop a kiss onto her nose. There would be time later.

Chapter Fourteen

Adelaide

Anna is a very beautiful woman. She is very sweet, kind, chatty. She's the kind of woman I would have loved to have a conversation with, a rapport, but I can't help but wonder if she's sleeping with my husband.

Andrei is distant, not that it's any surprise. He won't touch me because of my wounds, which are healing nicely, or so the doctor says. I'm trying to play the perfect patient, because the truth is I hate being in hospitals. I hate not being able to do anything. It's awful.

I like moving around. I love being active. Sitting on the sofa for most of the day with a blanket, only leaving for bathroom breaks, is so freaking boring. I hate it.

What I also don't like is how vague Andrei is being. I can't remember that day. I'll sit for hours thinking about it, trying to understand where I was, why I got shot. Andrei won't allow me to see Leo, and if he comes to the penthouse, Andrei makes sure he's not close. The constant questions I had were driving me crazy.

"Here we go, a coffee and a cinnamon bun. Please be gentle, I baked these last night. My son, Luke, absolutely adores them. I had to sneak these two past him."

This is news to me. "You have a son?"

"Yep, two sons and a daughter. Luke is my youngest. I also have Ricky and Patricia."

Anna has her phone in front of me and starts to show me pictures of her kids. I see one picture of them as young children, and then the other as they were older.

"Beautiful," I said.

"Tell me about it. Little terrors the lot of them,

but they bring me so much joy."

I frowned. "Do they know you work for Andrei?"

Anna had told me she worked in one of the casinos when she arrived on the first day. I did think she was a whore in one of his brothels, and they had come up with an elaborate lie to claim she wasn't. I had to wonder if she was doing this to get into Andrei's pants. Everyone wanted him. I understood it. The man was a catch, and I had felt jealous. I don't know if it was getting shot, the crap with Bethany seemed to have died down, or what. My emotions were all over the place. I felt like crying one moment, laughing the next.

I was so tired as well. The doctor had said it would pass with time. All I had to do was heal.

When it came to Andrei, my feelings were all over the place. I felt so many different things, and not all of them were good. I hated the control he seemed to have over my life. It was so unfair, and the moment I thought like that, I couldn't help but feel childish at the same time.

"Yes, of course. They all know I had to do whatever it took to take care of them." Anna clicked on her phone and then showed me a picture. "That there, is my husband. Fucking asshole he is." She closed her cell phone and threw it onto the coffee table, making me flinch at the sudden loud noise. "He was addicted to gambling. Did I know this? Hell, no. I was at home raising our babies, thinking he was doing everything to bring home the bacon, and what do I find? He's gambling away our money, our everything, until he skips town, leaving me with all his debts. It's why I went to Andrei Belov. I needed money and fast, and other than selling my body, I showed him that I would be a damn fine investment in his casino." She shrugged. "The debts are nearly paid off. Mr. Belov dealt with the loan sharks who wanted to pimp me out on the street, and I was able to provide for my family. That is the most important. Family."

"You sound like a wonderful mom," I said. She did. My mother wouldn't do anything to help me. She was more than happy to use me to get what she wanted.

"I know you don't like me," Anna said.

"It's not that." I groaned. "I'm sorry. You must think I'm a real bitch."

"Not at all. I'm used to people acting like this. Even before I worked for Andrei, when I worked at the hospital, I had nurses who thought I was getting special treatment. I seem to create a lot of anger by just being myself. It can get very ugly at times."

"Have you had encounters with other wives?" I asked.

"No, I don't fuck married men. There are plenty of single men who enjoy my company, or at least like to be distracted by me when they're losing money."

"What happened to your husband?" I asked.

"I don't know. I'm still married to the little weasel, but not for much longer. I'm working to get a divorce. I will never tie myself down to a man again. Never." Anna smiled. "Not that there's a problem being married."

This made me laugh. The big ring on my finger, and the fact I was Adelaide Belov, declared my married state. "Don't worry. I'm not going to take offense."

"In all honestly, Mrs. Belov, you have an amazing husband. He is nice."

This surprised me. "No one calls him nice."

"I know. I mean, he is nice so long as you don't end up on his bad side." Anna laughed. "I guess I have a soft spot for the man. He was nice to me and he didn't turn me away. He helped me get back on my feet."

There were not many people in the world who'd call Andrei nice.

"He is a man full of surprises."

"He loves you," Anna said.

Now I had heard enough.

Pushing off the blanket, I shake my head. "You don't have to do that. You don't need to lie."

I was getting tired again, but I had to do something.

Anna put her hand on my arm. "Please, don't hurt yourself."

"I need to use the bathroom," I said.

"Okay, but I'll be here waiting."

I had no doubt about it.

Andrei didn't love me. No one loved me.

I kept a wide berth away from the windows, going to our bedroom, and then into the bathroom. Even though I didn't expect her to follow me, I still made the effort to lock the door and leaned my back against it.

Reaching my hands up, I rub at my temples and feel a sickness swirling in my gut. I hadn't tried the cinnamon bun, and I hated to be rude, but the thought of food didn't appeal right now. I stepped away from the door and went to the sink. Gripping the edge, I look at my reflection. I was paler than normal.

I'd thrown on a pair of sweatpants and shirt. Lifting the shirt, I see the bandage covering my left shoulder, just over my heart. The doctor had told me that it had missed by a few inches. So close to death. The doctor came every other day to clean the wound and to check on it. With the shirt pulled up, I look down and see the one covering my stomach. This was healing quite quickly.

I was healing fast, but my mind was where I was having the real problem. My memories felt like they were destroying me. Well, they weren't real memories, just passing silhouettes that gave a hint of what might have happened.

For some reason I see Nathan. I had gotten a text from him on that day saying he was going away for some business and wouldn't be back, but he'd keep in contact. He never called. All I got were random texts asking how I was. It was strange.

Nathan didn't know I had been shot, but the way he asked, I felt like he *did* know. Was he there? What was I missing? Then Leo. Why wasn't Leo able to take care of me anymore?

What about Andrei? He was far more attentive, but I had to wonder if that was down to guilt. Did he shoot me? Did Leo put my life in danger?

What was I missing?

The doctor also was vague as well. People were keeping secrets from me and I found that harder than ever before.

I drop my shirt, splash some water on my face, and head back toward the main living room, but I stop when I hear Anna on the phone.

"You know you're not supposed to call me like this," she said. There's a chuckle. "You pay for that privilege." Another pause. "Am I looking forward to your big cock?" Anna looked toward me, but I'm hidden, so she doesn't notice me. "Well, Eric, I can tell you that I am." She let out a moan. "Yeah, I am, I want you so badly right now. Would you make me suck it?"

I'd heard enough. Stepping out from behind the wall, Anna spotted me, her face bright red as I walk into the kitchen.

"I've got to go."

Grabbing a glass from the cabinet, I fill it with water. I hear her coming into the kitchen.

"You heard that."

"Kind of hard not to."

"I'm sorry, Mrs. Belov."

I spun around to face Anna. "Have you ever fucked Andrei?" I asked.

"What? No. Of course not."

"Do you know if he ... has any other woman or women visit him while you're at the casino? Someone from one of his brothels?"

"No. No. He doesn't. When he comes to the casino, it's to work. Nothing else."

I press my lips together. "Then we don't have a problem." I nod at her.

Anna smiled. "I'm sorry. I don't usually accept calls but one night Luke had an accident and I was working, and well, Eric was ... there. It just sort of happened that he got my private number."

"But you enjoy talking with him?" I asked.

"Yes. I do, a lot. I'm not looking for a relationship. It's just ... sometimes, it's hard to keep the line straight, you know. Eric's a good man, but he's a workaholic. Rich, and he doesn't like having to work to screw a woman. I'm probably one of a dozen women. Not that we've had sex or anything." She frowned. "I know what you heard, but ... we've ... I've not ... it's all been in banter, you know. It's kind of fun."

The happiness dims from her eyes, and I hate myself. Going to Anna, I put my arms around her and pull her close, holding her tightly. I don't know if this Eric is a good guy or not. He is trying to get her to have sex, so for all I know, he isn't a straitlaced guy. He might be trying to string her along. I don't know. I don't have all the answers, but what I refuse to do now is to add to her heartache.

Anna, like me, is trying to navigate this world

we'd both been plunged into. Me with marriage to a Bratva brigadier, and her because of her husband's gambling. We were involved now, and even if we were both totally different, she was the first person who seemed to offer me friendship.

Bethany wasn't here to destroy it.

Rather than push her away, I hold her a little tighter. She might not be my friend for any other reason than Andrei paying her, but for now, I can fool myself into thinking it was something more.

****

Andrei

I stare across the room, hearing the sounds of pleasured moans. Leo is on my right, Terrance, my left. All my men are stationed around the room, and the women were providing enough distractions to the customers.

Ivan was no longer in my territory, but I still had a job to do, and as I glance down at my watch, I see he is late. I don't like when people are late.

Sipping at my whiskey, I hold my cell phone within my grasp. The temptation to look at Adelaide is strong. The doctor told me she had made a full recovery. With her listening to his advice and resting, the wounds had healed nicely.

The doctor had told me there were some lasting effects from the pregnancy, but they would go away in time, once her body realized she was no longer pregnant. I'd not allowed him to tell her she'd been pregnant. There was a lot she didn't know, and for now I wanted to keep her in the dark.

I was aware of the texts Nathan had sent her, which I didn't like, but there was nothing I could do to stop them. They had been friends some time now. She had no idea he was a hired hit man.

I was starting to feel that Adelaide was a fucking magnet to problems. It was turning into a task just to keep her alive.

The man I'd been waiting for, entered. He wasn't wearing his leather cut, as he told me he wouldn't. Evil Savages MC wouldn't be seen here. Not in a Bratva brothel.

Rage, the VP, was the man I needed to see, to come to some arrangement. Ive had already taken Lottie into his territory, and I had a feeling Ivan was preparing his plans for her. The man looked positively vicious. I'm surprised he's not the prez of the Evil Savages MC. My men had done their workup on him, and he wasn't one to be messed with. Rage wasn't his name out of coincidence. It was said he was a man with a very short temper, and the moment you set him off, even the Devil himself quivered in fear.

He was large. Scary-looking motherfucker.

But then, so was I.

Rage sat down at the table, and I already knew he'd assessed the room and figured exactly how to escape if this went south.

Neither of us spoke. Each of us were watching each other, trying to decipher what the other was up to. I knew what I wanted, but as for Rage, I needed to know his agenda, and fast. Was he going to be a team player, or would he become another problem?

I snap my fingers at Leo and my guard leaves and heads toward the bar.

"Drink?" I asked. I didn't have all day to sit around and chat.

"Whiskey," Rage said.

His voice was gruff.

Leo came back with two drinks, placing them both on the table. Rage didn't reach for his and neither did I. The whiskey here wasn't as good as the stuff I had back at home. I didn't want to think of home as that took my thoughts to Adelaide.

"Let's cut to the fucking chase rather than measuring our dicks," Rage said. "You want something from me. What?"

"I want Demon's head."

"Not going to happen. Try again."

"Do you think what he's doing with the club will allow you all to live?" I asked.

Rage laughed. "I'm in your territory right now and I'm still breathing."

"For now, you're alive because I will it, but at any moment with the snap of my fingers, your life would be mine." I hold my fingers up and snap them.

"You think I'm afraid of you, pretty boy?" Rage asked.

"I think you should be." I point at my body. "All of this, it's fucking fake, and that's why you're showing me respect right now. It's why you're not wearing your colors, and why you agreed to meet with me. Some of my men believe you would rather work with me than against me."

"I should have known there were rats in the club."

"Do rats make sure your club survives?" I asked. "Because from where I'm sitting, Evil Savages MC's days are numbered."

Rage sits back, stares at me for a few moments, and then reaches for his drink. "I'd heard about you, you know. Before you got all big and powerful."

There's no need to ask about what. I'm quite aware of my reputation. I'd lived it so I know exactly what is said about me.

"You ran from your father."

This did make me smile.

"They say you weren't his kid, that he beat you within an inch of your life. That you can take a great deal of beatings. People think you can't be killed," Rage said.

"Do you believe the stories they make up to scare little kids?" I asked.

"I know what I see, and you're a man who is one scary motherfucker. I have to wonder why you decided to talk to me rather than Demon. He's my prez. I follow him."

"But you don't agree with him. When the rumor of Ivan Volkov's death got to your club, you didn't agree with attacking my territory. Trust me, Rage, I can wipe your club out without a care in the world, but that's bad business. I have no interest in a war between us. I'm aware of how big your club is, how far it's spread." I could kill them all, and it would certainly provide me some good sport for a while, but I wasn't interested in that.

Killing the club off wouldn't work. Not for me. I had a feeling I would need them down the road. Cutting off good men and potential alliances wasn't good. Ivan knew that, and so did I. Even when my father beat me, I watched him work. He was a shrewd businessman and refused to take revenge if it would affect the Bratva.

The same goes here. Demon was one poisonous cog, but Rage would make a better prez. I just needed to remove the rusty cog.

"So, you know you wouldn't win," Rage said.

This made me smile. "They did say you were a dreamer. I would win. As you say, I can't be killed."

"Those are the scary stories people tell their kids to be afraid of you. I'm not afraid of you, Andrei. You're a man just like me, and I have no interest in hearing your bullshit."

He stands up, just as I knew he would, and I wait as he takes two steps. Picking up my whiskey, I mutter over the glass, "We have Lottie."

I make sure to use the nickname he's always used for her. The tension in his back rises. He's pissed off. Good. So am I.

Rage turned and stormed back to me. His hand swiped the glass off the table. Cheap whiskey spilled to the floor.

"What the fuck are you talking about?"

"Hasn't Demon told you we've taken her? That's a surprise because he does know she's missing."

Rage's jaw clenched.

"I guess he sees her as collateral damage." I tut. "I thought you liked her." Not romantically. Rage cared about Lottie as if she was his own daughter.

"She is no part of the club. You have no right to take her."

I drain the cheap-ass whiskey, swigging it back, hating the bitter taste as it slides down my throat. I'm not the kind of man who likes cheap things.

Standing up, I put my hands flat to the table, and glare right in his face. Both of us are hanging on by a thread, wanting to reach for our guns to take the other out, but we're also prepared to see what happens next.

"We have taken her, and if you want to see her alive, then I suggest you come to a decision and fast. Demon doesn't give a flying fuck about her. We've already reached out. Showed him what we know."

"I don't believe you. Demon wouldn't allow that."

Reaching into my pocket, I pull out the single photo we'd taken of Lottie, tied up, crying. We'd forced her to scream for this picture. Her face is scrunched up, and she looks very afraid. I almost feel sick about what we'd done, but it doesn't last. This is part of the job. Lottie is another cog, one that will have a very good life, if this goes our way.

Throwing the picture on the table, I stand up. "When you realize what's at stake, give me a call."

This time I leave, but I don't look back. Going straight to my car, I climb into the back and wait as Leo and Terrance climb into the main seats. My cell phone goes off and I see Ivan is calling me.

"How did it go?" Ivan asked.

"He's got the picture. He's loyal at the moment to Demon but he didn't like that we have Lottie. He'll call."

"Good. So, now onto our next topic of business."

"Nathan is getting close to Oleg. The fighting rings are proving to be his only way of building a reputation." Which is already a violation of what Ivan wanted. The fighting rings had to go. Ivan hadn't allowed them as they served as punishment, not as a way of earning money, at least not in Oleg's territory.

Ivan had put in different rules for all his brigadiers. Some of us could have fighting rings, others could not. It was to stop certain competition between his men. Ivan had once said that he watched how other Bratvas fell. Men were pitted against each other, rather than rising as one.

"That is not what I was talking about. You and Adelaide need a honeymoon," Ivan said.

This made me pause.

"There's no time to take a honeymoon."

"Every woman deserves to have one."

"Now is not a good time."

Ivan laughed. It sounded forced to me. "There is never any time, anywhere, to take a vacation, let alone a honeymoon. Don't you realize our lives are all limited, Andrei? You need to learn to live a little."

"I cannot leave. Not with Oleg or Ive, and especially not with Rage."

"You can and you will. Rage made a quick decision and we're going to make him pay for it. We will not be jumping through any Evil Savages MC hoops. Lottie is with Ive. At the moment she's safe, but if they attack, her life will be over."

This is news.

"They will attack my city," I said.

"I will be taking over your city while you're gone. I've already made the arrangements, and have all the necessary foods and details on my private island. You and Adelaide will have each other. The staff know not to be seen or heard, unless you want them. Trust me, you and Adelaide need this."

Running a hand down my face, I want to argue with him, but this wasn't a suggestion. Ivan was giving me an order. This was the first time he'd done it to me in a long time.

"There will be plenty of time, Ivan," I said.

"And I've said you are to take a honeymoon. Your plane leaves tonight. I hear the forecast is for hot weather, so go and enjoy the sunshine for a little bit. Show me that it's possible to be happy."

This makes me even more tense. The life within the Bratva was not fun, but Ivan always seemed to find the positives. He was a ruthless son of a bitch, but I did hear a rumor that there might be someone in his life. Again, it was a rumor. There were always whispers and gossip that followed him. I doubted any of it was true.

If Ivan wanted me to go on a honeymoon, then I didn't see a reason to put it off. Ivan controlling my territory was a scary fucking thought. I had nothing to hide. My loyalty was to him and him alone, and I would never betray him.

He'd given me the chance to exact my revenge, and I had taken it, gladly. Seeing my father fighting for his last breath was in fact a memory I treasured.

Hanging up the call, I smiled. It was a sick treasure to have, because right beside it was taking my wife's virginity, and knowing no other man was ever going to touch her.

I was a sick fucking bastard.

Chapter Fifteen

Adelaide

A honeymoon.

On a private island.

No one around for miles.

To many, this was the dream—to finally be alone with their spouse. Andrei and I had been on Ivan's island for two days. I don't know how he did it, but he'd been avoiding me. Like now. We enjoyed breakfast together and he'd looked down at his cell phone, and left without a word.

This was not a honeymoon. This was just another prison, only a little bigger. And incredibly beautiful.

I move toward the balcony that's just off our main bedroom, and put my arms on the ledge. I look out over the large island, surrounded by the ocean. There was a small dock, which allowed the plane to land, as well as for small boats. There was even a small yacht for Ivan to go out and enjoy the ocean.

Beautiful.

Serene.

Calming.

Stepping away from the balcony, I walk back into the main bedroom. The silence of the island was shocking to me. It had been a long time since I'd been able to really think. Closing my eyes, I listen to the sounds. Living in the city all my life, there was no such thing as real silence. There was always some noise and strange sounds in the city, and people were always so close.

Opening my eyes, I go toward the cabinet and make the decision that I'm going to go for that swim. Andrei's not around, so it's not like I have to be self-conscious in my swimsuit, which is one piece.

I pull my summer dress over my head, toss it to the floor, and wriggle out of my bra and panties. Then I step into my swimsuit and slide it up my legs and over my body. I don't linger on the scars from the bullet wounds. The doctor had promised me I'd be able to have children again, which was an odd way of putting it. *Again*? I didn't even have one child. The moment he said it, he looked like he was going to be sick.

I ease down the bathing suit, and look at myself in the mirror. The scar isn't ugly. The surgeon who worked on me had done a wonderful job. I'm shaking my head, because I know looking at the scars doesn't help bring back any of the memories. I slide my suit back into place, don't look in the mirror again, and head right down to the small pool. There was no way I was going to swim in the ocean.

The main caretaker of the house had warned that there had been some great white shark sightings, so yeah, this ass was not going near any ocean. Stepping up to the pool, I look inside the water, take a deep breath, and then jump, sinking down. I allow the water to take over, and then I charge toward the top, breaking the surface, lifting my head up. Sliding my hands through the water, I move back and forth, and then I start swimming up and down the length of the pool.

After some time had passed, I move so that I'm staring up at the sky, enjoying the warmth of the pool, thinking back to that day. Leo had been with me, I'm sure of it. Something had happened, that meant he couldn't guard me anymore. An image of me in the kitchen, and some sleeping pills I'd discovered flashed in my mind.

I drugged Leo. Why?

"You need some lotion on," Andrei said, pulling me out of my thoughts.

Why did he always have to be there when I was thinking? The man seemed to know when I was dwelling on that one day, and I didn't like it.

Standing up in the shallow end of the water, I wipe the water from my eyes and shake my head. "I don't need any lotion."

He sat down on the edge, putting his feet in the water and tutted. "You are being a little stubborn."

"Why did I drug Leo?" I asked.

Andrei's good at keeping his emotions in check. He is a very difficult man to read, but that didn't mean I hadn't been watching him to see if I could find a way of understanding the man I married. It was subtle. The slight tensing of his shoulders. The way his hands clenched on the edge of the swimming pool.

"I did, didn't I?"

"I don't know what you're trying to prove here."

"I'm not trying to prove anything. Did you know the doctor said I could have a child again? Don't you think that's rather odd for a doctor to say?" I asked.

"Doctors say strange things all the time. I wouldn't read any more into it than normal."

This made me laugh. "And then of course, there's the way you act. You don't want to be around me since that day. What happened?"

He frowned at me. "I don't want to be around you?"

"Have you figured out that people don't seem to like me? You should have been with Bethany. My family didn't even care enough to come and visit me in the hospital."

"Don't ever say her fucking name!" His voice is hard and stern.

"You were going to marry her."

"Her name doesn't even deserve to be spoken

from your lips. You will have nothing to do with her."

"Why? Why? Why?" I can't help yelling the last part. He's imposing all these restrictions on me and I don't know why. "Why isn't Leo my guard? Why are we here? Why are you so angry with my sister?"

"Because she's the one who arranged for you to be fucking shot!"

This made me gasp and I physically jerk as if I've been hit again. "*What?*"

"She wants you dead, Adelaide. This doesn't come as a surprise to you. As for your parents, I wouldn't allow them to come close to you. They have shown their loyalty to Bethany one too many times. They will never get near you. You did drug Leo that day, and that's why he cannot take care of you, and he's alive because I knew once you remembered, you wouldn't be able to live with yourself if I killed him for his carelessness."

Tears fill my eyes.

"And you were pregnant," he said.

This one makes me gasp and my hands go to my stomach. "What? No! That's not possible."

Andrei slides into the pool and comes close to me. I don't even bother to fight him as he cups my face and tilts my head back. "I wasn't going to allow you to ever find out, but you are so fucking persistent about that day."

"I was pregnant?"

"Yes."

"And I lost it?"

"Bethany stole that from you."

"Is Nathan alive?" I asked. I have flashes of him all the time.

"There is something you need to know about Nathan."

What Andrei tells me, shocks me to my core and I

shake my head. At some point, I try to pull away from him, but Andrei holds me tighter, refusing to let me go. Nathan was—no, *is*—a hit man, and now Andrei won't tell me where he is or what he's doing.

"But … he's my friend?" I don't know why I'm questioning it.

"Nathan is your friend. That I can guarantee you. He will not do anything to harm you, and he has, in his own way, been taking care of you for a very long time."

Tears trail down my cheeks, and Andrei swears, swiping at them.

I no longer want a swim.

"I need to go," I said.

He holds me even tighter. "I'm not letting you go anywhere."

"Why didn't you tell me?"

"I didn't want you to feel any pain, Adelaide. You were shot in front of my eyes."

As if Andrei had told me all the pieces, slowly, like a puzzle, I put it all together, and I remember what happened that day. The anonymous text. The warehouse. Seeing Nathan, broken and bruised.

"Why were you beating him?" I asked.

"I found out he was a hit man and he was best friends with my wife. I had to know who he was, and what he's capable of."

"You didn't think to just ask?"

"People lie, Adelaide. That's what I know."

"Or they keep the truth from you," I said. "Will you divorce me?"

Andrei cups my face and tilts my head back. "What?"

"I wasn't able to give you a child. Do you even want me anymore? I know you and Ivan have a deadline for getting me pregnant."

"Stop it," Andrei said. "There will be more babies. You are not damaged or broken."

"Why do you even want to have kids with me?" I sniffle. Shaking my head, I pull away from him. I feel the loss so damn hard, and it's a struggle to hold myself together. I need to get away from him.

He reached out for me again, but I step away and move toward the edge of the pool. I grip the edge and haul myself up, but I feel so fucking heavy.

I had been pregnant. Pregnant and then shot. I wanted children when I was a lot older. I thought I'd feel relief, but I didn't. Sadness consumes me.

I'm not even able to lift myself out of the water and Andrei is there, once again. He is not my knight. He is my forced husband, but his arms surround me and I sink back against him, as the enormity of what I lost hits me.

A baby.

I was going to be a mother.

A tiny bundle of happiness. That's what I could have had, and like always, Bethany couldn't even stand for me to have that. Did she know? How could she have known? I didn't even know, so that meant she just wanted to kill me. There was no other reason to attack me. I hated her.

"Have you killed her?" I asked. My voice is distant, cold, and I'm shocked by it.

"Not yet."

Andrei carried me out of the pool, and I wrapped my arms around his neck as he walked to the house. No one is around so I feel I can speak freely with him. "Will you kill her?" I asked.

He paused and looked at me.

Our gazes meet but I don't look away. I don't back down.

"Do you want her dead?" Andrei asks.

I open my mouth and close it. *Do I want her dead?*

Pressing my lips together to stop them from wobbling, I nod. "She won't stop until I'm hurt or dead. She killed my child. My baby."

"Adelaide." He coughed.

"I ... what if I get pregnant again and she has a temper tantrum? What if she kills my child? What if I can't protect her? I know Bethany is my sister but she's a monster. I can handle her, but I will never allow a child of mine to deal with her." Just the thought of it made me feel sick.

"You are already protecting our child," he said, and a smile curled his lips. It wasn't forced, natural, and this time it wasn't scary.

I put my palm to his cheek, and he turned to look at me. Andrei was handsome. He was the kind of man who would create wars, finding out all the secrets by bedding women.

He was my husband but I didn't consider him mine completely. Nothing and no one was ever mine. People were not things to be possessed.

"Always," I said.

****

Andrei

The first week of our honeymoon didn't exactly go as planned. There was business at home to take care of, and I had no choice but to be available for it, at a moment's notice. Ivan was handling everything, and I think his presence was scaring the fuck out of everyone. He did have a way about him that terrified most people.

Rage had been reaching out, and as per Ivan's instructions, I hadn't responded, ignoring the calls, and then focusing on my wife.

Adelaide had cried that first day, for our baby. Seeing those tears had broken my fucking heart. The desire to kill Bethany was strong, but seeing the pain on my wife's face helped me focus. What I needed was to wait for Nathan to get close to Oleg. My suspicions were that Bethany had reached out to him, or possibly Demon, and in doing so, she had put Adelaide in danger.

I stare down at my sleeping wife. Today had been a good day. We'd spent it together, playing some chess, which she was bad at. She had no strategy for winning. She loved moving the pieces around the board, and making up names for them. I loved this woman. She had no idea how fucking much, but I had a feeling Ivan did. It's why he meddled, why he changed Bethany to Adelaide.

I hadn't slept with Bethany, not once. She had tried so many times. She knew a baby would have cemented her place as my wife, but I'd not been able to do it. I fucking hated the slut.

When Ivan first told me of the arrangements, I'd been fucking terrified of seeing Adelaide again. The first time I saw her after she'd helped me, I thought she would remember, but she hadn't noticed me. Not that I blame her. That day on the streets, I'd been dirty, looked homeless, and I'd been cut up. She had helped me, no questions asked, and it was the first time in my entire life anyone had ever given a shit about me.

It was so fucking lame, I know. I'm a forty-year-old man, but this young woman cared. She loved, she … called to me. Reaching out, I stroke her hair back from her face. She is the only woman I have ever craved and not taken. I've watched her from afar, keeping an eye on her, while having a parade of women by my side.

Ivan had known all along, I know he had, and he'd made sure I finally got the woman of my dreams.

He would act like it didn't matter, like it was all one giant coincidence, but I knew differently. Ivan wasn't stupid. He had his spies everywhere. At all times he needed to make sure his men were loyal to him, which is how his suspicions about Oleg came about.

Adelaide releases a sigh and turns toward me. The negligee she wore was way too loose for her. Since being hurt, she had lost a little weight, and I didn't like it. I loved Adelaide's curves. I had never been a man who liked skinny women. They were way too breakable, and it also reminded me of a time in my life I would rather forget. I'd been starved myself. Denying myself the simple pleasures of life was never going to happen.

The top of her negligee had fallen open, showing off her full, ripe tits. Seeing them, so beautiful and on display, made my dick ache. It had been too long since I had felt the pleasure of her pussy wrapped around me. Sliding my finger from her face, I stroke down the curve of her neck, down her chest, and stroke across the mound.

Another moan escapes her lips, and I smile. Gliding across the bud, I stroke the soft flesh and it immediately hardens beneath my touch. Adelaide's body knows who's the boss, but she doesn't know it yet. This body is mine.

I stare at her face and wait, touching her, wanting her to wake up and not be afraid. Her breathing has changed so I know she's awake, and as her eyes open, they stare right at me. There's no fear there.

She licks her lips and I slowly lower, taking the bud into my mouth, sucking it. Adelaide gasped and arched up. Moving my hand across her chest, I hold her in place, flicking my tongue even as my teeth hold her in place. Another moan, this time guttural and deep. Letting go of her nipple, I glide my tongue across, taking her other tit into my mouth, tasting her. Stroking my hand down her body, I grab the edge of the blanket and pull it off, exposing her to my gaze. She's not wearing any panties and the negligee has rolled up her thighs.

Moving between her legs, I take the edge of the fabric and lift it up. Adelaide helps me by sitting up, holding her hands above her head, and then I toss the negligee to one side, letting it fall on the floor.

Her hands fall behind her, holding herself up, and I capture her face then take possession of her lips. I try to tell her with my body rather than words what I feel for her. But I don't know if she understands. Adelaide is such a stubborn woman, and she's been hurt so much by those closest to her.

Breaking from the kiss, I trail my lips down to her neck, sucking on the tender flesh, hearing her slight intake of breath. So sexy. Nipping at her pulse, I move down, going to her breasts, drawing them together, and licking at each nipple in turn. She had such juicy tits. Pressing my face against them, I kiss each mound before working down, kissing her stomach, even the scar she now has.

I grab her legs, spreading them open as I move between them, staring at her pretty pussy. I ease open the lips of her sex and stare at her clit. The opening of her pussy is so tempting, but I don't touch her there. My primary focus is her clit.

Using my tongue, I start to tease her, working between her legs, stroking, watching her reaction as I work her pussy. My name spills from her lips, and I can't resist her anymore. Going down her slit, I stroke her entrance.

All mine. No other man had tasted her. Touched her. Adelaide was mine, all fucking mine. Plunging inside her pussy with my tongue, I work my fingers across her clit, feeling her pulse around my tongue. I want her to be dripping wet, but I also want to feel her come on my dick, that tight cunt squeezing me for every single drop of my cum.

I'm like a man possessed. I can't help what I want. I just know I want it, and I want her.

Bringing Adelaide to the edge of orgasm, I hold her on the brink, but not allowing her to spill over, I lift up, getting into position between her spread thighs, and then working my dick between her wet slit, I nudge her clit with the tip before going to her entrance. Staring into her eyes, I don't look away, as inch by inch I sink my cock inside her slick cunt.

"You feel so fucking good," I said. "Do you like that? Do you like my dick inside you?"

In answer, she nods her head, and I can't help but smile. This woman is so fucking perfect. I don't know what I did to deserve her, but I'm not letting her go. She is mine. All mine.

With my dick to the hilt, I take her hands within mine, locking our fingers together, and hold myself in deep, relishing the feel of her tight warmth surrounding me. So good.

There is nowhere else I want to be than with this woman.

"Andrei?" She wriggled against me, and I know exactly what she wanted.

Letting go of her hands, I sit up, but with my dick still inside her. Caressing from her neck, down her body, going between her legs, I start to stroke her clit. Tiny movements at first, and I grit my teeth because the pleasure is so fucking intense. She's so tight.

With each touch to her clit, I feel her excitement start to build and I have no way of knowing if I will last through her orgasm.

Adelaide lets go, and her cunt is so incredibly tight as she milks me. I watch her, mesmerized as she finally loses control, giving herself up to the pleasure. She is so stunning.

I wait for the aftershocks to subside, releasing her pussy, and then I hold her hands in place. Starting off slow, I take my time, pulling out so only the tip of my dick is within her tight walls, and then I start to thrust, building up my pace, fucking her harder, driving in deeper.

Adelaide's moans fill the air, and I don't hold back. There's no need to be in control anymore. I give myself over to the heat, to the pleasure, and fuck my wife the way I want to. I make love, and pound, and have it all. Even as I plunge in deep, filling her womb with my spunk, I know it's not enough. I need to have her again.

My dick needs a moment, though, and I collapse over her. When I realize she has all my weight I go to lift off her, but Adelaide surprises me by wrapping her arms around me, keeping me close. With my face against her neck, she doesn't see my smile, but I fucking love it.

Adelaide could have the world with me.

Lifting up, I stare down into her eyes. There are no tears. She gives me her sweet smile, and I know I'd gladly take it. Whatever this woman offers, I would take.

"I will never let anyone hurt you again," I said.

"I know."

There's something in her gaze and I'm not sure exactly what, but I don't like it. Does she not trust me? Does she not believe me?

"Adelaide?"

She kisses me instead and rather than question her about her response, I take the kiss, feeling my cock start to thicken once again. I want her. When do I *not* want her?

Not fucking her on our wedding night had been a nightmare. The only reason I hadn't was because she had looked terrified. Bethany had scared her once again. That little bitch was getting in my way, and the only way to remove her was to kill her. I was going to do it.

I'd take great pleasure in ending her miserable existence. Then Adelaide would be free.

Chapter Sixteen

Adelaide

I think we're watching a porn film.

Curled up on the sofa, I'm acutely aware of my husband, especially as the couple on screen are … well, there's no doubt about it, the guy is fucking her, or at least it looks like he is. They had been having sex all throughout the movie, and the truth is, I wanted Andrei. I pressed my thighs together, hoping to stop the ache that had started to build between them.

Our honeymoon was nearly over, and the past week had been a dream. Waking up to Andrei, making love into the morning, then of course we'd made love throughout the day. I always got the sense that he was holding back.

The couple on the screen was not holding back. Glancing down at his crotch, I saw that he was aroused. I enjoyed making love. I loved it when Andrei touched me. My body came alive under his touch.

Pressing my legs together, I tried not to think about my own needs, and instead watched the movie, but there was no actual storyline. A couple just having sex, arguing, fighting, making up, and then when I saw his hand dive between her legs, I just couldn't take it anymore. Even as every part of my mind was screaming at me not to do this, I found myself straddling my husband.

My hands on his shoulders, Andrei held my ass and smiled up at me. This man had a sexy smile. I'd not seen it before, but on the island, he'd let me see another side to him, and the truth was I liked this man. I didn't mind the Andrei back on dry land, but this one was different. He was more playful. I knew it was because no one was around to see him. He was safe here. We were both safe. No one knew where we were other than Ivan.

"What's the matter, Adelaide?" he asked.

"Do you miss fucking random women?"

This made him frown.

"Not what I was expecting," he said.

"Have you been with other women since we've been married?" I'm not sure if I want to know the answer to that question but since I already asked, I don't see a point in backing down now. What if he says yes? I'm almost terrified of what he's going to say, but I wait, expecting the worst.

"What is this about?" he asked.

Was that a yes? Did he not want to tell me the truth?

"You make love to me and you're kind and gentle. Bethany said—"

"Enough with fucking Bethany," he said, growling out the word. His grip on my ass tightens. "I was never with her. I never put my dick inside her. Bethany doesn't know what I like in the bastard bedroom, and she never will. I've also not been with any other woman since we've been married, Adelaide."

He's angry but even as he snarls the words at me, I can't help but be a little bit happy.

"You've not been with any other woman?" I asked.

"Do you want me to repeat it in Russian?" he asked.

I shake my head. There's no point. I didn't understand any other language. "My mom warned me that you might take on other women. That I might not be good enough for you, and that I should consider that a blessing."

"For fuck's sake. What is it with your parents? Your mother doesn't know me. She will never fucking know me." He lets go of my ass but this time he seems to be massaging the cheeks. I like it.

"So…" I press my pussy against his length. "You don't want it rough?"

"Adelaide, are you wanting to be taken, to be fucked, to feel my cock pounding inside you?"

I sink my teeth into my lip, not sure if I could speak those words. Could I? Did I? I was so confused. Instead of saying a single word, I nod my head. I'm aroused. I enjoy making love, but I know there's more to be had.

"I … I don't want you to go to anyone else," I said.

This creates another frown.

Dropping my hands from his shoulders, I feel like a fool. I shouldn't have done this, but since being on our honeymoon I'd come to realize a couple of things. I liked Andrei. Not because he was attractive, but when he wasn't having to be a brigadier, he was a lot of fun to be around. I loved swimming with him, playing chess, even cooking with him. He hates tofu, but is more than happy to cook it with me. He doesn't mind taking long walks down the beach with me, holding my hand, basking in the moonlight. He's actually a nice guy. Don't get me wrong, I know he's not just a nice guy. The ink on his body told its story.

The never-ending list of scars that I saw looking past the ink. Even if I stroke his body, the ink can't hide the ridges and scars. There is one that does make me curious, but there was no way he could be that homeless man from the time I volunteered at the hospital. I'd taken a small first aid course as I was trying to figure out what to do with my life. My father, fed up with my nagging, arranged for me to have a work experience week with them.

I discovered I loved helping people, but all that blood and death was too much. I'd not pursued medicine. Shaking off the memory, I brought my focus back to Andrei.

"Adelaide, I'm not a mind reader. Tell me what you want."

Would it be that simple?

He'd laugh in my face. Men could do whatever the hell they wanted. He was Bratva. No one, not even his wife, got the choice. What did I have to lose? I was his wife. He could beat me but Andrei hadn't raised a hand to me. I wasn't afraid of him, at least not anymore.

"I don't want you to sleep with any other woman." I already knew about the brothels the Bratva owned. The women who were bought and sold. There was always going to be parts of his life that I didn't agree with. I couldn't change them. Taking his hand, I place it against my breast, not sure if this is the right way to go about what I want. "I only want you to have me," I said.

Even as I speak the words, I sound selfish. Is it wrong to want my husband to myself? To not share him with another woman? What if he had a mistress? A woman he was already in love with.

Andrei let go of my breast and I honestly thought he had someone, that this conversation was useless, but he gripped the back of my neck and pulled me down so that our gazes were on equal level.

"Adelaide Belov, there is no other woman. There is no one else I want." His lips brush against mine. "You are the only woman I want, and the only one I will ever have."

His words shock me.

Kissing him back, I cup his face. "Then take me however you want me. I don't want you to be afraid. I'm not going to be scared, Andrei." The time for being afraid has long since passed. There is no reason to fear this man. We've been married over seven months now, and other than a few cruel words and being ignored, he's not hurt me.

"Oh, Adelaide, you have no idea what your words could do to a man." His hands glide down my back and he tenses, tearing the negligee from my body with such ease. I never wear any panties for bed and as his hands go to my ass, I sigh. His touch always feels so good.

It's shocking to me that at one point, I actually felt afraid of him. Bethany's power over me is over. I won't be afraid of anyone else, especially not her.

"But, I am going to be the only man that ever knows this." His fingers wrap around my neck and he tightens his hold, not enough to cut off air, but firm enough that I know he's the one in charge.

He pulls me close, smashing our lips together. So powerful as our teeth clash. My hands go to his shoulders and he breaks the kiss, tutting.

"No, arms above your head."

I frown but do as he said, lifting my hands above my head.

Andrei leaned back, his gaze still on my breasts, and when his hands graze across my flesh, I gasp. He withdraws. "I want your eyes on me."

I open them up as he touches me. It's so good. I can't stop myself from wriggling against his hard cock. I'm so wet already.

Andrei lets go of my tits, sliding his hands around my body going to my ass. "I don't know what I love more. Your tits or your ass. Both are more than a handful. Your pussy goes without question, Adelaide. So tight and wet. Are you wet for me right now?" he asked.

"Yes." There's no point in lying.

I'm aroused and I want his touch. I've never felt

like this before.

"Good, show me." I'm about to ask him how when he instructs me. "I want you to lie down on the coffee table, spread those pretty legs open wide, and then hold your pussy open so I can see you."

My face is so hot. His words should humiliate me, but they don't. I like this side of him.

Hearing Anna speak to Eric the other week had gotten me thinking about my and Andrei's sex life. I didn't want it to be boring.

Nibbling my lip, I look at the wooden coffee table. I'm not sure Ivan would appreciate me breaking it.

"Do you think it would hold me?" I asked.

"I wouldn't have asked if I didn't think it."

His voice is deep, with an edge to it, almost as if he is close to losing control. Is that because of me? I sit down on the table and stare at him, waiting. Slowly, I lean back, getting comfortable, lifting my feet onto the table, spreading my legs. I'm nervous but aroused, and I'm more curious to see what Andrei is going to do.

"Very nice," he said, standing up.

He's wearing sweatpants, and I hate to say it, but he even makes the baggy clothes look sexy. Who could have thought sweatpants would be sexy? I sure didn't.

Andrei pulls his shirt up over his head, throwing it onto the floor, and then shoves his pants down. He's not wearing any boxers and so his cock springs out. He's long and thick.

I can't look away as he grips himself, tight and firm. He slides his hand up and down the length, and I wonder what he'd taste like in my mouth.

Licking my lips, I return his gaze. "I'd like to suck you," I said.

He growled, stepping forward. His hand is going to the back of my neck and moving close, within touching distance. His other hand is wrapped around the base of his dick, and he's holding it for me.

"Then have a taste," he said.

I press my tongue to the head and withdraw. "I don't know what I'm doing."

"You're doing everything right."

Wrapping my lips around the head of his dick, I suck him into my mouth and draw him in.

"Oh, fuck!"

I stopped. "What?"

"Your mouth shouldn't feel so good."

I can't help but smile, putting my mouth back on his cock and sucking him in, tasting him.

Humming around his length, I start to bob my head, loving how he fills my mouth, but suddenly he pulls out and his lips consume mine. His tongue plunges inside and I meet him, tasting him, wanting to deepen the kiss.

Andrei pulls away again, and this time he kisses down my body until he gets to my pussy, and then his tongue dances across my clit. I gasp, saying his name, repeating it, as he strokes over the pleasured bundle of nerves. It's so intense, I can't think straight, not that I want to. He feels amazing.

He goes down to my entrance and plunges inside, repeatedly, but it's not enough. Andrei knows what my body wants and needs, and he brings me to orgasm, sharply, quickly, but he's not done with me.

Andrei moves me so that I'm on my knees. He grabs my ass, spreading the cheeks wide, and he lets out a groan. I gasp as he gives my ass a slap, and then he's balls-deep inside my pussy. From this angle he feels harder than ever before, hitting right to the hilt where it's almost too painful, but so damn good.

His hands go to my hips, holding me in place,

keeping me there as he starts to pound harder and faster.

I know I'm close to orgasm again, and he pulls out, and then we're back to where we started, where I'm straddling his waist. Only this time, he's inside me and I'm gripping his shoulders as he tells me exactly what to do. I'm riding him, fucking his cock, enjoying every single second of pleasure, and I don't want it to end.

Andrei licks his fingers, moves them between my thighs, and starts to play with my pussy.

I'm so close that all it takes is a few strokes and I'm coming, screaming his name. He follows me, his hands digging into my hips as he floods my pussy. I feel every single pulse as he comes, and I wonder if we are going to make another child together.

****

Andrei

"What is this, Andrei?"

I smiled as I moved toward my wife. The island had been a dream and I had to say, I hated being back in the city. I'd been looking for a house, somewhere away from all the distractions of life, far from the penthouse. I'd found this beauty, in the middle of nowhere, enough land for us to build whatever we wanted, and this beautiful seven-bedroom house, complete with an en suite.

Ivan sent me the details for it. It was going for a great price. I'd already purchased it, but after a brief look at the details, I just knew Adelaide would love it. There was a great deal of security, and I was already making the necessary choices for the men who'd be guarding my wife.

"It's a house," I said.

"I know it's a house, silly, but I was wondering why you've brought me here." She spun in my arms and tilted her head to the side, eyes wide. I don't know how she got prettier every day, but she did.

Kissing those tempting lips, I smirked. "What do you think?"

"Are you planning on buying this place?" she asked.

"It's ours, if you want it."

"What about the penthouse?" She frowned.

"I've still got the penthouse, but we need a real place. Not one that has marks on the floor showing where you can move. I've watched you. You can handle heights to a certain point. I did look at a bungalow, but I've got to have me some views, baby." I kissed her nose.

"Your work is more important. Don't you have to be present at all times?"

"I am present at all times. It doesn't matter where I live. This means we can invite Aurora and Slavik over."

"Don't forget their little girl," Adelaide said.

How could I forget? Ivan had been raving about the little brat. I was happy for Slavik. Delighted for him, in fact. The next generation was starting, and it was good news. The Volkov Bratva was not going to die out. Ivan's ways would remain and I was hoping it would grow.

But, Slavik having a little girl got me thinking about the child we'd lost—the baby Bethany had taken from me. Adelaide hadn't been far enough along and I didn't ask the doctor to find out the sex or any of that shit. I don't even know if it was at the stage when the sex was determined. Didn't they all start out as girls? I didn't know fucking biology that well. Just enough to keep people alive long enough to cause them the most pain. I knew a lot, but not enough about babies and shit. Anyway, I couldn't help but be a little jealous. Slavik had a girl. I had nothing. And Bethany was still alive.

I had my spies on her. She was a fucking whore

who was blowing through the funds her parents had given her. As for her parents, their company was still struggling to hold itself together. They were draining funds and losing viewers faster than anything.

"Yes, their little girl," I said.

"Andrei? What's wrong?" she asked.

"Nothing is wrong. I just … it's good news for them."

"Are you disappointed I'm not pregnant?" Adelaide asked.

She had started her menstrual period that very morning, and I knew there was no chance of another baby right now. I wasn't disappointed, not really. I saw that she was in pain. Running fingers through my hair, I saw the sadness in her gaze, and I couldn't live with it. I went to her, cupping her face. "Look at me. I am fine and I don't care if we're pregnant or not."

"What if … what if I can't?"

"You can."

"I heard what Ivan said, within two years."

"Don't worry about that."

"You might get a new wife."

"Not going to happen." I kissed her hard.

I wanted to say more, but as I started, my fucking cell phone rang, pissing me off. Annoyed, I tried to ignore it, but Adelaide pulled away.

"You need to answer that."

What I needed to do was be there for my wife, not constantly be at the beck and call of everyone else around me. It was Ivan, though, so she wasn't wrong. I did need to take the call.

"Andrei," I said.

"I know it's you. Why say that?"

I rolled my eyes. "What's wrong?"

"I need you to arrange the meeting with Rage.

Have him come to your penthouse suite."

"Not fucking happening," I said, stepping away from Adelaide.

"Pardon me?"

I close my eyes, realizing what I just said. "I'm not having him come anywhere near my wife."

"She loves the house, doesn't she?"

I glance back at Adelaide who'd gone to sit on the bed, giving it a little bounce. "I don't know."

Ivan tutted. "You clearly didn't sell it well enough."

There were moments like now, where I would have gladly throttled Ivan Volkov. The man could be so fucking annoying and I knew he did it on purpose. He was a meddling fucker. He'd not gotten to where he was in life by not meddling. I was so fucked off with it.

"I'm talking with her."

"Tell her how nice it would be raising a family. How she can have Aurora come to visit. Their kids could be friends and all of that."

I step out of the bedroom so she doesn't hear. "Ivan, that's not the best course of action. I'll deal with it, but we can't meet at the penthouse suite."

"Rage needs to know we mean business. He also has to think we trust him."

"Which we don't."

"I trust him more than I do Demon. Now, if he comes to your penthouse suite, that is a sign of respect and trust."

"It's a sign of stupidity."

"So, get Adelaide loving the house and we'll see how everything else plays."

He hung up, of course. That was what Ivan did— gave instructions, and left me to deal with everything else. The guy was exhausting at times.

I dropped my head, taking several deep breaths. Adelaide had been attempting meditation. Since the attack, she occasionally had panic attacks. She didn't know what they were driven by, but I'd heard the methods and started to use them myself.

Anything that stopped me from killing my boss was a fucking bonus.

I enter the bedroom again but Adelaide is nowhere to be seen.

Seeing as I already paid for the house, I had the keys and there was no need for a realtor. Leo and Terrance were out front. No one else should be in the house, but fear raced down my spine. I called out her name, but she didn't respond.

Rushing downstairs, calling her name again, expecting the worst, I heard her calling out that she was in the kitchen. Breathing a sigh of relief, I made my way into the kitchen and found her with her hands spread out on the counter.

"This is a nice space," she said. "It's big. You could host family dinners. Invite some friends over. Are you thinking what I'm thinking?"

"Fucking you on every single counter?"

She giggled. "No, we're not thinking the same thing. I'm thinking Thanksgiving and Christmas. How about Halloween? We could decorate this place for when or *if* we have children." I close the distance between us and wrap my arms around her.

"*When*, Adelaide. *When* we have kids." I'd not been one for special occasions. I'd never celebrated a single Christmas or Halloween, or Thanksgiving. None of them had been important to me. Survival had. Kissing the top of her head, I breathe her in.

"I love the place, Andrei."

"Good."

"But you need to go, don't you?" she asked.

"Yeah, I do." I don't want to let her go.

This is crazy. I'm not the kind of man to act this way, but the thought of leaving my wife fills me with regret.

"I'll be fine. I'll be here," she said. "I can't go back to the penthouse, can I?"

"Not today."

She nodded. "You already bought this place, didn't you?"

"How did you know?"

"The closet, you've already started to fill it with your suits." She put her hands on my hips. "When will I get to see casual Andrei? Will he come back?"

"He will. He's already here." I kissed her temple, not wanting to leave her alone, but also knowing there was no choice.

Ivan expected a meeting and I had to contact Rage. Assuming he wasn't pissed off from being ignored. While I'd been on my honeymoon, Ivan had been sure to send pictures to Rage of Lottie's progress. Ive had eventually allowed her to shower and change, but even those images had been used to help our cause. The young woman was clearly special to Rage, and that was coming in handy right about now.

"Go," Adelaide said, letting me go. "I'll be here, waiting."

I kissed her again. "I'm leaving Leo," I said.

She had asked me not to be angry at him. It wasn't Leo's fault, and I doubted he would accept any beverage from her anytime soon.

I have no choice but to leave. As I do, I order Leo to keep an eye on my wife. Terrance is already seated in the driver's seat as I climb in the back, cell phone in hand. I contact Rage and wait. Three rings and he picks up.

"What the fuck took you so long? If anything happens to Lottie…"

"You are not in a position to question me," I said. "Lottie's survival will depend on you, Rage." I give him the location of the penthouse. "Be there in an hour. If you don't, then I can assume you don't care what happens to her."

Hanging up my cell phone, I slide it into my jacket and sit back. There is no relaxing for me.

Having Rage in my penthouse is not the ideal situation for me. He is still a member of the Evil Savages MC, and for all I know, he could be playing me. I don't trust anyone. Never. My penthouse would be tarnished after this.

Terrance drives us to the penthouse and I see Ivan's car is already in my slot, so Terrance parks in the closest available space.

Ivan is the boss. He knows what he's doing, but I have to wonder if I should question the man's sanity.

Arriving at my penthouse suite, I walk in to find the place tidy. There's nothing out of place, and Ivan is sitting at the dining room table, shuffling cards.

"Did you arrange it?" he asked.

"I made the call. He should be arriving in twenty minutes."

"Excellent. Can I interest you in a whiskey?"

I shake my head and take a seat opposite him.

"Did she like the house?" Ivan asked.

"Yes. You knew she would."

Ivan smiled. "There's a lot I don't know."

"What are you going to do?" I asked.

Ivan didn't speak. He flicked the cards over, one by one, and then gathered them up. "I don't see the addiction to cards. The winning part, I get, but all numbers on some card never appealed to me. People waste so much of their money on the flick of one of these bad boys. Do you get it?"

"We're talking about cards?"

"No, we're talking about the addiction cards causes."

I had no words. Ivan always had the most random thoughts. Sometimes I wondered if they dropped him on his head when he was a baby. Would that give him an excuse for his weird ways? I didn't know.

"Do addictions make sense?" I asked.

"Addictions make sense, if you think about the body's response to what's going on around it. The happiness, the endorphins that are released. It's a powerful drug." He sighed. "But now I'm bored." He put the deck of cards down on the table and stood up. "Is this guy known for being early or late?"

"I have no idea. Do you want to talk about Oleg?"

"No."

Ivan's the boss.

"How are Aurora and the baby?" I asked.

Ivan and I rarely made small talk. Until Adelaide came into my life, it had always been business. We weren't close.

"They're healthy," Ivan said, running a hand down his face. As he did so, I noticed the way he leaned slightly to one side, as if he had some kind of ailment. Like a bruise.

"Are you okay?"

"Fine."

He wasn't talkative today. Maybe I should have let him be his usual charming self and talk about the deck of cards for no good reason.

My thoughts drifted to Adelaide and I had to wonder what she was doing. I'd not yet installed any cameras so there was no way for me to steal glances of her on my cell phone. Not that I would with Ivan watching me. He already knew I kept a close eye on her, and he didn't need to see my obsession in person.

Finally, the doorbell rang and I went to open it. Rage was on the other side, looking mightily pissed. He raised his fist, but I saw it coming, blocking it. Terrance knew not to get involved even as Rage kept on coming.

"You take his daughter and fucking leave, you pieces of shit. You have no right. She is not part of this. She has never been part of this."

His rage was admirable. In between the blows, I struck out, slamming my boot against his leg, which made him stumble, and this time I charged him, ramming him against the wall and then wrapping my fingers around his neck, cutting off his air supply. Dragging him down to the floor, I stepped over him, wrapping my entire arm around his neck, using all the force I could to keep him there. I held him tight, not letting him go.

His hands gripped mine, but at no point did he beg. This was a club leader. A president. Not that piece of shit Demon.

I wasn't going to kill Rage. I held him still. "Lottie is alive. She's still breathing and right now I believe she's living a pretty cushy life. No harm has come to her, not a single bit. Do you understand?" I let go long enough for him to nod his head. "I will keep fighting you if that's what you want, but then she will pay for your sins. Got it?" I asked.

A single nod of the head and I let him go, stepping back.

Ivan simply clapped his hands as if it had all been part of a play. I didn't think that was necessary, but I didn't tell him that. Instead, I step back and allow Ivan to take over.

"This woman … does she belong to you?" Ivan asked.

"Lottie is a sweet girl. An innocent. She would never hurt a soul, and she has no right to pay for her father's sins."

I watched as Ivan tsked. "Don't get me wrong, I know she's a sweetheart. I've heard the rumors. Actually, I've seen the evidence. Lottie is not loved by the club. She is loved by you, and it would seem only you."

Rage slumped. It was a small action but I caught it.

"Lottie … don't hurt her. She is still club."

"But Demon told me to kill her."

I watched as Rage's hands clenched into fists.

"She is Demon's child but…" Rage dropped his head. "He has never been able to love her. He sees her as a murderer. When she was born, her mother didn't make it. She died in the room in Demon's arms. Lottie never stood a chance."

"But you take care of her."

"Because her mother begged me to," Rage said. "Before she gave birth, she had this weird feeling that something bad was going to happen. I don't fucking know what it was. I figured she was on something. Demon always liked to keep his women docile. The spirit she had was dying away, and she begged me to take care of her daughter. Lottie was left. Demon wouldn't even allow the club women to take care of her. He built up the lies surrounding her mother, told her she was nothing but trash, all her life. She was starving, dirty, and I took over her care. I raised her."

"So the truth is, you're her father?"

Rage shrugged. "I guess."

"You'd die for her."

"In a heartbeat."

"How interesting."

I always hated it when Ivan said that. There was nothing interesting about any of this. This was a man who clearly had a fatherly connection to the young woman. None of it was interesting. He took care of her, and during that time he formed a bond. Nothing to think about.

"Let Lottie go."

"I can't do that. You see, Demon has already told me to kill her, and I know for a fact he's got a grievance with me. Do you really think he's going to accept the daughter he can't even care for, to live?" Ivan asked.

"I'll take care of her."

Ivan snorted. "Look, no offense. I get that you're an incredible human being and all that, but you must see how futile it would be. Demon would kill you. Demon would kill his daughter regardless of the cost."

"What are you proposing then?"

Ivan slapped his hands together and smiled wide. "Proposing is a funny word, don't you think?"

I shake my head. He's all for the dramatics.

"You want to marry Lottie?" Rage asked.

"Not me personally, but I have a man who will take care of her."

"She's eighteen," Rage said.

"So, Demon has washed his hands of her, and do you think it's going to be difficult for me to get a marriage license? Hate to brag, but I am kind of the big deal in the Volkov Bratva."

I had to wonder what the previous Bratva Pakhan would think of this. Ivan didn't act or rule like any other Pakhan. I imagine it's why he'll be around for a long time. No one can truly know what he's thinking all the time.

"Lottie doesn't deserve this."

"My man isn't so bad. He's a little rough around the edges but no harm will come to her as his wife. He's my brigadier. Trust me, her life will be saved."

Rage didn't like it. I couldn't blame him. Thinking of a daughter, I couldn't help but imagine a little baby girl with Adelaide's sweet features running around the house. It made me smile, just a little, and then I composed myself. Now was not the time to be getting fucking sentimental, or hoping for a future that might not happen.

"What do you need from me?" Rage asked.

"It's quite simple, you need to find out where loyalties lie in the club, and when Demon dies, you kill those who follow him."

Rage cursed.

"You need to become prez of the club," Ivan said. "If you don't, then I'm going to kill you all, and I'll throw Lottie into the mix for good measure."

The calm negotiating man was gone. In his place was the cold monster rarely seen. It had been a long time since I saw the real Ivan unleashed. There were times I had to wonder if I imagined seeing the cruelty within him. He would do it, even if it wasn't his plan. If Rage didn't agree, Evil Savages MC would die.

"If I agree with this," Rage said, after a moment's hesitation. "I'm not going to be your fucking toy. I'm not going to be at your beck and call."

"Precisely. We will have an agreement and you could say we'll be a family, of sorts."

Rage sighed. "I want to see Lottie first."

"Not until the day of the wedding," Ivan said.

"I need to know she's safe."

Ivan clicked his tongue and then pulled out his cell phone, typing on the screen.

"Lottie," he said.

There was a pause and I waited. Rage stepped a little closer, and I reached for my gun but Ivan shook his head at me. Seconds passed, minutes, and then he clicked on his cell phone and held it up.

"H-hello?"

"Lottie, sweetheart?"

"Rage?"

"Yeah, honey, it's me."

"Are you coming to get me? Please, Rage, please."

Ivan tutted. "Now Lottie, tell the kind man, are you hurting?"

"N-no."

"Good. Are you being fed?"

"Y-yes."

"Good. That will be all."

Ivan ended the call and Rage charged at Ivan, who with a quick jab of his hand had choked Rage, who fell to the floor.

"Lottie is safe and well. Do we have a deal?"

Rage had his hands against his throat.

Ivan tutted. "Come on, I didn't hurt you that badly."

It took Rage a few minutes but he got to his feet and agreed. Ivan held his hand out and Rage looked at the greeting. I waited. Rage shook his hand and stepped back.

"There is one thing," I said. "I want to know when Bethany came to you."

Rage frowned. "Who the fuck is Bethany?"

Chapter Seventeen

Adelaide

I love the house. It's spacious and warm. There isn't a lot of furniture but Andrei had already told me to go shopping for some, which is why I was dragging him from store to store, forcing him to help me choose. With my hand in his, we walked into the third one and I knew Andrei was getting fed up. I had the color palette in my hands, and we started to look at the sofas.

"You know I can pay someone to do this," Andrei said.

I stare down at the cream sofa, and sink into the seat. It's not quite fluffy enough. I know it's weird but the best way to choose a sofa is to test it out with your ass, by actually sitting in it.

"I know. You can pay anyone to do anything. You've told me enough times, but I don't want to ask someone to pick out my furniture, Andrei." Patting the seat beside me, I wait. "I want us both to choose stuff for our place. Is that too much to ask?"

Andrei grumbled but sat down beside me, taking my hand in his, locking our fingers together. I can't help but look at the Volkov ink on his hands.

On one of the visits with Aurora, I noticed she had a band around her wrist. I'd asked her about it, but she had clammed up, saying it wasn't important.

"I like this one," he said.

I wriggle my ass from side to side and tut. "No, it's not comfortable enough. My ass will ache from sitting in it for too long."

"Doesn't everyone's ass ache from sitting too long?"

I wave my hand as if to ignore his statement. "You know what I mean."

"No, if I did, we'd have bought the sofa we saw an hour ago."

"Ew, that was green, and wouldn't have gone with the room."

"Ugh, I don't care about that."

I chuckled and walked up to him, putting a hand on his chest. "And what if Ivan thinks about it? What if he cares how a place looks?"

"He doesn't. Trust me."

"Are you so sure?"

He looked ready to talk, but then he stopped and I smiled, going up on my tiptoes and kissing him.

"See, just enjoy this." I take a few steps and realize I'm being unreasonable. "Actually, if you don't want to pick out furniture together, then I completely understand. I know you're very busy."

"You're doing that thing again."

"What thing?"

"That thing that makes me feel guilty."

I raise my brows. "I didn't think a *brigadier* could feel guilty." I make sure my voice is quiet so no one heard what I called him.

In response, Andrei laughed, pulled me into his arms, and kissed the top of my head.

"If this is what's going to make you happy, then consider me happy."

Wrapping my arm around him, we walked around the store, trying out new sofas. At one point, we were all alone, and Andrei reached for me, forcing me to straddle his waist, right there.

"What are you doing?" I asked, laughing.

"Simple. We need to test this sofa out for all eventualities, and I can promise you, all sofas are going to see my dick inside your cunt." He ran his hands down my ass and drew me close. I felt the hard ridge of his cock pressing against my pussy, and it made me gasp. I'm so taken aback by the pleasure.

Andrei sinks this fingers into my hair, which I have left down, and he kisses me, hard. I love his kisses. Cupping his face, I'm lost in the sweetness of his lips, but at the sound of a throat clearing, I jerk back and couldn't believe we'd been caught. Andrei had no such problems.

"Sorry you had to see that," he said, with a wink. "But I think we found the sofa." He patted the chair. "This is the bad boy we've been looking for."

"Excellent, sir. Would you be interested in the whole set?"

And that's how we left the store. Buying two sets of the sofa and chairs, one for the main living room, and another for the penthouse.

We weren't done. We picked out beds for the three bedrooms. I insisted because those would be the guest bedrooms for Ivan and then one for Slavik and Aurora.

While Andrei dealt with the payment, I did wander around one of the stores and came to an ideal example of a nursery. Yellow walls, a neutral color. A crib, a rocking chair, a small white cabinet with diapers, and creams peeking out.

I tense up as arms wrap around my waist, and I know from the scent of his cologne, it's Andrei.

"Hey." He pressed a kiss to my neck.

"Hey. It's beautiful."

"It is. We can buy it if you want."

"No. It's bad luck. I'm not even pregnant."

He nipped at my neck. "But you might be."

That we could. I was too nervous to take a test. My last menstrual cycle hadn't lasted long and it had been so light. I didn't want to know.

"Would you want a boy or girl?" I asked.

"Don't care, just so long as it's healthy. We're going to have to find names and do all that boring stuff."

I can't help but smile. "You don't like names?"

"What do I name our kid that won't make it hate us?"

This I found adorable. He was worried about what our child would think of us based on his or her name.

Leaning back into his embrace, I thought about it. "You could give him your name."

"Andrei Junior, no thanks. Trust me."

"Is there a name you'd like?" I asked, tilting my head back.

"Don't take this the wrong way but I haven't thought about it."

"I know. I haven't thought about names either. I've thought about having a baby in my arms, but names are so ... final."

Andrei rubbed my arms. "Come on, let's go and get something to eat. My treat."

As if it would be anyone else's.

Leo and Terrance were with us today but neither opened my door as Andrei was there, helping me inside.

I sat down, and thought of a name. "Billie?"

"For what?"

"A boy or girl."

"Not happening."

"You don't like the name Billie?" I asked.

"No, I don't."

I rolled my eyes. "How about ... Raymond."

"No."

"You're not being very helpful."

"I like the name Lucifer."

"You're not being fair now." I nudge his

shoulder, but I can't stop laughing.

"What about Bell?"

"To ring?" Andrei asked.

"You're not being very helpful," I said, taking a deep breath.

"I am being very helpful." He took my hand and locked our fingers together. "I'm telling you all the names that are not going to work. How about Lucille?"

"I like that name, but no." I sighed. "We're not even pregnant and we're arguing about names."

"You being pregnant is completely inevitable," he said.

I smiled and he cupped my cheek and kissed me. Staring into his eyes, I had this overwhelming feeling to tell him that I loved him. It came completely out of nowhere. I didn't say the words but I did come close.

Sinking my teeth into my lip, I held the words back. Did I love this man? Could it even be possible? He didn't love me. I was a job to him. He'd married me on boss's orders.

Andrei moved his thumb to my lip and tugged. "Don't bite that," he said.

"Why?"

"Because it makes me want to do a whole lot of wicked things to you." He kissed me. It started out gentle, and then he pressed harder against me, trailing his tongue across my lips, and when I opened, he plunged inside. I moaned his name, wrapping my arm around his neck, holding onto him, not wanting to let go.

His hand moved down my body, gripping my hip.

Cupping his face, I kiss him back, not wanting it to stop. He's not touching my pussy, but I desperately want him. All too soon, he broke the kiss, lifting up and away from me, and I miss his touch the moment it's gone, but it's a good thing he did so. We're at the restaurant.

He kisses the tip of my nose before climbing out of the car, rounding the vehicle to open my door. My face is all hot. I don't question Leo and Terrance. I never saw the two men eat, but I knew they did. Andrei takes my hand and leads me into the restaurant. The maître d' stumbles when he catches sight of Andrei.

Within minutes, we're at a table, a waiter taking our drink order, and menus being given to us. I hold my menu and stare at Andrei, a little shocked.

"What is going on in that crazy head of yours?" he asked.

"Don't you see the way people react around you?" I tried to discreetly look around the restaurant. It was rather busy.

The customers didn't care who we were, but I saw the waitstaff, and some of them pointedly looked our way.

"I own this restaurant," Andrei said.

"You do?"

"Yes. I own a lot of businesses. It was all part of Ivan's plan. We have a lot of companies to our name." He winked at me. "Does that surprise you?"

"Yes, and you know how to run them?"

He tutted. "Of course. Ivan Volkov would only ever have the best men on his team."

I liked this side of Andrei. He was playful, sweet, kind, charming. He was easier to understand and so approachable.

Looking at the menu, there was a lot of yummy food on offer. I noticed the vegan selection, and I didn't know what to have. The pizza sounded so good but then the lentil Bolognese sounded delicious as well. My mouth watered. In the end, I settled on pizza while Andrei had the steak with roasted vegetables.

"This is nice," I said.

Andrei reached across the table, taking my hand. "If you ever want to come here, let me know."

"Do you have the best chefs as well?"

"Only the best works for me."

"Did you always have a vegan menu?" I asked.

"No," Andrei said. "I came to the restaurant the day after I found out you were one, and I got all of my restaurants to include a vegan menu."

"You did?"

He nodded, lifting his water and taking a sip.

I'd declined the wine that was going to be poured for me, and had a soda instead. They still poured the drink in a wineglass, and I raised my glass with his.

"It was good for business. People go through fads all the time. It would seem vegan is the new thing to be right now."

I smiled. Some people went through fads, others did it because they wanted to. I was the former.

"Tell me about yourself," I said.

"What do you mean?"

"Did you always want to be … you know?" I asked.

Andrei didn't let go of my hand but I saw the scowl slowly settle into place. He wasn't happy. There was anger in his eyes.

"Adelaide, there is no choice in this life. Once you're born into it, there's no getting out. My father was born into it, so was I. There was no choice for me. This was going to be my life, regardless of whether my father wanted me or not."

"Do you miss your father?"

"No."

It was so final. Not a single hesitation.

"Do you miss your family?" he asked.

"Mine are not dead."

"True, but you don't ask to see them."

I stare at our hands and think about what he said. "There's no love lost between me and my family. They don't care about me. They never really did." After what Bethany had done, I'd not given them a thought. They didn't even come to see me in the hospital, so thinking about them, I didn't care. "Was it easier?" I asked. "With him being gone?"

"Yes, in a way, but you have to understand that he had to die in order for me to be here today."

I squeeze his hand, and we pull apart as the waiter brings our food. It smells delicious. My mouth waters. The pizza is quite large, and I know I'm hungry enough to demolish it all. Picking up a slice, I take a large bite and close my eyes as the flavors hit my tongue. Ripe tomatoes, garlic, onion, and lots of herbs. It's what I love and I can't resist taking another slice, another moan leaving my lips as I do.

"This is so good," I said, opening my eyes to find Andrei staring at me. "Here, take a bite. Trust me, it won't hurt you. It's just real good pizza."

He looked highly doubtful but I waited and he took a bite. I saw the small hint of surprise as he licked his lips. My husband liked my vegan pizza, who would have thought it?

Just as I was about to offer him another slice of pizza, the sound of gunfire rang out, bullets flew through the room, and I screamed. Andrei grabs me, pushing me to the floor, his body covering mine. His hands go to my ears, but I press my hands to my own, hoping he will protect himself. I don't know what's happening. It's frightening. Deafening.

****

Andrei

An attack was imminent. I shouldn't have let my guard down.

My only concern was getting Adelaide to safety. The attack took less than five minutes. I got the manager to account for everyone in the restaurant. There were no casualties, just a couple of wounds.

Adelaide and I were the main targets. The focus was on us, which told me someone within the restaurant had been asked to give our location. I got Adelaide to her feet and walked her out of the back of the restaurant where Leo and Terrance were already waiting.

Before I put Adelaide in the car, I force her to look at me.

"Are you okay? Are you hurt?"

"I'm fine. I'm fine. What about you?" Her hands go to my arms, holding me.

"I'm fine. There's nothing wrong."

I quickly glance over her body and see no cuts, no bruises, nothing. She was fine. I got her to safety. Leo and Terrance had been waiting around the back, per my instructions, in case we need to leave privately, but of course, doing this meant they weren't there to see who attacked.

"Take her home," I said, looking at Leo.

"No, no, no, I'm not leaving you," Adelaide said.

"Baby, you cannot be here for this, okay?"

"But, what about the cops?"

"I'll deal with them."

"Andrei?"

I cup her face and pull her into my arms. She's scared. I get that. Shaking. I don't care that my men are seeing me like this. If it had been anyone else, I'd have told them to get their fucking shit together, but everyone else, are not my wife.

"I've got to go and see what the fuck happened.

They could come back."

She shook her head. "Then come with me."

"I've got to do this."

Tears filled her eyes. "Please."

I slam my lips down on hers, kissing her. "I'll be fine. This will be easier for me if you go home. Please."

I hate seeing her cry, and I wipe the tears away from her face, not wanting to be the cause, but knowing I am. Whoever attacked me today was going to pay severely. I was having a good, quiet day with my wife and they had come and fucked with it.

Adelaide holds onto my hand and I have no choice but to help her into the car. My heart, for the first time, is pounding. Is this what I thought it was? Did Adelaide care about me? Was she worried I might die?

I wasn't sure what it was, but I kissed her and then looked to Leo. "Nothing happens to her, understood?"

"Yes, sir."

I step away from the car and watch it drive away. Terrance is by my side. "This was an inside job," I said.

"Sir?"

"I was the only target. Whoever did this knew I ate at this restaurant." I didn't believe Adelaide was the target. This time, I was.

I was annoyed that she had to experience that. Someone was going to pay for instilling fear into my wife.

Entering the restaurant, I take a few steps in and the manager Clifford is there. "Sir, follow me," he said.

The cops would be arriving soon. Hopefully it would be someone on my payroll, and if not, they would soon arrive to deal with this mess. Heading into the back of the restaurant, Clifford takes me to the security rooms, where we have multiple cameras set up. I'm a stickler for security.

Watching the screens, Clifford leans forward and brings up the moment I enter the restaurant. Adelaide is with me and I'm not paying attention to anyone but my wife. This is a first for me. I never allow pleasure to come before business. The maître d' on the front desk changes, his stance becomes tense. He takes us to our table and leaves us alone.

I follow his movements, tracking him. The moment he's back at the desk and out of earshot, he pulls out a cell phone and looks back, talking to someone. After a few seconds, he ends the call. Time passes, and then, the moment the gunshots hit, he takes off, running out of the restaurant.

"I want his name and details now," I said.

I'm full of rage. This could be anyone—the drug dealer I took care of for Bethany, the Evil Savages MC. I wouldn't put it past Rage to double-cross us. People were always after their own agenda, and right now I was so fucking pissed. I'd kill them all. I would have the streets dripping with blood if I had to. They nearly hurt my woman. There was no way anyone would get away with this.

I wanted to kill.

I wanted to hurt.

My thirst for blood was so fucking strong I could taste it. I was hungry for it.

Clifford arrived with the man's details and I opened them up. It gave his address, which I had to wonder if it was real. Marcus Knight. I didn't recognize the name, and glancing at his picture, none of his details rang a bell. I had nothing to do with this man, and he shouldn't be trying to kill me, yet that was exactly what he was doing, and now I was pissed off. So fucking pissed.

The police arrived and it was someone on my payroll. I gave him a few tips, and then left, leaving him to clean up the mess. This is what I paid people for.

There was already another car waiting. One of the soldiers had brought it at Terrance's request. I sat in the passenger seat as he drove, and I looked through the file. Pulling out my cell phone, I took a snapshot and sent it to my main computer guy, Edmund. He worked at the casino. He could crack any code and find all the dirt that was needed. He had a thing with numbers as well. I made sure he was protected. He was a good guy.

He used to be part of the Italian mafia, but because of his slender frame and the fact he faints at the sight of blood, they tried to kill him. I found him, killed the men who were about to take the final shot, rescued him, and he'd been loyal to me ever since.

Within minutes, my cell phone rang.

"What do you have?" I asked.

"Okay, so this guy makes next to nothing as a maître d' at one of your restaurants. However, an hour ago, fifty thousand dollars has just been wired into his account, but this is where it gets interesting. The wire comes from Oleg Pavlov's territory, Mr. Belov. Someone in his territory paid for him to do something."

I know exactly what he paid for.

"I want you to run a check." I give him Bethany's name and Edmund hangs up after he says, "On it."

I press my cell phone against my lips. I need to call Ivan but I don't have all the facts yet.

Terrance pulls up at an apartment building that had seen many fucking better days. It's crumbling. Men and women are on street corners. The scent of poverty is heavy in the air. I'd lived in part of this world long ago.

Climbing out of the car, the men notice me, recognize me, and scatter. This is what the Volkov do.

They instill fear. It didn't matter the gang, they knew we had more power. Usually, it was only men with little dicks who wanted to prove a point or thought they could overthrow our power. None of them were here today.

Stepping up to the building, I tilt my head back. Marcus had made a very bad decision. Entering the building, I notice the elevator isn't working. Not that I'm surprised. In places like this, elevators were always the first things to go. Diapers, used condoms, needles, dollies, and teddy bears decorated the stairs. The stench of piss and shit were heavy in the air. It was a smell I'd not encountered for some time, and it made me sick to my stomach, but I kept moving.

Marcus Knight lived on the fifth floor, and I had to wonder if Adelaide would still mark the area she could or couldn't move to. I hadn't gotten the floors cleaned in my penthouse. I rather liked the line she had given me.

We got to the fifth floor and there was no one around. Arriving at Marcus's door, I see it's partially open and someone is inside. I smiled. I couldn't help it. Pressing the door open, I see Marcus scrambling around his apartment. He doesn't notice me and I watch him. This man helped to nearly kill my wife. I stare at his body and all I want to do is hear him scream. In a place like this, no one would report it.

"Now, is that any way to pack a suitcase?" I said, alerting him to my presence.

Marcus spins around, catches sight of me, and literally pisses himself. He drops to the floor, hands over his head.

"Please don't kill me. Please. Please."

The apartment is a shithole. Mold is growing on the walls, and there appear to be old stains from a water leak. One of the windows has been smashed. This is not a place to be lived in. However, it does give me an idea for a business venture.

Going inside the apartment, Terrance grabs Marcus and slams him into one of the wooden chairs, but it was old and not designed to hold too much pressure, and it collapsed. Eventually, Terrance pushes him into a threadbare chair and holds him down.

I stare at Marcus. He's weak, and he's pissed himself again. The scent coming off him suggests that he might have also shit himself, which is so fucking nasty. I'm used to this reaction, though. He's guilty. He knows what he's done.

My cell phone rings and I see it's from the casino.

"Any news?" I asked.

"Bethany took a flight over two weeks ago, and other than landing in Pavlov territory, no one else has seen her."

"Thanks."

So there is a connection. What I don't know for sure is who reached out to who. The Evil Savages didn't help put a hit on my wife. That was all Bethany. She would have met Oleg because of me.

All the brigadiers were at a function. Adelaide hadn't met them all yet because Ivan had changed my wife after Bethany had been introduced to them.

Now I'm pissed off. I should have killed Bethany. This is what we needed, though. Oleg was no longer loyal to Ivan. That piece of shit was going to die.

I needed to contact Ivan. This is where it got a little trickier. Ivan wasn't always easy to get ahold of. He might have heard about the attack on the restaurant. He had spies everywhere. I called his number. Nothing.

Marcus had started to beg for forgiveness and even prayed to whatever would help him. In the end, I had no choice but to call Slavik.

"What do you want?"

"I need Ivan." I didn't tell him about Oleg or give any details. Ivan hadn't given me the green light to alert other brigadiers to what we had discovered.

"Hold on," Slavik said.

I heard movement and then minutes later Slavik hung up. I didn't have to wait long before Ivan rang my cell. He was in Slavik's territory. I could only guess he was besotted with the little girl they'd had not long ago.

When Adelaide eventually gives birth to our child, I don't want Ivan to start dropping by for more random visits. Not that I had anything to hide from him. I never did.

"What's going on?" he asked.

I give him a rundown of everything that happened, from the attack to Bethany's last known whereabouts, to the man in front of me.

"Put me on speakerphone and question him. I'll remain silent," Ivan said.

This is fucking news to me. Ivan can never be silent. He's the kind of man who always has to get involved. I put him on speaker and hand my cell phone to Terrance.

"Now, Marcus, you want to live, right? To get to use that fifty grand."

"Please, please, please, I don't … I don't … I was told that if you ever came into the restaurant I was to call this number and tell them exactly where you were." Marcus started to sob. "She told me it would change my life."

"A woman told you?" I asked.

Marcus nodded. "She said it was important. I had no idea they were going to kill you. I swear. I swear."

"What number?" I asked.

Marcus's hands shook so much and he did piss himself again. I didn't even know anyone could hold that much fucking urine without drinking in-between. He handed me his cell phone and I didn't want to touch it, but I had no choice. I'd be bleaching my hands by the time I was done here.

"The last number I dialed."

I didn't recognize the number.

"Anything else, Ivan?" I asked.

"Clean up. I'm on my way." His voice was clear.

I pocket Marcus's cell phone, and then pull out my gun. Terrance holds him down and I put a single bullet through his skull.

"Burn it," I said, leaving the room, and pressing the fire alarm as Terrance starts a fire.

Screams fill the air, and before Terrance and I even make it out, the flames have already engulfed the entire floor. The people who live in the building are all outside, staring up. No one pays us any attention, all caught up in the chaos and drama of their homes being set up in flames. Once it was burned to the ground, I'd build it right back up. Another business opportunity coming my way.

Chapter Eighteen

Adelaide

I'm pacing the floor waiting for Andrei to either call or to walk right in the front door. My hands shook as I held my cell phone. I hadn't called him, even though I wanted to. I want to make sure he's okay.

Leo won't leave. I've told him not to worry and to do something else, but he won't listen. He continued to stand guard.

"Is he okay?" I asked.

"I would have gotten a call if he wasn't," Leo said.

"That's not comforting."

"Why don't you sit down?"

I shake my head. "No. I can't sit down. Someone shot at us."

"Mr. Belov knows how to deal with this, Adelaide. He is perfectly capable."

"But someone wants him dead." I look at my cell phone, stop, and turn to Leo.

"Someone always wants him dead."

Tears fill my eyes. "That isn't good."

"I know. This is the life he leads. This is not the first, nor will it be the last attack on his life. This is what happens."

I move toward the stairs. My legs had started to ache and I dropped down onto the second step. "That's awful."

"He's used to it."

"I highly doubt that. I don't think anyone in their right mind could get used to having their life constantly in danger." I put my hands on my face and attempt to wipe my eyes, to clear my thoughts, but nothing is happening. "I don't know how you can be so calm."

"I have no choice," Leo said.

Alone with him, I feel the guilt at what I did to him. "I never said sorry."

"You don't have to apologize."

"Don't be like that, Leo. I betrayed your trust and I am sorry. You must hate me."

I know I hate myself for doing it. I'd found the sleeping pills days before I had given them to Leo. At first, I'd thrown them in the trash, but then I had the feeling I was going to need them, and I did.

"I don't hate you."

"I hate myself. Drugging you like that was awful. I didn't even think of Andrei being angry at you."

"He should have killed me," Leo said.

"But he didn't."

"Because of you," Leo said. "So we're even."

This made me want to cry even harder. "Have you ever thought it might be because you're a good man and soldier to him? Saving you might not have had anything to do with me."

Leo shook his head. "That's not how this works. Andrei spared my life to help you."

I still didn't believe it.

"Have you heard anything?"

"Are you not curious as to why?"

I looked at Leo and pursed my lips. "I'm not sure I know why."

"He loves you."

"You're wrong. Andrei doesn't have feelings for me. I'm his wife, and he was forced to marry me."

Leo laughed. "Haven't you realized yet that Andrei doesn't do anything he doesn't want to do?"

"But Ivan is the one in charge."

"Yes, he is, but Andrei didn't fight him on this, and everything he's done shows he loves you. He is in love with you."

I rub at my temple, a little uncomfortable. "I think you're wrong."

"Do you love him?" Leo asked.

"That is none of your business."

"Funny, I would say you are in love with him because you didn't want him to leave you."

"Maybe I was being selfish and I figured if he was with me, he'd be an easier target." It was all lies.

"No, I believe you love Andrei, and you were terrified of anything happening to him, which is why you begged him not to go back. You are in love with him."

But that didn't mean he loved me. I wasn't one to dwell on old emotions, but years of being second best, constantly made to feel like I didn't measure up to Bethany's standards, hit me so fucking hard.

These feelings were not fair. I didn't want them. I hated them.

Bethany wasn't better than me and I certainly stopped comparing myself. My parents hadn't loved me. Friends had easily abandoned me for the more fun-loving sister. They never gave me a chance.

Wrapping my arms around myself, I tried to hold on for dear life because the truth is, I was in love with Andrei. I don't know if it happened on our honeymoon, or when, but it was there, blaringly obvious, and I was unable to deny it.

He'd somehow gotten under my skin, worked his way into my heart, and now I couldn't stop.

"There's no guarantee he'll make it home tonight," Leo said.

I didn't like that. He had to.

"Then I'll wait right here until he does." I fold my arms determined to wait for my husband.

Even as I stare at the door, desperate for him to

walk through it, I can't help but be reminded of that moment the gun went off. I'd been so happy. Andrei had wanted to spend the day with me. He'd woken me up this morning, stroking my body, arousing me, getting me ready to take him. He'd made love to me. It had started slow and gentle, but it was like he couldn't get enough of me, and he'd gotten rough, commanding, and I loved every second of it. Even now, I'm sure I can still feel him on me, inside me.

Resting my hands on my thighs, I keep my gaze on the door. After making love, we'd taken a long shower. He'd washed every single inch of my body, taking care of me, before we'd gone down to breakfast. It was while eating my way through a selection of fruit he'd told me I had him for the day. Our house didn't feel like it, and I knew it was because we had to put our mark on the place, with furniture. No home was complete until you made it your own, and that was what I'd been determined to do.

Even as he griped, I made a note of anything that gained his interest. I'd been able to order a couple of lamps, and he rather liked this globe-shaped liquor cabinet. I thought it was ugly, but Andrei liked it. I'd hoped he'd put it in his office, but I wouldn't mind if he asked for it in the sitting room. This was our space.

Some people would call me crazy. I'd started to set up this life with a guy in the Bratva. I was a normal girl, well, as close to normal having a model mother and a father within media could be.

He had to come through that door.

Pressing my lips together, I felt so tired.

"I'll keep watch, Adelaide. Go to bed. Get some sleep."

"No."

"Adelaide?"

"No. I'm staying right here."

Leo stands by the stairs, not moving. Every now and then, he asks me to leave, but I can't do it. I have to wait. Andrei had to walk through the door.

I only look away to glance down at my cell phone to see if I'd missed a call. Nothing.

Waiting is torture. I don't know how anyone could live like this. The hours ticked on. Leo tried to get me to eat and drink, but I refused. I can't even stomach food right now.

The sun sets and the hours continue to tick by. At the sound of a car approaching, I stand up and wait. It could be anyone. The guards changing for the night shift. Andrei. Terrance. Was it Ivan to bring me bad news that he'd not made it?

Steps sounded through the door and then it opened. I threw myself at Andre, wrapping my arms around him, breathing him in. Holding him, convincing myself that he is in fact real and I'm not imagining it. His arms are so strong as they wrap around me.

Leo and Terrance disappear as Andrei picked me up and carried me across the room toward his office. Pressing my face against his neck, I smile, just so damn happy he's here. He's with me. He's not going away.

"What's the matter?" he asked.

"Nothing."

"Adelaide, talk to me."

"I … I was scared." He dropped me onto the edge of his desk and I lifted my head to look into his eyes. "I don't want anything to happen to you." Running my hands down his chest, I rest my palm over his heart.

"Nothing will happen to me."

"You're not invincible, Andrei. Look what happened today."

"That is business, babe. It's like that. People want

me dead."

"How can you live like this?"

"I was born living like this. I told you my own father, well, the man who claimed to be my father, wanted me dead before I was even born." He cupped my face. "I'm used to this and I know how to survive."

I press a kiss against his palm. His thumb reached out, stroking across my bottom lip. Opening my lips, I suck his thumb into my mouth, staring into his eyes. He groaned. Sliding my hands down his body, I grab the belt buckle and tug it.

Andrei doesn't do anything. He's leaving me in charge and I take it. Opening the button, then the fly, I shove his trousers down his body and touch him through his boxer briefs. Andrei had been teaching me how to touch him to drive him wild. I knew what his body liked.

Pushing my hand beneath the boxers, I gave his length a squeeze, and he released a hiss. Slowly, I start to run my hand up and down his length, and now Andrei, not satisfied, grabs my shirt and tugs it open.

Buttons flew all over the place and his hands go to my breasts, cupping the mounds. "Fuck me, you're beautiful."

His mouth goes to my tits, kissing each curve, before he reached around the back and flicked the catch of my bra. The lace was gone, replaced by his hands, cupping my flesh. I don't stop working his cock, but he pushes my hand out of the way to go for my trousers.

I have no choice but to push my hands down and lift my ass up so he can get them off, and once again he shreds my panties as if they are nothing. It won't be long until I no longer have any panties left.

The moment his palm touches me, I feel my arousal start to peak. He pressed two fingers against my clit, stroking back and forth, making me gasp and moan.

This feels so good. I don't want him to stop. But he does, to push his fingers down to my entrance, and he slams both fingers inside my pussy.

"So fucking tight." In and out, he pushes inside, working my body to a fever.

I rock against his hand, and then he kneels down, and his mouth is right on my clit, sucking at it. His teeth are biting down, causing me some pain, but not enough to stop the pleasure. I feel my orgasm start to build. I scream his name, and then his hands are on my waist, pulling me to the edge of the desk.

"Watch me, beautiful," he said.

I stare between my legs. He grabbed his hard cock, rubbing the tip against my pussy, sliding up and down my slit, grazing across my clit, which was still so sensitive. I almost can't take it and then I see him go to my entrance and watch as he disappears inside my body. Inch by inch, I see and feel him. He's rock hard and so wide.

When there is nearly half of him inside me, his hands go to my waist, holding me in place as he slams the last inches inside me, and he goes in deep. I feel him almost at my stomach, he's that large, but it feels good.

"Lean back. I want to see those tits bounce. Every time I'm working at this desk, I'm going to remember what you look like naked, open, begging for my cock."

I moan as he pulls out and then slams in deep, taking me by surprise by the sheer depth of his cock. I don't think I can take much more, but staring into his eyes, I know I can take anything. He starts to pound inside me, fucking me harder, the depth of the thrusts making my tits bounce with each hard push. I loved it.

"Wrap those legs around me. That's it, take all of me, Adelaide," he said.

I love hearing my name on his lips. I give myself

to him, not wanting to be anywhere else but with him. I'm all Andrei's. He is who I want. Just him, no one else. I don't know how it happened, and I'm a little afraid at how easy I fell, but there's no escaping it. I was in love with him.

I was in love with a monster, but I didn't care. My only concern now was how to tell him. A new wave of fear hit me. Not of my love for Andrei, but what had happened to me in the past. No one from my past was near me. Not my parents, certainly not my sister. No friends. No Nathan. Nothing. No one. I was all alone. Was it me? Was I unlovable? And that was what held me back. If I told Andrei what I felt, would it push him away?

No one else mattered to me in the past. They hadn't touched my heart. I was in love with Andrei Belov, and to even think of him walking away shattered my heart into pieces.

****

Andrei

"Well, we don't need hard evidence to prove who's responsible for providing the hit man," Ivan said.

Edmund was not a guy to do his work by halves. After I got off the phone with him about Bethany, he'd gone and done some digging, had gone as far back as a year ago. When Bethany was engaged to me. Oleg and my ex-fiancée had been meeting up right under my nose. I didn't care about the betrayal, not of Bethany fucking another man. What I didn't like was the deception against Ivan.

All the information was right in front of me this whole time, but I'd been too focused on other details. Ivan's death, the attacks. At the time when I was engaged to Bethany, I had to deal with her parents, as well as a fallout with the mafia. I'd been in Slavik's territory, and that was when Oleg and Bethany had struck.

I had a feeling their plan was to kill me. Bethany was the malicious type. I'd figured she would have poisoned me, and with Oleg's help, they'd have gained my territory. Framing the mafia in the process.

"Any word on Nathan?" Ivan asked.

"Not a word in two days," I said, and even as I hated the son of a bitch for the close relationship he had with my wife, I also felt responsible for him being missing. The man was a trained, hardened hit man. Edmund had gone hunting for information on him, and even with him being in Oleg's territory, he'd been able to find out that Nathan had been taken from one of the fighting rings.

Right now, I was on edge. If Oleg had Nathan, he suspected something, and I put this down to Bethany. She would have been the only one who'd know who Nathan was. Did she know he was a hit man, or was that just a bad coincidence?

"We've got to get Nathan out," I said.

"Yes. Adelaide would be pissed right about now, but I can safely say she wouldn't forgive us for getting Nathan killed." Ivan stood, hands on his hips.

"Us? You care what my wife thinks?"

"Adelaide is a good woman, Andrei. Why do you think I chose her?"

This made me laugh. "You always intended for me to have Bethany. She was far more suited."

"Really? Is that what you think?" Ivan laughed. "You're supposed to be this brilliant mind, but there are times I think you're as thick as a fucking plank."

I glared at him.

"You think I didn't know about the little woman you were keeping an eye on? Why you would sneak away in a piece of shit car to blend in with everyone, just so you could have the pleasure of watching her." Ivan rolled his eyes. "Please, you wore your heart on your fucking sleeve. I intended for Adelaide to be yours from the start. Who do you think put pressure on her father? I don't need that man or his company, but it makes it easier to have friends in certain areas. You never know when you might need them, and I wasn't going to burn bridges. Picking Adelaide would have been too obvious. Bethany, with all her crap and bullshit, and her addictions, was the obvious call. I just had to wait for her to fuck up, which she did. Her greed was her downfall. What I didn't anticipate was her hatred of her sister." Ivan sighed. "She probably realizes that Adelaide was the one most adored. Let's face it, the only reason her friends abandoned her was because Bethany threatened and blackmailed them. Adelaide has a natural way about her that draws people to her. Poor woman doesn't even realize it. Her family fucked her up bad."

"Have you noticed you're helping broke and damaged girls?" I asked.

Ivan glared at me.

"First, there's Aurora. She was considered second best, right? Not worth anyone's time. Ugly and all that. You gave her to Slavik. Then Adelaide, again, ignored, unloved. Pushed to one side as if she didn't exist. Now we move onto Lottie. Not wanted by her MC president father. Beaten regularly, from what I could tell." I'd seen the scars on Lottie's body. I had to wonder if Rage knew about them. If he did, my time doing business with him would be numbered. "The three women you originally chose—Irina, Amanda, and Sofia—they're not even around anymore. They're socialites, with no real pain or problems."

"Your point being?" Ivan asked.

I shrugged. "I don't have a point. I just find it

curious is all."

"Let's get back to business. I don't have time for this." Ivan stared down at the images Edmund had gotten for us. He'd also drawn a whiteboard of time stamps to clarify everything. "Oleg has nothing to do with Evil Savages MC, so we can use them. I've already set up a meeting with Demon. It goes down tomorrow night. Rage is aware of the details."

As am I. We're meeting at the docks, as per Ivan's instructions. I'd already made the necessary arrangements. Rage heard of Demon's plan to attempt to overthrow me and take back the city, but what his men didn't know was the suicide mission. He planned to take a group of his men, kill them, make it look like Volkov was responsible, and that would bring his other chapters there to come and fight. Fucking coward.

I don't mind taking responsibility for men I've killed. They'd probably do a sloppy job of it as well.

Rage was pissed off, because Demon intended for Lottie to die as well. He wanted to try and frame his daughter so it looked like she was a rat, and that way, when we gave her back, she'd answer to the club. All rats ended up dead. I didn't like Demon. Never had. We were enemies from the start, and now I was going to take great pleasure in killing the bastard.

It was a shame he wasn't going to get to see his club become our allies. I didn't know how long that would last, but I was open to it.

"With Demon and his followers gone, we need to use the MC to get into Oleg's territory. It's the only way to sneak in." Ivan looked at the paperwork.

"What do you think Oleg wants?" I asked.

"Power. He wants my seat. He didn't like being a brigadier, and he didn't like being picked sixth." He clicked his tongue. "I had my doubts about him, but he showed loyalty to me. Greed, that nasty fucking bastard, got the better of him. Now he's going to know real pain."

"You know he saw the same thirst in Bethany. She has to die."

"She will. They all will die. All of those that follow Oleg will fucking die." Ivan slammed his palm down on the table. His body was physically shaking with the rage consuming him.

I stay still, not that I'm afraid, but I know he's angry. I heard about the redheaded whore who'd turned on him. There were a lot of rumors surrounding Ivan's fake death, but the only logical explanation was that someone close to him turned on him. Since then, I'd noticed Ivan had withdrawn a great deal. He no longer stopped by for personal visits. He kept to himself. I had to wonder if he still visited Slavik. I know he went to see Aurora and the baby, but staring at him now, I know something is different. He has changed.

Ivan lifted up. His hands were clenched into fists and his jaw so tight I thought he was going to snap his teeth.

"Tell me, Andrei, why are you loyal to me?" he asked.

His words took me by surprise. I didn't know how to answer them. I stare at Ivan, not exactly sure what he wants to hear.

"Volkov, what is this about?"

"First Cara, now Oleg, I have to wonder why my men follow me. Is this the start of the end? Is this where people start to turn on me?" Ivan asked.

There was no emotion to his voice, or to his words. He was simply stating a fact. There was … nothing.

"I follow you because you're the right man for the job," I said. "I'm loyal because unlike other Pakhan, you earned it. You showed me who you are, and you rewarded that loyalty by allowing me to kill the very man that tried to take everything from me. I have no interest in taking your seat, Ivan. I'm happy to keep you in it, and anyone who tries to remove you is my enemy."

They were not pretty words. They were the truth.

"Even though I dragged Adelaide into this world? If it wasn't for me, she wouldn't have gotten shot, or lost the baby."

"Without you, she wouldn't be in my life. I couldn't stand Bethany. You knew that, but you had to make it work. Adelaide is my gift. I see that, Ivan. I will treasure her, always."

"She has to earn her place and her ink."

"I know."

She hadn't proven her loyalty yet, but I knew Ivan liked her. Adelaide hadn't run scared. She was a fighter, I knew that.

"I suggest you go to her. There's nothing more that can be done. We've got everything in motion." Ivan slapped my shoulder and within half an hour, I'm back in the car, heading home.

Not to the penthouse. To our country home, with the bedrooms I wanted to fill.

All I want to do is look at Adelaide, but I can't do that, because I've not been able to get the security cameras installed. My plan was to take her out on a date for an entire day, allow it to be her choice on what we do, and while that was happening, the house would be fully installed, so no matter where I was, I could look at her.

I missed her.

Pulling out my cell phone, I go to my images and pull one up of Adelaide sleeping beside me. She didn't know I'd taken this. There are a lot of pictures she doesn't know I've taken. Each one near and dear to my heart. I fucking love her so much.

"I ... I'm so cold."

I can't help but remember the moment she collapsed in my arms, capturing her the second after she'd been shot. My world felt like it had come crashing down. From the moment I first saw Adelaide in that alleyway, helping people, she had gotten under my skin. She was the one weakness I had in my life, the one secret I had successfully kept to myself. Only I hadn't. Ivan had known. There was no way anyone else had known.

I'd played my part well with Bethany. Behind closed doors the truth had come out. Bethany knew I didn't want her, but she had no idea that I wanted her sister from the start.

Running a hand down my face, the moment I see my front gates, anticipation rushes through me.

I want to see my woman, right fucking now.

Chapter Nineteen

Adelaide

I didn't want to love the house, but I do. It's not too high that I can't enjoy parts of it. I've not gotten a marker to ruin the floor, giving myself a no-go area. It's childish to still be afraid of heights, but it's a feeling that has never faded.

Walking around our house—and it does feel that way—is so freeing. I finally feel like I belong. I don't care about the guards anymore. At first, seeing them with their weapons on hand was absolutely terrifying. It was a constant reminder every single day of the life I lived. Being a brigadier's wife, part of the Bratva. There was no getting away from it. This was my life and to be near Andrei, I knew I had no choice but to remain here.

Whenever I thought of a marriage or a husband, Andrei wasn't the man that came to mind, but my feelings for him could not be pushed to the side. Even though he had been cold to me in the beginning. I knew I had fallen in love with the attentive, sweet man he had shown me in recent weeks.

Leo had once told me that Andrei couldn't afford to be kind. That there were people always looking to hurt, to kill, to take him from me. I couldn't allow that to happen. It was rare for me to get the opportunity because he always had his guard up, but one lone night, I'd watched him sleep. Seeing him like that, I'd been overcome with a need to protect him, to take care of him. So, regardless of him not loving me, I knew I was going to love him enough for the both of us, and I was happy with that. Content.

Walking downstairs, I smiled just thinking about him. What was wrong with me? My feelings made no sense at all. I couldn't wipe the smile from my lips, because it felt so good to finally be able to accept that I was in love with Andrei Belov.

The front door opened and as if my thoughts conjured him right out of thin air, he moved toward me. There was a look in his eye I'd never seen before, and I didn't know if I should be afraid of him or not. He stepped up to me, and I didn't flinch as he raised a hand, and then gripped the back of my neck, tugging me close, and slamming his lips down on mine. I gasped, putting my hands on his stomach, and slowly reaching up, wrapping them around his neck.

He lifted me up as if I weighed nothing and then proceeded to carry me up the stairs toward our bedroom. He kicked the door closed and then let me go on the edge of the bed. Staring up at him, he stepped back, removing his jacket. I stood, and followed his direction, stripping my clothes from my body in time with him. We were both naked, and then our bodies crashed together, the heat radiating between us.

Andrei's arms surround me, pulling me close. One gripped my neck, and the other moved down, going toward my ass, which he gripped tightly, making me moan. The hard ridge of his cock pressed against my stomach. I felt the pre-cum as he was so slick. He moved me back, so I had no choice but to fall to the bed, and he pressed me down, breaking the kiss as he trailed his lips down my neck. He didn't waste time, going from my pulse down toward my breasts.

He pressed them together and I loved it when he didn't seem to be able to get enough of me. It was a heady experience. He sucked at each of my nipples in turn, lavishing each one with attention, making me crave him even more. I was hungry for more of him. I didn't want it to stop, but Andrei had other ideas. He kissed down my body, going toward my pussy. Even before he got there, my legs were open to accommodate his body, and he groaned. His hands went to my knees and hovered just above my sex. "Fuck, I love your pussy," he said.

I smiled and then cried out as his lips went straight to my clit, sucking at the swollen bud. It felt so good.

He moved down, going to my cunt, plunging his tongue inside, once, twice, three times, before moving up, going to my clit. Each touch brought me closer to orgasm. With his tongue on my nub, he used his fingers to plunge inside, stretching me out, making me moan and beg for more. I couldn't control it.

There was no holding back as he hurtled me toward an orgasm that shook me right to my core. Even before my release was over, he moved up between my thighs, and I felt him as he slammed inside me.

This wasn't gentle. This was consuming.

He took me so hard and so strong. Grabbing my hands and pressing them either side of my head, holding me down as he fucked me hard. I wrapped my legs around his waist and whimpered his name, wanting him, craving him. I was drunk on my need for him.

Andrei fucked me harder, slamming into me, going as deep as possible, his gaze on me as he took me. Something shone within his gaze. I didn't know what it was, but he didn't look away. I was his sole focus and I loved it.

"You're so fucking beautiful." He growled out the last. His face pressed against my neck as he found release. It was over so quick, it took me by surprise. We're both panting and his weight is on me, but I love the feel of him. He still held my hands down and I licked my lips. "I'm not done with you yet," he said.

I loved the sound of that.

He lifted his head to look at me. He released one

of my hands to capture my cheek. Did he want to say something? I don't know what's going on but then he brushes his lips against mine, and everything fades away.

Andrei doesn't pull out of me and I moan as he presses deep within me again. I don't know how it's possible, but he is still hard.

Time passes. Neither of us speak.

He kissed me again, slowly this time. There was no rush in his movements and I'm addicted to the feel of it. I don't want him to stop. I want to be with him so completely. I wonder if there was a way for us to freeze in time in this moment, where there is nothing bad about to happen. We don't need any more heartache. We're together and it is calm and peaceful. We have each other and nothing could ever go wrong.

"I … I…" I don't know if I can say the words. Would he laugh and mock me? "I enjoy living here, Andrei. Thank you for buying this house."

It's not what I truly wished to say, and he looked at me with such disappointment. Was he hoping I'd tell him I loved him? That I wanted to stay with him?

I'm so confused.

****

Twenty-four Hours Later

I don't know what happened. One moment Leo and I were driving back home after going to the shelter, and the next moment, our car was being forced off the road. Tears flood my eyes as I recalled what happened next.

Leo had gotten out of the wreck first, and then helped me. The seat belt had been stuck, and I'd been upside down. He'd warned me that the moment he cut the belt, I was going to fall and I had to break it somehow, which I did. Again, it was all a bit fuzzy. He'd pulled me from the wreck, but the danger hadn't ceased.

We'd been forced off the road for a reason. They'd shot Leo, four times. His body jerked with each bullet and I'd screamed. He'd tried to protect, ordered me to run, which I had done without question.

I had so much guilt when it came to him, that to disobey him just didn't sit well with me. So I ran, until someone shoved me to the earth, pulling my arms behind my back, and then forcing my head down. His hand had covered my mouth, preventing my screams. I couldn't recall a time I'd been so afraid before. Even my wedding night hadn't left me like this.

Bound up, stuffed in the back of a truck, I scented the oil and gas that surrounded me. No one was in the back with me. I was alone. They'd put a gag in my mouth, and a horrible bag that smelled like rotten fish on my head. My heart raced and the urge to vomit came over me multiple times. I couldn't believe this was happening.

Just last night I thought about how peaceful it was. How much I wanted to stay within our tight little bubble where nothing would go wrong, and now I'm with an enemy of Andrei's. Or was it Andrei?

I didn't know anymore.

I curled up into a tighter ball, trying to control my fear. I wasn't just a random woman off the streets. My life, my name, I'm connected to the most feared Bratva in the country, and I wouldn't let my husband down by showing fear.

Letting the tears dry, I attempted to calm myself by deep breathing, by trying to convince myself that everything was going to be okay. Andrei would come and find me, but why would he? If I was with his enemy, he'd be able to get rid of me.

Ignoring the horrible thoughts running through my head, I attempted to focus on the now. On listening to the van as it moved.

"I'm going to be fine. I'm going to be fine."

I didn't believe a word I was saying. How could I? We'd been traveling for a long time. I wasn't a fool. The longer we traveled, the further from home I got.

What about Leo? Was he alive or dead? He fought so hard for me, ordering me to leave so that I could be safe. Did they mean to harm him, or was I the target? I had so many questions. No answers. Andrei had warned me that I'd become the enemy, and people would want to hurt me just because I was associated with him. I had believed him, but I figured it wasn't important. It was now.

Why hadn't I thought about defending myself? Why did I have to be weak? I hated myself in that moment. I was so damn tired of being like this. If I made it out alive, I'd make sure I found the means to protect myself.

Closing my eyes, I waited for the journey to end, hoping I'd understand what was going on and why I was taken. Part of me hoped Andrei was doing this as a test, to show me that I could be hurt at a moment's notice. If so, I was going to be pissed with him.

The van came to a slow stop. The small jerk of the vehicle let me know the hand brake had been applied. Fear raced down my spine and threatened to cause me a panic attack. I couldn't allow that to happen. I needed to be calm. I felt anything but calm.

I heard voices and then the door to the van slid open, and I was pulled out of it. Their grip was so tight, there would be bruises. I was pushed to the floor and then the hood that bound my head was removed. Keeping my gaze on the floor, I clenched my hands into fists. No one within the Bratva showed weakness or fear. I wasn't going to let Andrei down now, and slowly I lifted my head.

I became aware of three things. One, my very best friend Nathan was hung from a chain. Two cuffs were wrapped around his wrists, another his neck, and he was bleeding. There were marks all over his body and I didn't know what could have caused it. The second, my sister, looking like a queen. She had this smug smile on her face that usually meant there was going to be trouble. Three, a man I vaguely remember being at my wedding. I think he was one of the brigadiers, but I didn't know which one. There was a similar tattoo that Andrei had across his knuckles, but this man had it around his neck.

"What's the matter, sis? Shocked?"

Ignoring Bethany, I focused on the man by her side.

"So this is the woman that will bring Andrei in line?" he said, coming a bit closer. I didn't like the way he looked at me, almost assessing in his gaze, as if he saw something he didn't like.

The closer he got, the stronger the impulse to hurt him became. If my sister was involved, this couldn't be good.

"You've not had any work done," he said.

"Oleg, enough, please, she's not worth your time, other than to get Andrei here. Trust me, she is the key."

Oleg Pavlov, one of Ivan's brigadiers. I don't know his story or why my sister is working for or with him, but either way I knew this was bad. So fucking bad.

"What lies has my sister told you?" I asked.

He laughed. "So she does speak."

"Whatever she has told you, trust me, it won't end well for you."

"Shut your fucking mouth," Bethany said, advancing toward me.

"What is it you want now?" I asked. "Money?

Drugs? A place as a brigadier's wife? You threw all of that away in a goddamn orgy."

Bethany went to attack me but Oleg stopped her, shoving her back. "Enough."

My sister obeyed, which was a shock to me. She never did anything for anyone. He'd denied her the pleasure of hurting me, which told me something even more terrifying was in store.

"Be strong, Adelaide," Nathan said.

My gaze jerked to his and I cried out as someone struck a whip right across his body.

"You don't like that, do you?" Bethany said. "The same is going to happen to you."

"Let him go," I said, ignoring Bethany, pleading with Oleg. "I don't know why he's here. Why are you doing this?"

Oleg tutted and came closer. "No, I don't suppose you do know anything about this. Thrown into this world because your sister couldn't keep her legs shut." He held his hand up as Bethany attempted to yell at him. "You're a slut and don't even pretend to be anything but." He turned to glare and snap at her, before bringing his attention back to me. "But you, now you have been a bit of a mystery. Andrei has never shown a single moment of weakness, until you."

"I'm nothing," I said.

He laughed again.

"If you think you can use me to get Andrei to bow down to you, or give you what you want, you're mistaken. I'm nothing to him. He was forced to marry me."

"Trust me, it took some convincing, but I have known Andrei Belov for many years. The moment you walked into a room, his gaze was on you. At your wedding, you were never out of his sight, and then of course was the rumor that he wouldn't even allow a guard to get close to you. I can see why." His gaze roamed down my body.

"She's a fat fucking bitch. Don't you look at her like that!"

Oleg stood and backhanded my sister. "Do not ever disrespect me again. Your place is to be silent, or I will send you to sleep with my dogs, understood?"

Blood seeped at the corner of Bethany's mouth, and I kept my gaze on Oleg. I didn't know what the hell was going to happen. Leo was hurt badly. Nathan, I don't even know why he was here, but he was also bleeding. This was a trap. Andrei wasn't going to come and save me. He had his whole territory to think about.

"I think it's time for us to send a message to Andrei," he said.

He clicked his fingers to a soldier and ordered him to come closer.

I didn't like this.

Nathan started to thrash in his binds and I watched as they covered his mouth, landing blows to his body. This couldn't be good. My hands were still tied. I couldn't fight back.

Oleg moved behind me and pulled me to my feet by my hair. A scream left my lips, and then he hit me hard, sending me to the floor, dazed. He wasn't done with me as he pulled me to my feet once again. I couldn't stop the yelp as he pulled at my hair again.

"Andrei, I've got your pretty little wife. I suggest you come and get her, because she's just too tempting to ignore." His hand ran down the front of my body, and this time I did scream. I didn't stop, trying to fight against him, begging him to stop.

I hated myself, especially when he threw me to the floor, and then he was on top of me. Keeping my legs together, I looked at him with fear. His hands went to my neck and he started to choke me. I struggled against him, fighting with all my might, desperate for him to let me go, and when he did, I sucked oxygen into my mouth. Deep and hard, and desperate.

"He's not going to come," I said between pants. "Andrei will never come for me. He won't."

"We will see."

Chapter Twenty

Andrei

Oleg had taken up residence on the border between our territories.

I wasn't there to stop the attack. Rage had gotten word to us that Demon had changed the plan, brought it forward by a day. While my wife had been hunted down, I'd been with Ivan, watching as Demon and the rest of his men took their last breath. The deal was done. Rage, while I watched, was voted by his club to take over as President of the Evil Savages MC. To start peace once again between the club and Ivan, there was going to be a wedding. Lottie would be marrying Ivan's brigadier of choice, and as they were shaking hands, I got the call.

Leo had told me what happened. Told me his exact location where they'd been pushed off the road, but Leo hadn't stopped. He'd followed them, giving me the place where Oleg had taken Adelaide. My wife. The love of my life.

Ivan was with me, as was Terrance and even Slavik. They were there as I watched the video Oleg sent to me. I was already near him and my grip tightened on the cell phone. My hands were still covered in blood. Ivan and Slavik said nothing to me.

"He's dead," I said, finally speaking up. "I don't care what I have to do to make amends, I will kill him. He will die tonight." He hurt Adelaide.

Ivan nodded his head. "He doesn't know Slavik and I are with you. We will have to be careful about this."

I shake my head. "No."

"You want Adelaide to come out of this alive?" Ivan said.

"He wants my territory. Mine is the border

between the MC, the mafia, and the Cartel. That's what he wants. He's probably in talks with them to broker some kind of deal." I'd already figured out what Oleg wanted—power and money.

Attempting to remove Ivan gave him a shot at the crown, at the title of Pakhan. By taking my land, it would connect him to Ive's, which would bind three territories to him, and a whole host of power. Slavik's would be the hardest to take over as his was the most obscure. I guess he didn't see Victor or Peter as any real threat.

My hands shook with anger. Adelaide had once again been hurt. I would kill everyone involved with her death, including Bethany.

It didn't take a genius to work out that she was the one who pointed at Nathan, told of his true identity. I wonder if she even knew he was a hit man. Either way, she would have figured out he was working for us, and that would have put him in danger as well as Adelaide. Bethany was going to die today. It would seem today was a day for spilling blood. My enemy's blood.

"I go in first and alone," I said.

"That's suicide," Slavik said. "We can storm the whole building."

"No. That would put Adelaide at risk."

"Our main objective is to take out Oleg."

"If Aurora was in there, would you storm the fucking building?" I snarl.

Slavik reached for his knife but I was ready and prepared.

"Enough!" Ivan yelled. "No one is dying today, apart from Oleg and those who follow him. I will not risk Adelaide. Andrei is right, he doesn't know you and I are here. He will want to gloat, to bring Andrei to his knees, and you will let him."

I look at Ivan.

"He needs to believe you came alone. That you are desperate for Adelaide."

"I am," I said, through gritted teeth. "She cannot…" I have never begged for anything in my life. I've always been in control, but this wasn't about me, this was about Adelaide. "Please don't let anything happen to her. She is … let her live in peace if I don't make it out today." I lifted my head and stared at Ivan. "I beg you."

Ivan looked at me. "You really do love her."

"She is mine." That was all I could say. Adelaide was mine. Mine to love. Mine to cherish. Mine to honor. Mine to obey. All fucking mine. No one else's. I was hers in every single way possible.

"Then let's go and get your woman."

We found Leo in a ditch, far enough away from the abandoned farm where Oleg had taken her. There was an outbuilding that had been completely rebuilt, and looked like it had been changed to have storage.

Leo was pale, bleeding badly, and I knew he wasn't going to make it.

"I failed you."

I took his hand within mine. His grip was weak.

"It has been an honor to serve you, Andrei," he said.

He died right in front of me. I would take care of his family. Even though Adelaide had been taken from him, he had died serving me, and that couldn't be ignored. If he'd gone to the hospital, there would have been a chance for him, but instead, he'd followed my wife.

Nodding at Slavik and Ivan, I expected them to do their part. I stepped away from the ditch, brushed the dirt from my body, and covered in dried blood, I rolled up the sleeves of my shirt.

I was Andrei Belov, brigadier to Ivan Volkov and husband to Adelaide. My enemies would know real pain tonight.

Approaching the building, I see three of his men tense up and point their guns at me. Linking my fingers together, I raise them behind my head and look at them dead on. They were going to die.

They approached me and started to search my body, looking for weapons. They wouldn't find any, and they'd have to chop off my hands because my fists were all that I needed.

One of the men moved behind me, nudging at my back with his gun, forcing me inside. Entering the building, I saw that I was right. It still had the original features of a barn, but it had been converted to a storage room. There were concrete floors, high beams, and the windows were quite high as well.

I saw Adelaide on the floor and Oleg had a gun pointed at her head. I saw the bruise on her face but what surprised me was the shock in her eyes.

"I didn't expect you so soon," Oleg said.

"My man called me the moment you left," I said. I tutted. "I always knew you were sloppy, Oleg, but leaving my man alive, that was your mistake."

I tensed up as he grabbed a fistful of Adelaide's hair and pulled her to her feet. His arm went across her neck, holding her against him. I should have known he'd make a move like that. The fucker was a coward. He'd pay for each bruise.

"You've got a pretty wife, Andrei. How about I fuck her right in front of you?"

This time, I went to charge forward but one of his men shoved the butt of his gun into my stomach, forcing me to my knees.

Oleg laughed. "Did you know your wife didn't

think you'd come? She doesn't realize that you're in love with her. That you would die for her. That you would give up your entire territory for her."

I lifted my head but I didn't look at Oleg, I stared at Adelaide.

"Andrei, please?"

"I am in love with you, Adelaide. I have been for a long time," I said.

She gasped.

"The moment Ivan gave you to me was the happiest fucking day of my life." I turned to Bethany and snorted. "Still enjoying my sloppy seconds, I see. Trust me, the only thing she can do is suck dick."

"Fuck you, you piece of shit. You didn't even want a piece of this."

"Exactly, you weren't worth using," I said, but I had also just gotten Bethany to admit in front of her sister that I had never slept with her, nor would I ever.

Turning to Oleg, I wait. "What do you want?" I asked.

"I want you to kill yourself."

"Too much of a fucking coward to do it yourself?" I asked.

"Oh, no, I want Adelaide to know how much you love her, what you're willing to do for her. How low you're willing to go. Take off your shirt."

"Andrei, please don't."

I unbuttoned my shirt and a knife was tossed in my direction. Picking up the knife, I looked at Adelaide. I hold the knife to the flesh of my arm, and slice down. There's pain, but I don't show any.

"We met before," I said. "A few years before you became my wife. I had been in a fight, I was cut, and hurt. You were with some nurses, helping the homeless, and I had stopped to rest. You came to me, Adelaide.

You helped me when no one else did, and I fell in love with you then. You wanted me to go to the hospital. You feared what would happen to the wound if I didn't."

"That was you?" she asked.

I nodded. "I love you, Adelaide, completely."

"Then stab yourself," Oleg said. "Show how pathetic Ivan Volkov's men are. Let me see how weak you are."

I lifted the knife, ready to plunge it into my body. I knew where to hit so it wouldn't damage any organs or risk my life, but I didn't need to.

Slavik and Ivan stormed into the building and I chose the commotion to charge forward, taking Oleg down. Adelaide fell and even as I wanted to go to her, I couldn't. Punching Oleg, I landed blow after blow. He didn't get a single chance to hit me back.

Suddenly, a scream erupted in the air, stopping me. Oleg shoved me back. He was too weak for me to care about, but I saw that Bethany had grabbed my wife by her hair and pointed a very shaking gun at her head.

"She will die if you don't do as I say," Bethany said.

Her pupils were dilated. She was high on drugs and her hand shook so damn badly.

Adelaide's gaze was on me. Every now and then, she had no choice but to close her eyes because of the grip Bethany had.

I was trying to figure out how to save Adelaide, when I noticed her arm. Her hands were still tied together, but she shoved her elbow, jarring her sister in the ribs, causing Bethany to stumble. There wasn't much time. The gun dropped to the floor, and Adelaide was able to overpower Bethany.

I grabbed the gun, shot Oleg between the eyes, and then pointed the gun at Bethany. I knew if I didn't kill her sister right then and there, she would keep coming after Adelaide. I made the decision.

Adelaide could hate me, but enough pain and heartache had come to her life. With a single shot, I ended Bethany, right between the brows.

Adelaide, covered in blood, gasped and quickly jerked away from her sister. She got to her feet and turned to look at me. Her eyes were wide, but she rushed and stumbled against me. She collapsed in my arms, tried to hold onto me, but the rope around her wrists stopped her. Ivan handed me a knife, and I sliced through the rope. She wrapped her arms around me, and I held her tightly.

"I love you," she said. "I love you so much but I was so afraid to tell you." She started to sob.

"I had to kill her," I said. "She was going to keep coming after you."

"I don't care. I don't care." She pulled away and held up my arms. "You didn't have to do this."

I cupped her face, tilting her head back. "Don't you realize it yet?" I asked. "I love you. I will do anything for you. No matter what."

"Well, that was rather … fucking boring," Ivan said. He tutted and then looked to Nathan. "I better deal with him."

"Why is Nathan here?" Adelaide asked.

"That's a long fucking story."

"I have all day until we get home."

Home sounded so good right now.

****

Adelaide

Nathan was a hit man who now worked for Ivan Volkov. Andrei had been right. Nathan had nearly become Oleg's trusted ally when Bethany ruined it, telling Oleg exactly who he was.

Nathan had been tortured but had refused to give any information away. He was supposed to die with me in that converted barn.

My parents mourned Bethany's passing. I did have a lunch with my mother where she proceeded to tell me in detail what a huge disappointment I was. How ugly I was. How she wished she'd never given birth to me. That was the last day I had seen her, and I'd asked Andrei never to help my parents again. It may seem bitter, but they didn't deserve it.

Andrei left them for Ivan to deal with.

As for the sixth territory, Ivan had yet to pick a replacement and was currently dealing with all of Oleg's fuck-ups—Andrei's words, not mine.

Me? Well, I stared down at the ink I'd gotten. I don't know what I had done for Ivan to decide that I was now under the complete protection of the Volkov Bratva, but I had the same ink around my wrist as Aurora, the same ink that was on Andrei's knuckles—ivy surrounding a V. I liked it. Every now and then, it caught my eye and made me smile.

"What are you smiling about?" Andrei asked, coming back to the beach.

Ivan had allowed us the use of his island once again. He knew about the news I wanted to tell Andrei, and had insisted we use his island.

Tucking my hair behind my ear, I smile up at him. "Can't I just be happy?"

"Yes. We're surrounded by the ocean. We've had peace and quiet all day. I've made love to you every single chance I've had."

He moved in close to me and I press my hand against his chest, crawling on his lap, straddling his waist. I feel the hard ridge of his cock as he pressed between my thighs. I kiss his lips and trail them back toward his ear.

"I'm pregnant," I said.

Andrei cups my head, pulling my face back enough to look into my eyes. "Pregnant?"

"Yes."

He releases my face and puts his hands on top of my stomach. "Our baby?"

I nod. My throat feels tight as I watch him.

"I love you, Adelaide," he said.

I would never get tired of hearing that. "And I love you too."

Epilogue

Adelaide
Five Years Later

I never knew being married could be so amazing. Being Andrei Belov's wife didn't come without its problems. He was the brigadier to Ivan Volkov. His life was constantly in danger.

"Daddy!"

Spinning around toward the back of the house, I smile as soon as I see Andrei. His son, Phillip, immediately charges toward him.

Seeing father and son always made me melt on the spot. Andrei had been so terrified of being a bad father. He'd told me about his past. About what his father, who wasn't his father, had done to him. The price he had to pay for his mother's mistake.

I yearned for the small boy, wanting to take care of him myself, so I helped the man. I helped Andrei to realize that he wasn't going to be like his father. He was a better man. A kinder man.

When I gave birth to Phillip, he'd been so afraid to hold him. He feared dropping him, but once I showed him that he would give the world to Phillip, there was no stopping him. He helped with feedings, being there, giving me time to rest. The only job he tried to get out of was changing diapers, but I wouldn't allow that.

He was involved in every single step of raising Phillip, and he had not once raised his fist to our son.

Phillip was a good boy. Resting my hand on my swollen stomach, I wondered if Andrei would be the same with our little girl.

He didn't want me to get pregnant again. Giving birth had been a bit of a nightmare for him. He threatened all the doctors and nurses, who were only doing their jobs. As for me, I'd been in pain, but that had faded the moment Phillip was in my arms.

Andrei didn't forget.

He lifted Phillip, putting a kiss on his cheek before letting him down. Our son knew not to come between me and his father. It was the only time Andrei had scolded our son. No one, not even our children, would come between us.

Andrei wrapped his arms around me and kissed me. Even though his soldiers were near, he didn't care. He loved me.

When he pulled away, I opened my eyes.

"How are you feeling?" he asked.

"Better." I smiled up at him.

"I missed you," he said.

"You only went to get Anna and the kids," I said.

Anna had become my friend. I was not sure if Andrei was happy about that. He had promised me it was only because he was jealous and didn't want to share me. Not that I minded. There were times I loved having Anna over, because when she went home, he would become so possessive. Making love to me, marking me, telling me how much he loved me, and making me his all over again.

Only this time, Anna wasn't alone. Slavik and Aurora had come for a rare visit, and so had Ivan. We had more guests arriving as well.

This was our family. We were not related by blood, but we were here by choice, and I chose Andrei Belov.

****

Andrei

I hated having people at the house.

Adelaide wasn't mine when we had guests. She was the perfect hostess. I couldn't keep my eyes off her.

Pregnancy suited her well, and for that, I was relieved. I had been a good boy these past five years. After Phillip's birth, I had sworn to never get her pregnant again. Standing behind her, holding her hands, hearing her screams, the pain in her voice. It would stay with me forever, and what made it worse, I'd been the one to cause that. I hated myself with a passion.

Making love to her, wearing a condom, wasn't easy. I loved feeling her wrapped around me. It was only a matter of time before she caught again, and she had done so, and now we were expecting a little girl.

I didn't know if I could handle another pregnancy. Watching Adelaide in pain nearly destroyed me, and that was putting it mildly. I couldn't handle it, even though after she held Phillip, she seemed to be so fucking happy, like a moment before she'd not felt torn in two.

"You're quiet," Adelaide said as I made my way into the bedroom that night.

I stay quiet until I get to her and climb in the bed, resting my hand on her swollen stomach.

"What about caesarean? I asked.

"Andrei, I can do this. I can have this baby."

Lifting my hand to her cheek, I stared into her pretty eyes, stroking my thumb across her lips. "I know, I just … I don't know if I can stand it."

She covered my hand with her own and smiled at me. "You can handle this, and you will." She pressed her lips to mine and I breathed her in.

When we're in the confines of our bedroom, away from prying eyes, I allow Adelaide to see, to feel, to have absolutely no doubt how I feel about her. Too many people knew too much already. I couldn't risk her or our son, and now our daughter.

"I love you, My Adelaide."

"I am yours, only ever yours." She leaned in close and when I kiss her lips, I know I'm the happiest man in the world.

The woman I'd been searching for was finally mine.

The End

SAM CRESCENT

EVERNIGHT PUBLISHING ®

www.evernightpublishing.com